The Sun Jumpers

Ken Luber

Ken Luber

First published by Dog Ear Publishing
4011 Vincennes Rd
Indianapolis, IN 46268
www.dogearpublishing.net

ISBN: 978-1-4575-5046-1

This book is printed on acid-free paper.

This book is a work of fiction. Places, events, and situations in this book are purely fictional and any resemblance to actual persons, living or dead, is coincidental.

Printed in the United States of America

ACKNOWLEDGEMENTS

My heartfelt thanks to my editors, Robyn Conley, LaDonna Harrison, Reba Hilbert, Linda Langton Int. editors, and to the support staff at Dog Ear Publishing. And a special thanks to my readers, John Pat Anderson, Charles Buckman, Lenore Sazer, Shannon Hodgen, Shelley Parrish, Shannon Ng and Sandra Luber, all of whom have helped to clarify and enrich this story. And to my wife, Kathleen, for her persistent acumen and enthusiastic support of my work and to my sister Rochelle Devorkin for her unwavering encouragement. I would also like to thank the participants in my Idyllwild Writers Workshop for their love of writing.

CHAPTER 1

Darren stood at the kitchen counter, beating out "When the Saints Go Marching In" with a plastic spatula in his right hand. "Oh when the saints... Oh when those saints..." He bopped across the kitchen, craning his neck back and waving the spatula, as if the refrigerator and stove had joined the march one step behind him. Louis Armstrong growled through the CD player. He waited for the last drip through the filter and poured himself a cup of coffee. "Late night, Louie!" he shouted and ambled back through the dining room. He stopped in the living room, took a deep breath, and paused for a moment at the view outside the big picture window that faced the front yard. The sun had already left the LA sky. Low clouds still glowed with a ruby-gold tint. Seconds later, the clouds banged together in a timpani of thunder. "Come on in, saints. I need a miracle!" he pleaded as his gaze brushed the swaying palms.

"It never rains in Southern California." He scrunched his face, repeating the lyric, reassuring himself that bad weather wasn't going to screw up his early morning film shoot. He took a sip of coffee. "Yeow! Too hot!" he yelled. Six feet, two inches tall, he was bony thin and looked, when he walked, like the different parts of his body were constantly trying to reorganize and keep up with his gait.

The phone rang. He loped through the hallway, past the Monty Python, Adam Sandler, and Chris Rock movie posters, to his cubicle office at the rear of the bungalow.

"Yo!"

"Yo back." He heard his father's hard-edged voice crackle through the receiver. "How'd it go today?"

"Great! Super! We shot a lot of the background stuff. The mountains, a great hillside of yellow flowers…"

"I'm not making a Disney picture!" his father snapped. "This is a carpet commercial, Darren."

"Have I ever let you down? You just opened another big store in Tarzana. The carpet business is booming." Darren was laughing off his father's caustic tone that often made the red spot on his chin flare up. "Don't you think the commercials have something to do with that?"

"Don't laugh, kiddo. It's kept you in a damn fine lifestyle."

Darren wanted to say something like, *You don't have to remind me every time we talk,* but instead he buttoned up, slumped back in his chair, and said good-bye. The smile on his lips turned to relief.

He stared at the world map on his computer screen. *If I could go anywhere, where would I go? How far can you run from your father and still be his son?* He let the questions drift, unanswered, into corners of silence. His gaze skimmed the movie posters on his office walls. He thought of the years he had spent at film school and the dreams he had, how he opted instead to make commercials for his father's carpet empire and had lost touch with friends from his film school days. He was twenty-four years old, making more money than a lot of struggling writers and directors, but something was lacking. Something inside of him was as hollow as the rattle of thunder overhead. He reached over and listened to his voice mail.

"Darren, this is Dr. Greenberg. I've got to cancel our appointment for tomorrow afternoon. I'm setting it up for Friday morning at eleven. Unless there's a problem, don't bother calling me back. Bring a picture of your mother if you have one."

The therapist hung up. Darren had been seeing Greenberg for almost six months. The doctor was trying to help Darren understand how his mother's death, almost ten years ago, figured into his thorny relationship with his father.

He looked out the small corner window that overlooked the backyard. Raindrops spotted the glass. He rubbed the red patch on his chin as if it were the threads of a beard. He wanted to stay up all night and figure out exactly who he was.

His cell phone rang. He checked the caller ID. A smile rose on his lips as he leaned forward and answered. "Hey, sweetie, what's on the grill?"

"Darren, that's not cool. Either be more clever or answer with more authority."

"Well, I knew it was you, Dorsey. Cut me some slack."

"Where are you now?"

"In my office."

"Go into the living room and look out the window."

Darren got out of his chair and hustled through the hallway into the living room.

"Can you see the red Honda parked in front of your house?"

Darren peered through the streams of rain running down the living room window. "Yeah."

"That's me. I'm in it, D." She flashed the headlights. "I just leased it."

"Fantastic. Don't just sit there. Come on in. I'm just hanging out, staring at the cobwebs in my mind."

She said she had a meeting with a movie producer at seven. "We'll catch up tomorrow."

A swell of rain blasted against the picture window. Darren saw the red taillights shimmer through the glass and disappear in a watery darkness. He looked down at the mute cell phone in his hand. *She doesn't love me.*

He stared at the downpour thrashing across the front yard. *The saints aren't marching in in this weather. I need a miracle.*

CHAPTER 2

Through the billowing, fire pit smoke, Sita saw the vision. A long file of travelers covered in hides was fighting through a winter storm.

"The Antelope People!" she gasped. "Wait'll I tell Ty."

"Your long-ago ancestors," a deep voice spoke from behind her. "They left the forest caves to find a better way of life."

Again, Sita looked into the fire-tinged hologram. "Who are they?" She pointed to a small band of hunters standing at the edge of a forest.

"Those hunters you see are the forefathers of your clan, the Antelope People who refused to leave. They gave themselves the name Kishoki, for 'those who stayed behind.'"

The teenage girl shook her head. "We were wrong to stay behind. But what can we do now?" She folded her arms and sighed. "What can I do?"

She was only fourteen winters old, but she understood the impact of her ancient clan's refusal to leave their forest caves and follow their Antelope brethren. She looked up to the dark mahogany brown, bearded man, known to the Kishoki as Man Who Stands Alone.

"If you stay behind any longer," the shaman answered, "you will all die." His left eye, patched with iridescent feathers, stared into the fire pit smoke. "You have a great love for your people. I see that in your heart."

"Yes. Can you see my love for Ty too?"

The shaman raised his heavy gray brows and his voice turned to a growl. "The boy who makes fun of me and casts doubts on everything I say?"

"He doesn't really mean to. He's stubborn, that's all." Sita's voice grew apologetic. "Besides, he's very, very brave."

"He will have to be. The leaves in the wind tell me he is planning a dangerous journey."

"A journey without me? Impossible. The leaves are wrong." Her dark eyes lit in protest, but she didn't want to appear disrespectful in front of her teacher. "Where is this dangerous journey to?"

"Sh! You must go now." The shaman bowed his braided head. "You will help him on his journey. He is a brave boy, but he does not have your wisdom."

"I somehow knew that."

"Sh! again, Little One." Man waved his hand through the light. "I have shown you the power of potions, the meaning of dreams, and the wisdom to transport yourself, *star-stepping*, into other worlds. One day, soon perhaps, I will die and I want you to be the shaman of the Kishoki clan."

"Me?" Sita felt her brown cheeks redden. She clasped her hands against the leather strips that crossed her chest. Her voice seemed to come from a fire in her throat. "More than anything, I want to be shaman."

Man Who Stands Alone sprinkled a handful of seeds across the fire pit flames. The yellow smoke drifted into the winds of primordial history. "Your spirit is a holy flame," he said. "Where the elders only see shadows, you see light."

"I somehow knew that too."

"Sometimes words jump from your lips quicker than a hand on a hot stone!" he admonished her.

The dark-skinned girl caught her breath and stood silently.

5

"Go. The wind will tell you." The shaman walked past the luminous stalagmites to the back of his cave.

Sita raced through the tall grass and started down the steep cliff-side. Scrambling across the boulders, the thought that Man Who Stands Alone had said she was wiser than Ty propelled her with joy. *My mother and father will never believe this. He said I could be the next shaman. I can't tell them. No Kishoki woman has ever been a shaman!*

She slipped on her rump down several more stones, ripping a tear in her leather skirt and bruising her leg. "*Shnikee!*" she gasped, Kishoki for "yikes." A thunderous sound rose from the clearing below her. Sita heard shrieks, drum banging, and a loud chorus of jubilant voices.

Through the crossed branches of trees, she could see Ty's father, Star, march into the clearing. One end of a wooden pole rested on his husky shoulder. Several feet behind him the pole ended on the shoulder of her own father, Pau. The legs of a dead ram were lashed to the pole. Despite the weight of the ram, Star walked with a proud, upright gait. A string of brightly colored shells necklaced his chest across a pink crosshatch of scars.

Three more pairs of hunters followed. With no bounty to carry, they had turned their poles into walking sticks.

Sita shook her head. She was glad her father, as well as all of the hunters, had returned safely. Yet in her heart she knew: *One ram is not enough food for my people.* Her gaze raked the crowd for Ty.

With his long ginger hair tied in a braid down the back of his leather jerkin, Ty was easy to spot. After a few stumbles and quick steps, Sita was at his side.

The hunters passed and Star glanced over. A thin smile rose to his lips as he caught his son's eye.

Ko and Shum, Ty's buddies, *wings* in the Kishoki language, were tracking alongside their fathers, but Ty stayed back. His mother, Su, coming up behind the hunters, carried Star's spear.

Sita couldn't keep quiet any longer. "Not enough food... Did you hear me, Ty?" she repeated. "That's one ram, not enough meat to last us through one full moon!"

Ty jerked his head to the side. "I have a plan." Sita saw a sneer bridge his lips. His skin tone was darker than hers, and the color of his eyes, blue like the mountain sky, was unique among the Kishoki. "There are tribes out there, past the river forest, who have better tools, better food and ways of living."

"No one believes there are people out there."

"I don't care what the elders believe! I don't want to become a great hunter like my father." He shot his all too familiar, defiant look at Sita. "I'm going to find people who will help us!"

"The Antelope People left us long ago. I saw it in the shaman's fire."

"I will find them!" he shouted, ripping his arm away from her hand.

"Man Who Stands Alone told me..."

"I don't want to hear what he told you!" Ty fired back. "Why doesn't Man bring us food with his powers if they're so great? Why do babies die in the winter storms and forest beasts terrorize our families? Why doesn't Man kill the emmydactyl beast that almost killed my father? Does the shaman do anything except mix potions?" Without waiting for her answer, he turned away and strode into the crowd to embrace his father.

Sita sighed. *Why do I love such a stubborn boy?* Her gaze rose to a trail of ragged gray clouds passing overhead. Thunder swallowed up the sky.

It was ten thousand years ago, ten thousand years before man had tracked the moon. Across the clearing Sita saw women herding their children out of the light rain and back to their cave dwellings. The brief celebration was over. Then Sita caught a glimpse of Ty with his *wings*. They were following the hunters down to the River Gan. The shaman's mysterious utterance about the journey flitted again through Sita's restless mind.

"Ty!" She caught up to him and grabbed his arm.

He spun around with anger still ripping through his voice. "What are you doing here?"

"Don't be mad." She pulled him from the river path. "You told me you love me. Treat me like you love me."

"I'm with my *wings* now."

"Does that mean you have to act like a beast?" She stamped her foot. "Listen to me! You must see Man Who Stands Alone."

"I told you I don't need him. One ram is a pitiful show of the shaman's power."

"You don't know why things happen."

"And you do?" His blue eyes blazed at her. "Things happen because I make them happen!" He pounded his chest. "I don't need Man's help!" He looked down at a trickle of blood on her leg. "Go fix your skirt and wash your leg."

"Your stubbornness is a wall, Ty. It holds you back just like our people stayed behind when the Antelope People left."

"You're wrong. I'm not like my father or my father's father." He wiped the spittle from his lips and turned back to Ko and Shum. "Let's go! The rain is letting up."

Sita stood alone, watching the boys walk toward the river. *They think they're tough. They've never been a shaman-in-waiting.* Her gaze stayed on the head of an eagle, stained on the back of Ty's jerkin. *His plan is probably just as crazy as the color of his hair.* She folded her arms in a determined clutch. *Man was right. The more Ty talks, the more I see: how could he go anywhere without me?*

CHAPTER 3

Ty threw his arm around Ko's shoulder. "Are you going or not?"

"I'm thinking," the burly boy growled.

"When did you start doing that?" Shum snapped.

"Listen, no more goofing on each other." Ty raised his voice and looked between them. "We leave tomorrow. The rain will stop tonight. The hunters are back. Now we don't have to leave our mothers alone. Everything is falling into place perfectly."

"If I go, I'll take food for three moons, no more," Ko announced in his usual subversive growl. He added sternly, "But Sita doesn't go with us."

"No, no." Ty was adamant. "No Sita. Never. My boots will fall off first."

The clouds made Ko's amber skin appear darker. Black crinkly brows hooded his eyes. His forehead slanted back into a crown of slick black hair. Some of the elders joked that Ko had the strength of a beast and the brain of a stone. "I'm slow because my thoughts are heavy," he would tell them, rubbing the patch of hair sprouting on his teenage chin.

Ty looked over to Shum, shuffling along on his right. "This journey is only for Kishoki boys, Shum. A *kanta-wing* would cry all night in the forest."

"Exactly," Shum agreed. He would love to take one or two girls, *kanta-wings*, on the journey, but he knew the forest dangers were too great. "I'm taking my spear, that's it. We might have to fight a beast, maybe even the emmydactyl."

Shum was Ty's height and wore his shiny black hair in two long braids. His brown skin glistened in the shafts of light that poked through the trees. "Maybe I'll bring back a wife."

Ko stamped his feet, wiping tears of laughter from his face. "You've never even kissed a girl, Shummy. You're lucky if you bring back a girl rabbit."

"You'd be lucky if a rabbit kissed your ugly face," the spear boy shot back.

Ty threw up his arms. "Didn't you hear me? No more jabbing! The journey is to find people with ideas to help the Kishoki, not to waste our time trading insults."

"Truce!" Shum proclaimed.

Ty pounded out the words with a clenched fist. "We will not stay behind anymore!"

"No more!" Shum shouted again, in his habit of repeating Ty's proclamations.

Ko tossed a stick into the brush. "Enough about planning. Maybe no one is out there. No Kishoki has ever seen another tribe." He turned his gaze toward the river. "But we know where the fish are. Let's go swimming!"

"Wait!" Ty threw up his hands again. Ko was already bolting down the forest path. "He's always running ahead. He can't do that on the journey, Shum. We've got to stay together. I'm the leader." He paused, noting Shum's faraway look. "You want to swim too, don't you?"

"You?"

Ty shrugged. "Go ahead." He smiled to himself, watching his *wing* run down the muddy path.

The hunters' voices grew louder. Ty could hear his father shouting instructions to the men, performing the after-hunt ritual of butchering the ram, washing the meat in the river, scraping the bones, and cutting the hide into strips and swatches.

Ty turned onto a shaded fork in the path. He didn't want his father to see him. He knew that if Star saw him, he would call him over and nag him about the need to learn the hunter's trade. "It has kept us alive all these years," he could hear his father saying. *Barely,* Ty thought.

Ty hadn't expected the guilt that was creeping at the edges of his heart. River light flashed in his eyes. "I was born on the banks of the Gan," he mumbled. "And I was born to follow the river. I am not afraid. My journey is for my people."

A last shock of thunder broke through his thoughts. The trees shook with the scrape of branches and rustle of leaves. A long, yellow-ringed snake fell from the branch above Ty's head. He thought lightning had killed it, but then it slithered across his path. The snake craned its sleek body, glistening in the rain-soaked leaves. It twisted its bullet blue head toward him. Terror gleamed in its jet-black eyes.

Is this a sign of death? Ty wondered. At the same time, he remembered that Sita had once told him that the snake was also a sign of wisdom. Ty inched to the side of the path and picked up a heavy stick. *Are you death or my destiny?* He raised the stick to his shoulder. *What if we die on the journey? What if we get lost and starve to death or the emmydactyl rips us apart? What would I tell the fathers I hear chanting along the river if I were the lone survivor?*

The snake arched its body one last time and hissed, like a cynical laugh answering Ty's fears. Ty smashed the stick against the bark of a tree. The snake disappeared into the brush.

What would I tell Ko or Shum's mother? Would the elders banish me into the forest? Would I never see Sita again?

He had scoffed at the shaman's powers, ridiculed the wasted time Sita spent with the one-eyed holy man, smirked at his own mother's faith in the Man on the cliff. Now he wondered: *Could Man tell me that my wings will not die? That we will return?*

He raced back up the path. An old woman standing at the mouth of her cave shook her head and turned back into the darkness. From the shadows of a banyan tree, Sita stepped forward. Wind shook the leaves, sending a veil of raindrops around her.

Ty saw her lift her hand. In the curve of her silent lips, he heard the word "Go."

He raised his eyes to the summit of the cliffs. It was there Man Who Stands Alone dwelt in a grandiose cave with his powers, his potions, and his prophecies. Ty looked back to Sita. Again, she echoed the word and nodded. He clenched his fists and drew a fateful breath. Ten thousand years ago, a teenage boy took the first steps toward the twenty-first century and a confused young man on a mountaintop.

CHAPTER 4

The boy's eyes settled on Man deep inside the chamber. A blazing fire pit burned before the shaman, who sat majestically on a tall obsidian rock, like a black throne, etched with the flight of birds. Surrounding the throne were the skulls of the bear, the ram, and the antelope. Animal bones, bound and crafted into the shape of a huge golden shell, encrusted with brilliant stones, hung like a canopy high above the shaman.

"You are here...?" The shaman's voice cracked with a hint of disbelief. "Why?"

Ty pressed his fingers into his palms and raised a voice that tumbled from the back of his throat. "I'm going on a journey." He paused, hoping Man had not heard or had forgotten how often Ty had made fun of him and had disparaged his tribal ceremonies. "A journey with my *wings*, but I beg you not to tell anyone."

Man's dark face remained expressionless. A smoking branch of sage rested in his palm.

"Will I die?" The words popped from Ty's lips in a single breath, barely scratching the silence. "Will my *wings*, Ko and Shum, die with me?"

A bellowing laugh rose from the shaman's thick gray lips. "Die?" The shells and teeth embedded on his priestly vestment jiggled against his chest, as if they, too, were mocking Ty. He got to his feet. "You don't believe what I say." His laughter stopped, followed by a harsh whisper. "What good is it to tell you?"

"You are the shaman of our clan. Kishoki trust you."

"Not all Kishoki." The shaman narrowed his good eye into a violet beam directed at Ty. "You?"

Ty hesitated. He nodded rapidly. "Yes. I trust you."

"Now?"

"Yes, now. And forever if we do not die."

"Remember your words. You do not know who will follow me." The shaman tossed the burning sage into the fire pit and kneeled before the flames. "You will go far, farther than your father or any of the elders have ever gone. That is what I saw when you were born, when Star took you from your mother's womb and washed your blood in the River Gan. That is what I see again in the fire."

Ty's nerves were jumbling inside him. He needed to pee. His voice shot up. "But will we die?"

"Does the tree die?" Man answered, raising himself up. "Does the branch not turn to ash in the fire?"

It was more a riddle than the answer Ty wanted to hear. "Where is farther than my father has gone?"

"If I tell you, then it is no longer a quest, is it?" Man walked past the crystal-hard icicles that hung from the ceiling, shooting out golden wands of light across his path. "Why do you want to take this journey?"

"To find new people and ideas. Now, all we have is the hunt and fish in the river." Ty's voice grew stronger as he declared his purpose. "But when winter comes, and the snow is too high for my father to chase the ram and the river freezes, then we have no food. We are always near death."

The shaman kept his back to Ty. Many times, he had exhorted the Kishoki elders, including Ty's own father, Star, to move beyond the river cliffs. "You have the courage to make the journey?"

"I do."

The shaman walked deeper into the cave. "You love Sita."

"Yes."

"Love makes time small." Man turned and balled up his fist. "Time goes away. You will follow your blood." His fingers flew open, like the wings of a bird.

Time goes away, follow my blood. That's not a map. "I'm not a child," Ty stammered. "Why must you talk to me in riddles?"

The shaman answered harshly. "Because truth is a river with many streams!"

Man stopped at a basket woven of purple and silver reeds. It sat on a gleaming emerald stone engraved with patterns Ty had never seen before.

With his palm faced down, Man spread his hand. His lips moved, but Ty could not hear a single word. The shaman made a quick dipping motion as if he were scooping air from an empty canister.

He turned to the boy, walked back, and placed his hand over Ty's palm.

Ty stared down at a small golden shell. It, too, was inscribed with symbols he did not recognize.

"For me?"

The Man nodded. "Trust."

"Trust in what? In who?" His voice rose as questions tumbled from his lips. "In this golden shell?"

"In your journey."

Ty didn't want to leave. There was the chance that Man would tell him something more about his journey or explain the riddles, but a dizzying feeling inside his head, from the smoking branch or the radiant light, forced him to take several steps back.

"Son of Star, be wise." A smile broke through the shaman's craggy face. "You will need help on your journey. The morning moon will answer you."

Another riddle, Ty thought. *Can't he just talk straight?*

Clouds of smoke billowed from the fire pit. The image of Man disappeared in a golden-purple haze.

Ty turned and bolted from the cave.

By the time he reached the clearing, the dizziness in his head had lifted. The hunters had finished their work and gone back to their families. He looked for Sita but could not find her.

He peed and wondered where time had gone. Ty was certain he had been in the shaman's cave for only a short time. The sage in the shaman's hand hadn't even burned to its stem before Man threw it back to the fire pit, but the stone faces of the caves dimmed with a falling light. He saw Shum chasing a squirrel with a stick. He waved and shouted his name, but Shum never looked up, as if his friend hadn't seen or heard him.

Ty opened his fist and stared at the golden shell. Man made a trick with light and smoke, he thought. Man hid time in the shell. But why, he wondered. *How much time will our journey take?*

CHAPTER 5

Ty's mother was sitting atop a pile of animal skins, away from the fire, when Ty entered the cave. Her small dark figure was nearly lost in the plush of fur.

"Where were you?"

"Just talking with my *wings.*"

Su hadn't yet seen the summers of six hands, but already her face showed the creases of age. Like a child, she held up her arm. "Star brought me this. He made it at night when the hunters slept."

Ty gazed at the thin leather strips that circled her upper arm. Yellow and ivory claws hung from each strip. He turned to Star. "Pa, did you see an emmydactyl on the hunt?" The boy walked over to the cave entry, pulled the hide over the mouth of the cave, and secured it with heavy stones.

"Dead emmydactyl bones, long dead," his father grumped.

The emmydactyl, a mammoth bloodthirsty beast, prehistoric survivor of millennia, was as heavy as a mountain boulder, with slit red eyes and razor-sharp teeth. Its serrated front legs slashed its victims with powerful claws, tearing them to pieces. No Kishoki had ever killed an emmydactyl.

Star placed his hand across the scars on his chest. "Never try to kill the emmydactyl at its head," he warned. "Attack from the back. Emmydactyl can only move forward. Not this way." He moved his rough dark hands from side to side. "We will hunt together. Maybe on the next hunt, you will see. Only kill from the back."

"But if you saw emmydactyl bones, then someone had killed the emmydactyl."

"Hah!" Star grumped again. "There is no one else in the forest. Another beast killed the emmydactyl."

Ty was too caught up in his own urgent thoughts to argue with his father. He asked to use Star's tools.

"What for?" Star looked up from the fire pit.

"A stone for Sita." Ty touched the red stone that hung from his neck. "I want to shape it into a heart."

"Her mother doesn't trust you."

"I'm not making it for her mother. Besides," Ty added, "someday she will."

Ty didn't like lying to his mother or his father, but this wasn't really a lie, not a complete lie, he told himself. Sita had always wanted the red stone, and some day he intended to give it to her.

He spent the next hour grinding a small hole in his golden shell. He carefully brushed the golden dust onto his palm, but when he turned to pour it into a pouch, the dust disappeared. Like time, he thought, Man took the dust away. Ty removed the red stone from the leather cord around his neck and replaced it with the shaman's talisman, concealing it under his jerkin. Then, working the oiled stones, he sharpened his bone knife to a lethal blade. "In case I meet the dreaded emmydactyl," he whispered to himself.

Star was snoring at the fire pit. Su had retreated to her spirit chamber. Ty quietly put together the last stock of food for his journey, wrapped his provisions in husks, and lodged them in his fur roll-up blanket.

His father awoke, yawned, and stretched his thick-corded arms. He picked up a lit branch and carried it to the mouth of the cave.

"Wait!" Ty shoved the bedroll behind a woodpile and jumped to his feet.

Star pulled back a corner of the hide, and the two slipped out. They stood together, peeing into the bushes. Ty finished and looked up at the stars.

Star raised the burning branch, pointing it toward the moon. "No more clouds. No rain. We will sleep well tonight."

One of us will, Ty thought. He knew that darkness aided the forest beasts. Moonlight favored the *wings*.

Father and son slipped back into the cave. Star threw the burning branch on the fire and shuffled over to his bed. Su had already curled into the blankets.

Ty sat in his chair by the fire and watched the flames die. His heart pounded with excitement. The elders had laughed at him when the fish he tried to catch slipped out of the net he had made of vines. *No more*, he thought. *I will change their lives. They will laugh no more.*

From a distance, he could hear animals howling in the hills and an occasional snort from his father's heavy breathing. Then he, too, closed his eyes and felt the warmth of the golden shell on his chest.

* * *

Sita lay perfectly still, covered in furs in the darkness of her family cave. Her soft breathing joined the ebb and flow of her two sisters and brother asleep beside her. Her eyes were closed, but a dream took her to another world. She saw men and women in a large room surrounded by walls, parts of which were cut out so she could see the sky. Most of the people were white-skinned, but some were her color and a few with skin even darker. She admired the different colors of their clothes, especially the way they fit the women. The people were talking to each other and, as well, into small black devices they held in their hands. The language sounded nothing like Kishoki. Some of the meaning was clear, but most of it didn't relate at all to her life. Everything these dream-people did—the way they talked, the way they ate their food and walked—felt rushed to Sita.

She opened her eyes and shook her head. I was *star-stepping,* she thought. A slight wind brushed her cheek. She looked over to the thick hide covering the mouth of the cave. How could there be a wind, she wondered, when the entry was sealed with hides?

She crawled over to a circle of white stones built up and hidden with a leather wrap. The faint blaze from the fire pit afforded just enough light. Sita removed small clay vessels stored within the stone circle. She rubbed her sleepy eyes. Then, she opened three beaded pouches and hurriedly mixed powders from the vessels into each pouch.

* * *

Ty, keeper of the cave fire, wakened and looked over to his parents, huddled in their fur blankets. His mother moved her arm. He caught a glimpse of a yellow claw on the bracelet Star had given her. *He brought a gift for Su. I will leave the red stone for Sita.*

He stirred the embers in the fire pit and crawled to his bedroll behind the woodpile. Ty looped it on his back and made his way to the mouth of the cave. Then he looked back one last time across the glowing fire pit and lipped a silent good-bye to his parents. *Will the emmydactyl or another forest creature swallow me up?* he wondered as he turned to the hide that covered the mouth of the cave. *Is there someone else out there, someone brave and kind? Or am I just a fool and we Kishoki will die alone in the world?*

CHAPTER 6

Ty raced to the river cave. It was here that he and his *wings* had often made plans, traded stories, and talked about *kanta-wings*. "Shum, Shum," he whispered into the mouth of the cave. A hand on his shoulder sent him spinning around into Shum's gap-toothed smile.

"Let's go," Shum said.

Ty shifted his eyes from Shum's upright spear to Ko, with his arms folded resolutely and a haughty smirk on his face. "I knew you'd miss me if I didn't go," he growled. Both boys had bedrolls on their backs.

Before Ty could get to his feet, they heard a crackle of twigs and shuffle of leaves. A small figure appeared under the drooping riverbank trees. The face was shrouded in a leather hood that flared into a long, dark cape.

As the figure moved toward the cave, a ray of moonlight fell across a familiar face.

"Sita," Ty mumbled under his breath.

"Sita!" Shum and Ko exclaimed. "Why's she here?"

She approached with a bright, airy smile, as if the *wings* were expecting her. "I'm a long-step girl. Let's—"

Before she could finish her thought, Ty angrily grabbed her arm and pulled her onto the rocks along the river. "Why did you come? This is my journey!"

"Man Who Stands Alone told me I was going on a journey too."

"But not with us, Sita!" Ty leaned his face inches from her. "He never said this journey, did he?"

"This morning I awoke from a dream. And then the wind came."

"The wind doesn't blow in a cave!"

"But it did. That was a sign. Man told me to listen to the wind."

"Then go back to your cave and listen to it!"

As Ty started to leave, she grabbed his arm. "Listen to me. I couldn't fall back to sleep, so I went outside. I saw Shum and Ko sneaking into the grove. I knew something was up."

"Nothing is up for you except the sun! What if we all die?"

"I'm not afraid."

"And if an emmydactyl attacks us?"

"You will protect me."

"Stop fighting!" Ko waved his hand. "Sita's a big problem! Let's go!"

"Don't shout!" Ty stammered, venting his anger wherever he could. He turned back to Sita. "Where are you going to sleep? You don't even have a bedroll."

"With you. I always slept with you when we were small."

Ty slammed his hands in frustration against his sides. "I'm not small, you're not small." He was getting confused in his own feelings. He had always wanted to sleep with Sita, but with two *wings* accompanying him, risking their lives as well as his on a journey into the unknown, the possibility was out of the question. "We're big now!" he whined. "Your mother would make me as small as a frog if we slept together!"

Ty caught a glimpse of Shum, with his arms crossed and a silly grin on his face. "Not funny, Shum! Stare at your spear!" Ty jerked his head back to Sita. "The *wings* are laughing at me. You're making a fool out of me, and I'm their leader."

"I can help you, *masuqa*," the Kishoki word for *sweetie*. She whirled open her cape and softly trilled her voice. "Look. Woo, woo, woo." Ty stared at three beaded pouches attached to a cord around her waist. "These are good powders, Ty. Man Who Stands Alone helped me."

The shaman hadn't said a word to him about Sita or any *kanta-wing*. But it was twice now, in just a few breaths, that Ty had heard the word *help*, like a bell reminding him of what the old shaman had said: "You will need help on the journey."

He leaned back and turned his eyes to the fading moon. "Follow me," he said. He took two steps and turned back sharply. "You don't kiss Shum, no Ko. No woo woo!"

Ty caught a smile peek from the darkness of Sita's hood. Hastily, she followed his steps.

They pooled their food into one large pouch. Ko carried the provisions, as well as a water pouch. Shum took the rear guard. Ty carried the precious firestone. "Sita, don't talk. Make like you're not here," he commanded.

They marched into the silky gray dawn with only Ty's vision to guide them, Shum's spear-fighting skills, Ko's mighty strength, and Sita's mysterious woo-woo potions. They had no map, no idea of how far they would travel or the difficulty of their challenge. No idea whom they might meet or whom they might have to fight. Or if they would die in the angry jaws of a bloodthirsty beast.

CHAPTER 7

Light had flooded the sky by the time they reached the golden waterfall.

Ko looked up at the sunlit water tumbling over the rocks. Ty sensed a hint of trepidation in his friend's eyes.

"We've never gone further than this," the beefy boy muttered.

"This is just the beginning, Ko. I know there are tribes on the other side of the world."

Ko protested that no Kishoki had ever seen another man from any clan.

Ty looked keenly at his burly *wing*. "You're not afraid, are you?"

Ko thumped his broad chest with his fist. "Ko doesn't know that word. He is never afraid."

Ty waved Shum and Sita forward. Together, the four explorers stepped beyond the frontier of their prior forest journeys and into the unknown.

Ty was feeling confident and lighthearted. With his acrobatic balance, he quickly maneuvered over rocks and fallen trees, leaving his *wings* to struggle with nature's impediments. Would it take more than one moon or two, he wondered, to reach the river fork where the Kishoki world ended and the New World began?

Sita ended his thoughts, grabbing Ty's elbow and pulling him to her side. "When do we eat, Ty?" She nudged him harder, trying to loosen his tongue. "You'll be sorry. Why are you so mad with me?"

"I don't see you, I don't hear you. You are only a shadow."

"You are one dumb *wing*," she snapped. "Both of us were born on the banks of the River Gan. We crawled in the mud together and played in the rain and snow. Did you ever have a bump or a scratch when I didn't try to comfort you? Now you act like a toothless old man!" She pulled back the hood of her cape. "Look at me! I am the *kanta-wing* you love."

His cheeks turned red and he pulled his arm away from her. He hurried up the path. Ten steps later he heard her screams.

"Pull on your cape!" Shum yelled, reaching out to grab Sita's hand.

Her long leather cape had caught in a snarl of dead branches.

"Stop crying!" Ty shouted.

"It's my new cape! It's ripping!" Sita clambered out of the debris and looked down at the torn hem of her cape.

Ty shook his head, amused and annoyed that she would give so much attention to clothes. *But she always does that*, he thought. *Maybe she really is hungry. Ko and Shum are probably hungry too.* A half day into their journey, he didn't want to risk a barrage of complaints, much less a mutiny over empty stomachs. The leader raised his arm.

"Stop! We'll make camp here."

Sheltered by a canopy of trees, the exhausted *wings* sat in a circle, ready to enjoy their first meal away from the clan. Shum divided the portions of dried fish and berries. Ko passed them around. He stopped in front of Sita and looked over to Ty.

"She didn't bring any food," he observed snidely.

"She brought..." Ty paused. He could feel the eyes of his *wings* fixed on him. As much as he had fought against Sita joining them, it was no secret in the clan that Ty and Sita were bound to each other. His first major decision had to represent fairness, without a hint of favoritism. "She brought powder, better than food."

KEN LUBER

He struck a chord of confidence and shot a look to Sita, but he really didn't know what her silly *woo-woo* powders could do.

Ko grudgingly set a small portion of fish on the leaf in front of Sita. Then he went down to the river and returned with a pouch filled with cool water. Even Sita took sips under Ko's watchful eye.

Aside from Ko's occasional belch, the wings ate in silence. Ty hoped things weren't beginning to fall apart before their first night under the stars. "Let's go," he said, jumping to his feet, still sounding upbeat.

They passed stretches of tall yellow grass buzzing with black and purple insects and a long plateau of flat, saucer-shaped rocks. Clouds covered the sun and darkened the river. Ty looked up, hoping they wouldn't have to take shelter from a rainstorm. Caves, he knew, were filled with poisonous insects and venomous snakes.

He glanced back to see if Sita was still keeping up with Ko and Shum. Shum was only a few yards ahead of her, but Ko wasn't with either of them. "Where's Ko?" Ty stared in disbelief.

Shum scrunched up his face, as if he had to push out each word. "He went into the woods, passed you when we were at the big rocks."

"Passed me? Why? I'm the leader!" Ty clenched his teeth. "He's always running ahead." He kicked the stones around him and cursed himself for having urged Ko to come on the quest.

But when he turned back to the path, he saw a bullish figure crashing through the trees. Ko was racing back, twenty yards away. Ty could hear his gasping breath.

"Smoke! Smoke!" Ko shouted.

Ty's heart jumped. "How far?"

"On a big hill, not far." His sloped forehead glistened with perspiration. His dark, narrow eyes flew open with a mixture of sudden fear and feverish excitement.

Ty didn't hesitate. "Let's go!"

Shum raised his deadly spear. "Let's go!" he yelled, repeating Ty's command. "Forward!"

Ty marched with Ko across a barrier of logs tangled with vines. Both boys felt a rush of super energy.

"What color is the smoke?"

"White."

"See, Ko, I told you." Ty was grinning, feeling his confidence fly back. "We haven't even reached the fork and we're in sight of new people."

"What if they try to kill us?"

"Why think the worst? Why would they do that? We're just kids with some dried fish and berries."

"They might kill us to get Sita."

"Ty! Sita fell back again!" Shum shouted, pointing behind him. Sita was wobbling along the barrier of slippery rocks, her arms outstretched and flailing, like a tightrope walker teetering on her wire.

Ty gritted his teeth. *Ragnoki*, he whispered, a Kishoki expletive for excrement. *She just wants my attention.* He charged across the wet logs and rocks. *Why at a crucial time like this! Is this her way of helping me?*

"You're wearing dumb boots!" he scolded, reaching out to take her hand. He looked down at her water-soaked booties, trimmed with fringe and tiny pink shells. "You couldn't catch up to a dead snake in those booties!" He raised a foot. "See this!" Ty pointed to his own boot sole imbedded with small pieces of husk. "These are journey boots!"

Sita dropped her gaze to his antelope hide boots, laced halfway up his calves. "My boots are prettier."

Ty stomped his foot and shook his head, sending his ginger braid flying back and forth. He grabbed her hand. "This is no time for pretty! This is a life-and-death adventure! Ko has spotted signs of another tribe!"

By the time they caught up to Shum and Ko, the riverbank had smoothed to a grassy trail. "I'm going up with Ko," Ty barked. "You walk with Shum. He uses his spear like a walking stick. I'll get you a walking stick!"

Ty broke from the path, scrambled into the forest, and came back quickly with a strong, smooth, staff-like branch.

"It's bent," she said.

"It's good enough!" Ty slammed the branch into the damp earth and marched up the trail. *If bad men kill us to get Sita, she'll definitely drive them crazy before they lay a hand on her.*

"She's a problem," Ko grumbled.

Sita was becoming a stumbling block, figuratively and literally, every step of the way. She inspired only jealousy and resentment, especially in Ko, who, tough as he was, had never really had a *shagu*, a girlfriend, in all of his fourteen years.

"She's never gone this far along the river," Ty said, bluffing a weak apology.

"Neither have we," Ko grumbled. "But we're *wings*."

Dissension was the last thing Ty wanted, but he couldn't ask Sita to turn back without an escort. Even if she would agree to return to the caves, he knew she would only consent if he were the *wing* accompanying her. Without a leader, the journey was over and so was his desperate hope of finding help for the clan. "I will be laughed at again," he mumbled to himself.

But as they moved along, even though he trusted his burly *wing's* keen sense of observation, doubt was starting to rub his nerves.

"Where's the smoke, Ko? You said white smoke."

Ko snuffled up a breath of air. "The sky is too bright. Wait until it darkens more."

The line of the forest curved, opening to a grassy field. Ko jumped a few steps ahead, searching the hillside with his hooded eyes. "Maybe the men left and killed the fire."

"Maybe it was dust," Shum volunteered, coming up beside Ty.

Ko leaned on his heels with his meaty arms folded against his barrel chest. "I saw smoke! I know what dust looks like, Shummy. It's the stuff inside your head!" Questioning another *wing* was something that no one in the clan took lightly.

Ty raised his hands, fed up with one more sign of dissension. "No dust, no wind! No more talking about what might have been or could have been!" He turned his head, drawing their attention to the western sky. "Look," he said, pointing to a low stream of white clouds running just above the setting sun. "The sun is going down. We'll make a fire soon."

Sita caught up to Ty, banging her stick against the rough ground with every step.

"You're worried, aren't you?"

"No." Ty clenched his fists and looked straight ahead. "If I'm worried, it's only because you keep falling down or making Ko *fassi* (upset)."

"Who do you love more?" She banged her stick. "Ko or me?"

"It's not who do I love more. It's who do I need more."

"Easy answer. You need me."

"Ko is stronger than most of the elders." Without slowing down, he turned to her, his eyes ripping at her heart. "If an emmy-dactyl attacks us, what can you do besides scream?"

"You are one dumb *wing*," she hissed. "My mother was right. I'm crazy for loving you." She smacked her stick and her mouth flew open again. "You're frightened of the smoke, aren't you?"

"No. I want to see the smoke."

"Then make smoke, Ty. Show the smoke people that we are here."

Ko, on the other side of Ty, looked over. "What's she saying?"

Ty mumbled and shook his head as if whatever she said wasn't worth repeating.

"You told me you want to meet new people," she said, refusing to let the subject die. "Maybe the smoke people are a smarter people. Maybe they can help make a better life for the Kishoki!" Her voice was sharp, as insistent as the thump of her marching stick against the stones.

"Is she doubting what I saw?" Ko butted in, in disbelief.

Ty shook him off with a wave of his hand. The sky darkened. There was no longer any sign of smoke, even in Ko's eyes.

Ty raised his arm. "Time to make camp!" He looked over to Sita. "You must follow what I say. This is no time to be woo-woo, Sita." He took a step away and turned sharply back. "This is about saving my people!"

"But you love me."

"This isn't about love."

She raised a brow. "Oh."

Ty could see the hurt in her eyes was deeper than his willingness to understand. "I don't have time for this," he said.

CHAPTER 8

Ko dug a fire pit. Shum and Ty scraped the inside fibers of dry bark for tinder. Sita kept busy gathering sticks.

"Stay close!" Ty shouted to her. "There are monsters out there!"

"Like the emmydactyl." Ko raised his eyes, less charged with concern than with the pleasure of an eerie warning.

"*Kumbuti*!" Ty snapped, the Kishoki word for "shut up."

The *wings* spread out their bedrolls and huddled around the fire pit. Ty struck the firestone. A spark, like a speck of gold, jumped onto the tinder.

"It's going!" Ko shouted.

"We are the fire *wings*!" Shum boomed, raising his spear. "We are the Kishoki warriors!"

"We're not warriors, Shummy." Ko had a habit of correcting him. "Those are just old-time story words."

Around the glow of the fire, they ate their meal. Sita sat in the shadows, only a few feet from Ty. He regarded her as if she were a ghost spirit. No one spoke to her.

They clapped their hands and sang tribal songs, releasing the tension of their first nerve-wracking, exhausting day. Ty noticed that Sita was hesitant to join in, but he also knew that her love of music would soon win out. At first, she could hardly be heard. Quickly, the sweetness of her voice took hold and animated the songs, bringing the boys to follow her. They sang of the lost Antelope People and of love for the mountain spirits, the sunrise, and the moon.

Several times they repeated the refrain of a hunting song: "Cold not stop us, claw not stop us, river brings us home, river brings us home," softer and softer, until the *wings'* chant was a whisper. All one could hear was the haunting beauty of Sita's voice floating above the fire into the forest darkness. The boys were stunned into an enchanted silence.

Suddenly, Ko jumped to his feet, crying out, "We're dumb *wings*! Beasts can hear Sita!"

The boys gasped. Ko's harsh warning pulled them from a reverie to the lurking peril that surrounded the camp. Ko looked across the fire pit to Sita and cocked his head. What he had said was true, but it was his small victory over her, over preventing her from singing and gaining the *wings'* admiration, that he cared most about.

"Sita's voice is so beautiful," Shum said, protesting meekly.

"We sing, we die in the night!" Ko shot back.

"Ko's right," Ty acknowledged grudgingly. His father's chest scars and the emmydactyl's blazing eyes flashed through his mind. "No more songs. It's time to sleep."

Deliberately omitting Sita, the boys drew blades of grass. The duty of tending the fire and guarding the camp fell to the *wing* who pulled the shortest blade.

"I got it!" Shum yelled. "Warrior number one!" Quickly he put his hand to his lips.

"Shummy, pinch those lips shut," Ko growled.

Ty, the fire-keeper in his family cave, accustomed to waking after four hours of sleep, volunteered the second shift. He started to ease himself into his bedroll, two lengths of furry hide laced together. Sita crawled over to him. Their eyes met, inches apart.

"You first," she said.

"I sleep alone," he mumbled.

"Go," she prodded. "You are stubborn."

"You should have brought a bedroll," he grumbled, slipping between the furs. "I am not your father."

"I brought woo-woo powder," she reminded him. "I am not your mother. Move over."

She spread her cape across the top cover and wiggled her slim body beside him. Her long curls brushed against his face. He smelled her fragrance. He listened to the crackle of the fire and the scream of night birds in the branches. Then he felt the soft leather of her boot rub against his leg. It was gentle enough to have been inadvertent, an innocent brush of her foot, but he knew it wasn't. He knew that nothing Sita did was accidental.

He looked over to Shum, settled at the fire pit with his spear beside him. *He will see the fur move if I go on Sita*, Ty thought. *In the morning, my* wings *will talk, laugh, think badly of her.* He had seen enough of jealousy. He didn't want to give any reason for more.

"Go to sleep," he whispered to Sita.

It never occurred to him that she might be frightened. That all she wanted was the reassurance of his kiss. He listened a moment longer to the song of night birds. The heavy boughs of the trees had blocked out the moonlight, leaving only the glow of the fire. Then he, too, fell asleep.

A shuddering roar and agonized scream awakened the camp. Ty pushed aside Sita. "Stay!"

He leapt to his feet. He saw the terror on Shum's face and the paralyzing fear in Ko's eyes, standing mummy-like beside his bedroll.

The powerful beak-faced emmydactyl roared again, rearing on its hind legs to the height of Shum standing on Ko's shoulders. Its single ebony horn tore through the branches. Ty turned to a pair of red eyes glowing with the light of a thousand embers. It shuttled one pounding foot in step with the other, waving its long front legs, serrated with lethal blue spikes. Razor-sharp teeth hung behind its meaty lips, forming a rigid gate of death.

Shum's lips froze, his eyes locked on the scaled, black chest dripping with blood.

The emmydactyl had survived a brutal fight and was stalking the forest in a dizzying, angry mood for revenge.

"Knives!" Ty shouted, drawing his sharpened knife from his waistband. In a twitching adolescent hysteria, Shum pointed his shaking spear at the beast. "Knives!" Ty yelled again, urging Ko to release his horror and draw his weapon.

The journey leader reached for a flaming branch and stumbled to his knees. The emmydactyl lunged. Its saw-toothed arms slashed through the air with a murderous fury.

"I'll stay front," Ty yelled, scrambling to his feet. Trying to distract the beast, he danced from side to side, waving the flaming branch at the emmydactyl's bloodthirsty gaze.

"Go back! Kill from the back!" he commanded, repeating his father's counsel.

Ko and Shum cautiously edged into the darkness.

The emmydactyl roared again, bolting horn-first straight at the frail, shifting figure in front of it. Ty leapt sideways, tucked and rolled to the skirt of the fire pit. A bloody spray from the emmydactyl's wounds splattered the flames. The beast stumbled forward, smothering the fire. With a horrific cry it raised its mighty bulk and shook off the embers, showering the night with burning cinders. A choking smoke wreathed the wounded beast.

Ty crawled through the darkness to his bedroll. "Sita, run into the forest. Run!" he cried in desperation.

The bedroll was empty. Sita was gone. He lay helplessly sprawled on the ground, clutching the burning branch. He heard the stomp of the heavy-footed beast inches from his face. He stared up at the mask of death bearing down. The emmydactyl grabbed the torch with its saw-toothed arm and flung it, like a quivering matchstick, over the trees.

Ty was alone in the darkness, unable to move.

The demon blended into the night. The stench of its smoldering fur descended like a suffocating blanket. Ty gasped and coughed. All he could see were two menacing eyes bent on destroying him.

"Kill!" he screamed.

"We can't see!" Ko shouted back.

"Kill!" Ty screamed again.

Suddenly, the fire pit burst with flames. Sita was kneeling beside it, throwing her powders onto the smoldering embers.

The emmydactyl emerged from the darkness in a bright, hideous silhouette.

Shum raced ahead, rallying every drop of his adolescent strength. In one mighty, terror-fueled thrust, he plunged his spear into the beast's spine. The emmydactyl shot up, stumbling away from Ty. Gobs of pinkish-green slime spewed through the agonized howl that sprung from its lips.

Ty scrambled to his feet. Ko rushed to the monster's side and jabbed his knife into its softer flanges. Shum struck again and again with his spear, ripping out chunks of the beast's flesh. The crazed animal, weakened by his earlier battles, spun wildly, grazing Ty's arm. The boy staggered in pain but kept his balance. Ty leaped against the emmydactyl, sticking his hand into one of its jagged wounds. He gripped the bloody flesh, pulled himself up between a pair of flailing saw-toothed arms, and plunged his knife into the beast's narrow gullet. The emmydactyl gurgled and gagged on the slime in its throat. Ty sprang from his chest as the beast heaved, groaned, and collapsed across the ground.

With a running start and a triumphant cry, Shum thrust his spear into the corpse. "*Wings* forever!" he shouted, planting the spear like a victory flag on the black mound of butchered fat. The monster's spiked arms sank harmlessly into the earth.

Breathless and shaken, the boys stared incredulously at their conquest.

"Our first emmydactyl," Shum stammered.

"The first Kishoki emmydactyl," Ty reflected, hardly above a whisper, as if he were talking not to them, but to his father's ghost.

A deafening sound ripped from the emmydactyl's rump.

"Emmydactyl wind," Ko said, waving his hand under his nose.

"Emmydactyl stink." Ty nodded. "We must take the beast down to the river."

"First, I taste its blood," Ko grunted. He kneeled down and dipped his finger into a wide gash in the animal's hide. The boys watched him bring a bright crimson finger to his lips. "Blood makes me strong," he said. "Strong like the emmydactyl."

Ty and Shum, not to be outdone, quickly followed, dipping their fingers and licking off the blood. "We are bound together in the blood of the emmydactyl," the leader said. "Brothers forever."

"Brothers forever," Shum repeated. He looked directly at Ko. "Warriors forever."

Ty looked over to Sita. She was shaking her head in disgust.

The *wings* wrangled over whether they should eat some of the emmydactyl's meat or, at least, save a slice for their breakfast, but Ty was insistent. This was not the time to gloat or begin butchering the beast. They dragged and rolled the dead emmydactyl across the trail, downhill into the river, hoping the current would push the beast downstream, keeping the carrion stench and smell of blood far from the campsite.

Ty glanced at his arm. Blood dripped from his wound where the animal had slashed him. "You sleep," he told Shum, patting him on the shoulder. "You are a great spear *wing*. I will stay with the fire."

Shum wagged his head. A smile crept into his bleary eyes. "I will tell my children this," he said.

"You don't have any children," Ko reminded him.

"I will have great-grandchildren before a *kanta-wing* sleeps with you."

Ty took Shum's place at the fire pit. Sita brought water and carefully washed his wound.

"Ouch," he winced. The emmydactyl's mark felt like a burning stake had scorched his flesh.

He watched the budding shaman cover his wound with her powders and balm of leaves. She was tending his scrapes and bruises just as she had done since they were children crawling in the mud.

Ko and Shum wrapped themselves in their bedrolls, exhausted with victory, and fell asleep.

"You sleep too," he told Sita.

"I don't want to leave you."

"You have done so much already. At dawn we will start again. I don't know how far until we meet the smoke people, but we have to be ready. You rest now."

"You're right," she said and added with a smile, "but only this once."

He watched her snuggle into his bedroll. Then he looked back on the achievement of his *wings*. Neither Ko nor Shum had run away in the terror of battle. In the glow of the campsite fire, Ty realized this journey wasn't just about his vision or quest. "No," he whispered to the trees. Somehow, it was about feeling a sense of kinship, of brotherhood, of family—words the elders had used over and over when they taught the Kishoki youths. Now Ty felt those words. And this feeling, he realized, was as important to him, even more important than the quest itself. *I am a part of my* wings, he thought. *And they are a part of me. This is the reason for my journey.*

The fire crackled as if it were talking back, answering his thoughts. He looked over to Sita, asleep in his bedroll. Without the spark of light that she had brought to the battle with her powders, Ty knew that in the confusion of darkness, they would have all been killed and lain, darker still, in the beast's stomach.

She saved us. Maybe that's what Man meant when he said "help." Ty threw a stick on the fire. *Maybe he was talking about Sita.*

His gaze fell to the covered wound on his arm. The pain was already starting to subside. *My scars will be just as deep as those across my father's chest. The beast has tasted his blood, but Star has never tasted the blood of the beast.*

The dreamer boy leaned back. A sweet, lingering calm came over him. He touched the golden shell that hung from his neck. *Time sleeps in the shell.*

CHAPTER 9

Standing on the banks of the River Gan, Ko watched the fast-moving current. He saw no trace of the beast they had battled the night before.

"The river washed the emmydactyl downstream," Ty surmised. "Just as we planned." He smiled to himself, imagining one of the Kishoki women filling a water jar and seeing the furry black carcass bobbing on the current.

"But maybe it got stuck on the rocks," Shum piped up, "and never got to the clearing."

Ko winced. "You know, Shummy, sometimes you don't think of the possibilities. Anything could have happened."

"You shouldn't talk," Shum fired back. "You didn't even want to come on this journey."

Ko turned to Ty. "I never said I wasn't coming. Did I say I was definitely not coming, Ty? I just had to think."

"Think? That's a first!" Shum ducked, barely missing a swat from Ko's hand.

"Quiet!" Ty threw up his arms as they tramped along the river path. "No one's going to want to meet us if all we do is argue. We'll look like fools. We've got to stick together. We traded blood, didn't we?"

"Emmydactyl blood!" Shum stamped his spear.

"He started it," Ko growled. "I'm just wondering if that was a baby emmydactyl or a big daddy. We didn't even look to see if it was male or female. I should have cut out one of his teeth or a claw just to prove to the elders that we had killed the emmy-dactyl."

"You just said you didn't know if it was male or female, so you can't say *his* teeth."

"I'm just saying, Shummy," Ko looked to Ty, "tell him to shut his face or I'll lick his blood off my finger like I did the emmy-dactyl's."

Ty had stopped listening. He glanced back to see if Sita was keeping up. He thought he caught a smile from beneath the shadow of her hood. He didn't want to think she was laughing at him, but even he thought the *wings* were acting like children. *They're going to have to change their behavior when we meet the smoke people.*

Walking into the high point of the afternoon sun, their bodies no longer cast shadows. Their feet dragged. Ty searched the vistas for any sign of smoke.

"We rest now!" Ko cried out.

Ty looked over to Ko, slightly annoyed he had given the order. "I'm still the leader, Ko."

The boys settled on the rocks along the river and splashed their faces with the cool water. Ko refilled the leather water pouch.

"We're going to *tunga*, wet the trees," Ko announced. He and Shum went into the forest to relieve themselves.

Alone with Sita, Ty gathered his feelings and turned to her with an adoring, if slightly frazzled, look.

Without a word, she took his hand and led him into the rushing current. "You are doing well," she said. "Don't worry. Ko always grumbles and argues, but he is loyal to you." Carefully, she washed the wounds on his arm. "I saw the smoke," she said.

"You did? Where? Why didn't you say something?"

"Because Shum and Ko were squabbling and I didn't want them to start fighting about this too. It's only for you."

Ty cast an anxious look toward the hills. A glimmer of hope surged again through his spirit. Sita pulled him deeper into the river and pointed toward a slope of yellow flowers. Ty shook his head. "I don't see any smoke."

She kissed him on the cheek and whispered, "You will see." Again she told Ty not to worry. "You are going in the right direction."

They climbed onto the rocks and sat in the sunlight to dry. Sita applied a fresh balm of leaves to Ty's wound. The visionary leader looked over to Ko and Shum lying across the flat stones with their eyes closed and their arms spread behind them.

Ko licked his lips and smiled. "I can still taste the emmydactyl's blood." He got to his feet and lifted enormous rocks over his head, shouting, "Emmydactyl blood!"

Ty watched him heave the rocks backward into the current. He laughed and turned to Sita. "Look at—" She was gone. "Sita! Sita!"

"She's one big problem!" Ko howled from the rocks.

"She made the fire!" Ty fired back. "She saved us!" He scrambled down to the river, searching vainly for his Sita. "Let's go!" he yelled.

Dark fears gripped Ty's mind. Could an animal have abducted her while the *wings* were horsing around? For sure, he reasoned, he or one of the *wings* would have heard her screams. How could he ever return to the caves without her? Or live without her? "Sita!" he cried out.

They had traveled less than a few hundred yards when a massive outcrop of boulders forced them away from the river toward the hillside of golden flowers.

Shum hustled up beside Ty. "Sita always goes her way," he said, trying to be reassuring.

"But she saw what happened last night. We almost died. Sita doesn't even carry a knife!"

"Maybe she went to *tunga*," Ko guffawed.

"Or she found some berries," Shum added, optimistically. "Berries make the eyes better."

The drums of guilt and fear pounded in Ty's mind. How could he have been so foolish to think that his vision of a journey would bring joy to anyone when that same journey risked the life of one of his *wings*? No one, least of all Sita's mother, would believe how adamant he was in rejecting her appeal to join him.

"Sita! Sita!" he called out again and again, thrashing away the wild vines. He had asked Man about his *wings'* survival. He had never thought of asking about an uninvited *kanta-wing*!

Less than twenty feet ahead, sunlight broke through the thick foliage. Sita's bent walking stick lay across the trail. Ty's heart stopped. "Sita." Her name caught in his throat.

He raced to the stick and held it in his hands. *She complained it was bent. Maybe she went to find a straighter stick.*

He whirled to the sound of broken twigs. Sita stepped from behind the trees. "Not funny," he lashed out. "Where did you go?"

"I saw smoke. I told you."

"I didn't see it! And I'll never talk to you again if you go off without telling me!"

Sita smiled from beneath her cowl. "You don't mean that."

She grabbed his hand, ignoring the hurt look in his eyes. Then she veered into the tall meadow grass. It spread like a rippling green lagoon at the base of a steep hillside.

The boys rushed forward. "I saw the smoke first!" Ko yelled, trying to reclaim his lost discovery.

As they approached the hills, the ground beneath their feet grew soft and marshy. High, razor-sharp grass scored their arms.

"Roll down your sleeves, Shummy," Ko grumbled in a kind of paternalistic, irritated way.

The *wings* labored under the mounting heat of the sun and the sheer exertion of keeping their balance on the spongy terrain.

"Now I know why Star and the other hunters didn't go any farther than the river fork." Ty gasped, wiping sweat from his forehead. "This ground is too difficult to run if you're chasing a really fast animal."

Ko cried out, "I feel sick!"

"I feel the same!" Shum stopped to catch his breath. His gimpy smile had turned to grimacing pain.

Ty turned to Sita with a frightened look. "I feel dizzy." He grabbed the sides of his head with his hands. "My head feels like it's floating away from me!"

Sita looked over to the *wings*, bent, staggering, retching up a dark reddish bile.

It's the emmydactyl blood, she thought. *I'm the only one who didn't lick the beast's blood.*

"We're going to die," Ty whispered. His lips were swollen. His eyes burned. His face was turning green.

"Don't say that! Never say that!" Sita pulled back the flap of her cloak, revealing the three small, beaded pouches tied to her waistband. "Trust me," she said. "Sita will return."

She pushed through the tall grass. "Ko!" she cried out. "Shum!" Her eyes darted to a thrashing racket of broken stalks. Ko was reeling from side to side, flinging his arms, trying to mutter something. Instead of words, bile spilled from his lips. Sita commanded his attention and loosened the leather water pouch strapped to his waist. "I'll come back," she promised. *If my booties don't fall apart,* she thought.

Using her long cloak as a shield, she hurried through the razor-sharp thicket of blades. Ty was crawling on his hands and knees when she reached him. He was scratching the earth like an animal. Sita removed one of her beaded pouches and poured a mustard-yellow powder into the water. "Drink this, Ty." She dropped to her knees and held the water pouch to his swollen lips. The boy's glassy eyes stared back at her. "Drink," she repeated, tilting his head back with her free hand. "I am Sita, the shaman-in-waiting, and I love you." She heard the gurgle in his throat as the yellow liquid passed several times through his lips. "Good *wing*," she whispered. "I must find Ko and Shum. I promised."

Sita rushed back to the patch of trampled grass. Ko and Shum were shaking uncontrollably, reaching out, trying to steady each other. She dodged between them and thrust the neck of the water pouch into Ko's mouth. "Drink," she commanded. She yanked his head back by a lank of his tangled hair. "I am trying to help you! Don't fight me!" Sita watched him swallow several mouthfuls before she pulled the pouch from his lips. "Enough!" She immediately turned to Shum, who was clutching his mighty spear like a pole to keep from falling. "You must drink this," she instructed. Tears were running down his cheeks, but he wouldn't release his two-fisted grip on the spear. Raising the pouch to his trembling lips, Sita pleaded with him to open his mouth and let the water heal him. He took halting swallows. Then he removed his grip on the spear, let it fall, and held the pouch steady to his lips.

Ko, blinking and bouncing on his toes, had already stopped shaking. Sita watched the two *wings* drift aimlessly in a widening spiral, losing sight of one figure or another in the tall, spiky reeds.

Slowly, their bodies straightened. Ko stretched out his muscled arms and inhaled deep gulps of air. Shum raised his knees, kicked aside the stalks that encumbered him, and waved his spear triumphantly.

"The *wings* are back!" he howled.

"I'll go back to get Ty," she said. She turned and stopped before her second step. Ty was standing, perfectly still, a few feet behind her. His dark, handsome face had regained its color. His blue eyes flared again with alertness and light.

He didn't say anything, not even "thank you" or "good Sita." He turned to the *wings*, still rejoicing in their resurgent health. "We go!" he shouted.

He reached for Sita's hand and drew her close to him. The gesture said everything to her. She didn't need his gratitude. She understood this was his way, his silent acceptance of her shamanic powers. With quiet dignity, they started up the rugged hillside.

"I saw my mother's face, Shummy." Ko held up the narrow gap between his thumb and forefinger. "I was this close to death."

"Your mother's still alive."

Ko smacked his fists against his sides. "I was saying good-bye, stupid!"

* * *

The marshy grass gave way to the scent of the yellow flowers. *Was our sickness a punishment*, Ty wondered, *for traveling beyond the world we know?* He still felt lightheaded, just as he had moments before he left the cave of Man Who Stands Alone. With each step he took, colors melded together and swirled around him. The flowers burst into a universe of brilliant suns and golden shells. He gripped Sita's hand tighter. When he looked back at Ko and Shum, he saw their smiles waver like ever-increasing ripples in a pond. Their outstretched arms, as long as honey-gold fronds, reached toward him. The *wings'* eyes, glassy fixtures of light, floated in blue circles. The hill was growing steeper, the air thinner.

"What did we drink?" Ty's voice was hoarse with a creeping fear.

"You drank the woo-woo potion," Sita answered. "You drank the future."

"Future? What future?"

"When time falls over the stars, jumps over the sun."

He stumbled forward. He tried to grab her arm. "Where are you?" he cried out. "Don't leave me!"

"I am next to you."

He tried to focus on Sita, struggling to make distinct the slurred words from his lips. "Then you are bringing us here."

"Your vision-quest is bringing you here."

The sky was cloudless, blue, like the blue surrounding the eyes of the *wings*. Ty couldn't find the horizon. He felt as if a sheet of smoky wind was whirling through his brain. The earth cracked. Thunder roared through the soles of his boots. He clutched his stomach and held his breath. The wind inside his brain grew stronger, longer, swirling into a luminous ball, as if a thousand ghosts had exploded and all their filmy parts had gathered in his head.

He knew he was holding Sita's hand, but he couldn't feel her fingers. "I feel like everything is going away. My cave, my cliffs, my River Gan are leaving me."

"You're in the shot!" a voice bellowed through the wind. "Get out of the way!"

Ty and Sita froze. It was a voice! Ty recognized it was a human voice, but he had no idea what the sounds meant.

The *wings* clambered up behind them, breathless, filled with confusion and fear.

"The smoke people," Sita whispered.

The voice returned still louder as the wind died down. "Please move! This is a closed set! We're filming now!"

Ty shot a look to Sita. *"Who's that?"*

Her brows furrowed, but her voice, in Kishoki, was clear. *"Part of the future."*

CHAPTER 10

Ty looked toward the mountain, shouting in Kishoki, *"Who's that?!"*

"Who's that?" the *wings* echoed, just as spooked as Ty.

"We're shooting a commercial, kids. You're on private property!" A short, chubby man was trudging down the hillside. He wore something on his head hiding his hair, and it had what looked to Sita like a beak on the front shading his eyes. His baggy clothes were just as strange as his speech.

"I think they want us to go," Sita whispered. "I think—" She stopped in mid-sentence. "I think...I'm talking different." She blinked and looked over to the stranger coming toward them. *"I'm talking like I hear in my dreams,"* she exclaimed in Kishoki, *"when I star-step!"*

"It's over, kids. The joke's over." The chubby man waved a burnt stick. "Get your butts out of here or we're calling the cops."

The *wings* froze. No one understood what the man with white skin was barking, but some words registered in Sita's brain.

"I think he wants us to move," she said.

The man tapped the stick against his palm. Sita watched a thin stream of white smoke curl into the wind. The red stick was unlike any branch she'd ever seen.

"I don't know what kind of game you're playing, but you can't play it here. *Capiche?*" The man's eyes settled on Sita. She watched him raise a small, black-shaped rock, a *chikup*, the

47

Kishoki word for box, to his upturned lips. "Read me, Darren. We've got teenage boys, three of 'em, and one girl. They're all dressed up in leather with furry sleeping bags on their backs. Probably playing some kind of Dungeons and Dragons war riff. Knives, spears, that kind of crap. One kid's got dyed orangey hair."

"I can see them, Scottie!" A voice crackled through the black *chikup*, startling Sita.

The man shot a look toward the ridge. The *wings* followed his gaze.

Sita saw a tall, light-skinned man standing on top of a giant yellow rock of some kind. He waved his arm. He, too, had a black *chikup* in his hand.

"What do you want me to do, Darren?"

"Bring them up here," the same voice rattled back. "And we'll feed 'em. That'll keep them from butting in any shots."

"Roger."

"I'm always two steps ahead." Darren radioed out.

Sita and the boys watched the tall figure disappear.

"Two steps ahead," the short man snorted. "With his old man's dough, any one of us could jump two steps ahead." He looked over to the kids. "He's the boss."

"Boss?" Sita piped up.

"The director. You know, chief, *jefe*. He calls the shots."

Sita turned to the *wings*. "*He's the chief.*" She pointed uphill.

"Follow me. My name's Scottie. This is your lucky day."

"Scottie," Sita repeated, smiling. "Sita, Scottie. First sound is same." She mouthed the words silently again. Sita was beginning to pick up on the language. "Lucky day," she said, shooting a wink to Ty.

Scottie started up the hill. After a few steps, he looked back. Nobody had moved.

"Let's go! Jesus, you're getting free food."

Ko and Shum looked to their leader. Ty shot a glance to Sita.

"*Go*," she said in Kishoki. "*Scottie say to go.*"

They marched up the hill. Ahead they could see two long, high things with round black stones under them. The high yellow thing looked pretty much like the thing the man was standing on near the ridge. The smaller green thing was sitting under a tree. The *wings* could see holes in them, like big eyes, along the front, the back, and the sides. The holes were covered with something clear, allowing Sita and Ty to glimpse the empty insides. Sunlight flared off red crystals on each of their sides.

"*Where are we going?*" Ty glanced nervously at Sita.

She shrugged her shoulders with an uncertain look.

Scottie stopped at the smaller green thing. "This is the director's Jeep," he said.

"Jeep," Sita repeated. The language of her dreams came back again.

He opened the back end of the Jeep and lifted the covers off two large, flat *chikups*. "You can eat the food in these boxes."

"Boxes." Sita smiled. "*Chikups* are boxes."

"Whatever." Scottie shook his head. "We've got donuts, bagels, cream cheese, some slices of turkey, roast beef, and cheese." Scottie peeled off a slice of cheese and popped it in his mouth.

Ko nudged Shum. "*He's got yellow teeth.*"

Scottie froze Ko with a stern look. "None of that Pig Latin. And keep off the sushi. It's been sitting out since noon."

The boys crowded closer to the tailgate and stared at the shapes and colors of things the man was eating. They had just climbed a steep hill. Moments before that, they had retched up the food in their stomachs. They were starving.

Ko reached for a frosted donut. Ty's hand stopped him. "*Maybe poison.*"

"Go ahead, eat." Scottie jammed another cheese slice in his mouth and pointed down a dusty road. "Stay away from the set. *Capiche?* The director said I should feed you. No charge." He rubbed his thumb against his index finger. "No greenbacks. Get it?" The *wings* stared back with puzzled faces. Scottie swallowed the mouthful of cheese. "You guys could use some weight, except for—" He jerked his head toward Ko. "Mr. Munchies. Where you kids from?"

Sita hesitated, but she was eager to try this new language that jumped from her tongue. "We from caves."

"Caves?" Scottie raised his brows. "Like Magic Mountain? You doing a show there? Music?" He awkwardly wiggled his hips.

Sita had no idea what he was talking about or where the Magic Mountain was. "Where we?"

"Where we?" Scottie repeated. "Don't that take a verb? I pay taxes so you guys can learn something." Sita watched him squint his small brown eyes. "Are you guys on drugs?" Four faces stared back in silence. "Come on, I got nephews. I know the games. This ain't a holiday. You guys should be in school."

"*Where are we? Who are you?*" Ty blurted.

Scottie frowned again. "I don't take foul language lightly or any smart-ass code words. You should be grateful I don't have the cops up here hauling your butts away." He narrowed his eyes toward Shum, standing with his spear. "It ain't a gladiator flick, so don't get no ideas you're gonna be in it. The only one Darren sticks in these puppies besides his old man is his girlfriend, Dorsey." Scottie spit to the side. "And she can't act, except like an out-of-control blonde prima donna."

Sita got the words *Darren*, *old man*, and *girlfriend*, but she wasn't sure how they fit together.

Then, the tall, light-skinned man came up from around the yellow high thing. He struck the back of it, drawing everyone's look. "This is no way to break into the movies. Go YouTube. Hit the Web."

Sita looked up to the towering voice. Darren was the tallest person she or any of the *wings* had ever seen. His skin was even whiter than the short man who had offered them food, even whiter than the shaman's beard or the ceremonial ash that sometimes chalked the elders' faces.

"How old are you?" The tall man wore a red cloth knotted around his neck and a smile that seemed friendly to Sita, but not especially happy. His black hair lopped over his forehead. The *wings* could barely see his eyes behind a pair of dark flat crystals that flared with sunlight, like light off the river, every time he turned his head.

No one spoke. Not even in her *star-stepping* had Sita ever seen these dark crystals cover the eyes.

"I'm not asking you when you were born or who you ratted on Myspace."

Ty nudged Sita, who was staring at Darren. She was trying to understand the words flying out of the stranger's mouth.

"Did you see the public service commercial where the guy swings a bat at a lamp and almost hits his pop? Anger management. I directed that." Darren folded his arms, waiting for a reaction. He looked over to Scottie, who had just shoved a sesame bagel in his mouth. "Go see if the setup is ready."

He adjusted the knot in the red cloth on his neck. "We're shooting a carpet commercial. But remember the name, Darren Michael Davies. Someday you're gonna say, 'I remember when that man gave us free food in Topanga.'" Darren winked and checked a silver bracelet on his wrist. "Eat, I gotta run. Two more setups and we're history."

Sita watched the tall man follow Scottie up the dirt road. She glanced at the food. "He wants us to eat." She was getting used to her new way of speaking, but Ty's blank look abruptly stopped her. "*Sorry.*" She repeated in Kishoki: "*He wants us to eat.*"

Ko didn't hesitate. Ty's warning that the food might be poison flew from his mind as he hungrily took a bite out of a coconut sprinkled donut. "*Good, Shummy,*" he growled. "*Maybe I eat two. Better than a ram tongue.*" Flakes of coconut stuck to his sly smile.

Only Ty stood aside. He gave Sita another worried look. *"What happens to us?"*

"I don't know. We are far away. Far from the River Gan."

Ty glanced back to his *wings*. Shum was stacking roast beef and cheese on a chocolate donut.

"Good far away?"

"I don't know that either. But I know when I sleep and star-step, sometimes I come to a world like this," Sita answered in Kishoki and thought a moment longer. *"Where is the golden shell?"*

"Here." Ty touched his chest. He took a wary step back. *"You don't give Man's shell to the white man."*

"You are one dumb wing!" She stamped her bootie foot. *"I will never give away Ty's shell. Never!"*

Slowly he drew the golden shell out from beneath his jerkin. She studied the etched symbols. *"Let me hold the shell."*

"No." Ty jumped back.

"Man Who Stands Alone showed me what the shell marks mean. We talk Kishoki. Here man has different talk. He doesn't understand Kishoki." She put out her hand and rubbed the shell. *"Put your hand on the shell."*

Sita could see the hesitation and fear in Ty's eyes.

"We might never get back to the River Gan if you don't!"

As he was instructed, Ty covered the shell with his hand. *"Now you talk,"* she said. *"You talk,"* she insisted. *"Shell says, talk."*

"Time is in shell; no words are locked in shell!"

"Words are in time! Time is made up of words! Put your hand back on the shell," she repeated. *"Close your eyes and say what Sita says. Say, I am Ty, I am here, I am Sita's wing."*

"I am Ty, I am here, I am Sita's wing."

She placed her hand over his. *"Say it again."*

"I am Ty… I am here." He paused, frightened by the sound of words rising to his lips. *"I am Sita's wing."* His voice dropped, words blurted out, his eyes flew open.

"Do you understand what you just said? You're talking white talk. Now the *wings* must touch the shell. We are going to all talk white talk." She clapped her hands. A rainbow smile burst across her lips. "We are in the future world!"

"But who is this white man? Why are we here?" Ty looked over to Ko, who was licking the frosting off two sprinkle donuts stacked on his index finger. "How will we ever get back to the River Gan?"

CHAPTER 11

W heeling the Jeep Cherokee down the mountain, Darren slipped a CD into the dash player. "I'll drop you off in Santa Monica or West LA. La Cienega is as far east as I'm gonna haul you guys." He looked over to Sita, sitting in the front passenger seat. "I'm twenty-four years old. You guys better straighten up your act before it gets too late. I've already got a car, a house, a job."

Darren gave a quick glance to Ty and Ko in the rear seat. Shum was squeezed between them. Their eyes were shut, their hands clamped over their ears.

"Hey, dudes, I'm not the world's biggest Cold Play fan either, but give the guys a break. Uncover your ears and let the music in. The whole world ain't just rap." He turned down the volume on the CD.

"Everything fast," Sita said. "Everything new."

"I get it. They're a little carsick. Didn't Scottie tell you not to eat the sushi?" Darren flipped down the visor and cornered a sharp curve. "Wait'll your parents find out you got a ride with the guy who directs the Karpet World commercials. Just remember to tell them, I can't give them a discount. No discounts but all the rugs are on sale."

Sita shook her head: *He has no idea who we are.*

The *wings* were heading down a steep mountain road in a moving *chikup*, at a speed they'd never experienced, listening to a kind of music they'd never heard, all this managed by a man whose height, color, clothes, and language were as strange and startling to them as if a emmydactyl had dressed itself up like Man Who Stands Alone and sang Kishoki songs around a fire pit.

"This scary." Sita clutched her folded hands. Only she seemed to have grasped some glimmering of the world they had entered. She looked at Darren as if she were studying the veins in a leaf. A stubble of beard grazed his jaw, sloping to a soft chin. Sita had seen this kind of shadowy beard among *wings* one or two winters older than Ty. Even Ko was beginning to show hair on his face, but she had never seen the bare chin of an elder, all of whom, like her father, had shaggy beards. The gold-rimmed crystals across Darren's eyes made her wonder what he was hiding. They rested on a furrow just below his black brows, which came quickly together in a nervous twitch.

"What are you looking at? This?" Darren pointed to a reddish blotch along his chin. "It's eczema. I break out every once in a while. Nerves. Comes and goes. I hate when it happens on my face. Everybody and their mother either gives me a weird look or advice on how I can get rid of it. Stay away from sulfites and French fries."

He caught her blank stare. "You know, Sita, like acne. I had that too when I was jumping the high school hoops." Darren looked back to the traffic and jerked his neck. "Shooting film is no cool breeze, especially when it's for your old man. I'm seeing a shrink about it now. You ever have acne?"

He talks and twitches a lot, Sita thought. *Is this the way all white people are?*

"Acne? Pimples? You must have had one pimple in your life."

"Pimple," she repeated. "Pimple good?"

"Don't be nutty." Her answer made him smile. "Look, if you want to hang at my crib for a couple of hours, wash up, call your parents or email them, that's cool. But don't get it in your head that I'm the Holiday Inn, although my dad might be carpeting all their West Coast locations next fall. More commercials for me to shoot."

Ty nudged Sita's shoulder. "What's he saying?"

She peeked her face between the front seats. "Good English, cave boy. He's talking about pimples and shrinks, and he doesn't stop talking. Something is wrong with him." She looked back to Darren, still rambling on.

"In a few days I've got to show this carpet commercial to my father. That makes me nervous. You know, getting the old man's approval." He glanced up to the rearview mirror. "Do you dudes ever have a problem getting your old man's approval?"

Silence.

He tried again. "Have you ever been in a commercial?"

"What's a commercial?"

Darren gave Sita a sharp look. "Don't play dumb. My dad would flip if you were in one of his sixty-second spots. Think of it: 'Karpet World Meets the Original Rug Rats!' Do you guys sing?"

Sita answered with a gasp. Darren had just taken a tight mountain curve at fifteen miles above the posted speed, but it was less the speed than the view in front of her that made Sita shout, "Ty! Ty!"

Ty opened his eyes and craned his neck in the direction Sita was pointing. "Look!" she shouted.

"Big river!" Ty exclaimed.

"Big river," Ko and Shum mumbled, sputtering their new language as if they were coughing up hairballs.

Ahead of them, gleaming in the last rays of sunlight, was the Pacific Ocean, the biggest, widest spread of water the *wings* had ever seen.

"Big river! That's the Pacific!" Darren shouted back. "What's a mountain? Big hill? Ha! You guys are funny!" He smacked the steering wheel. "Funeee!"

"Funeee!" Sita repeated, clapping her hands.

She saw all kinds of "Jeeps," in different shapes and colors, behind them, in front of them, moving toward them. Two bright rays of light beamed from the front end of each Jeep.

"We are lost in starlight," Shum muttered.

Ko poked him. "We're swimming in light, Shummy. I feel like I'm in a shaman trance."

Sita glanced back again.

Ty sat stone-faced, managing one nervous question. "Where we going?"

"To a crib or maybe the Holiday Inn." She reached between the seats and took Ty's hand. "I'll tell you later. Breathe slowly. Take deep, slow breaths."

Sita was intrigued and thrilled by the miracles she saw. At the same time, a sense of caution and a protectiveness of her *wings* kept her from fully embracing the fantasy that was rushing at different speeds toward her. She had twinges of doubt about the power of her potions. It was only the night before the start of the journey that she had hurriedly mixed the shaman's powders, hoping that the combination of ground seeds and leaves and the measurements she'd used were correct. *There was so little light. I could hardly see.*

"Holy One Hand," she murmured. "I hope I did this right!"

She was certain that she, Ty, Ko, and Shum had landed in some dimension of the future. But Man Who Stands Alone had taught her that there were many futures. All of them were a part of her. *Which future is this?* she wondered.

"Is he taking us back to the River Gan?" Ty whispered.

"Maybe later. Just breathe."

She looked out the window, on her right. "What's this called?"

"The Pacific Ocean, Sita." Darren shook his head. "I just told you that."

"Pacific Ocean," she repeated softly. It rang no bell in her mind. "Darren, do you have *wings* like us?"

"Wings? Bird wings? Don't tell me you fly. Don't get weird, Sita."

"*Wings* are like..." She tilted her head, searching for the words. "Like when your mama and papa have a baby. That's it. Boy is *wing*. Girl, like me, is *kanta-wing*."

He let out a sharp laugh. "No way. I'm not ready for that. I've got a shrink, Dr. Greenberg. He says I should definitely wait before I have kids."

"Who's Dr. Greenberg?" Ty piped up.

"A shrink." Sita glanced back. "I'll find out what's a shrink, later. Keep breathing."

* * *

Traffic slowed to a crawl. Darren didn't want to insult the kids any more than he already had, but he was getting impatient with their lame questions and ridiculous shout-outs. He drummed his fingers against the steering wheel hub.

"Didn't this cave life you insist on describing have any kind of school?"

"School?"

"Learning. High school, middle school. What grade are you in?"

"No school," Sita answered, watching the golden headlights passing them.

"Don't tell me: homeschooled in the cave. Cave schooled!" He slapped the steering wheel and chuckled at his corny joke.

"Cave schooled is good," she shot back, not having a clue as to what she was defending.

"Relax, Sita. I wasn't laughing at you." Darren flipped open his cell phone and speed-dialed a number with his free hand. "Honey, pick up if you be there. Dorsey? I know the other night was just a little misconnection. No hurt feelings. It's a wrap on the shoot. We won't need you tomorrow. Besides, my pop's never liked the Godzilla idea." He glanced over to Sita, who was staring back, but he kept talking. "I might have company tonight, so we're iffy. But you're welcome to join if these guys can't get someone to pick them up. I think they're some kind of explorer's club or teenage rappers. Shout me back." He clicked off, slipped the cell into his vest pocket, and followed the bumper-to-bumper traffic through the tunnel and up the Ronald Reagan Freeway.

"You talk to someone not here?"

"My honey. But don't tell me you've never seen a cell phone. You're pushing it, Sita."

"Cell phone, cell phone, cell phone," she repeated softly. "I dreamed of a cell phone."

"What teenager hasn't?" Darren cracked, totally missing her meaning. "Okay, I admit it, Dorsey and I have had some bumps in the road. I'm talking it over with Greenberg."

"Who's Greenberg?"

"I told you, my shrink."

"What's that?"

"What's what?" Darren's voice was starting to tense up. He smacked the steering wheel. "That's it! You're really getting on my nerves now. You can't just goof on people. As soon as you step into my house, you're calling your parents. In fact," he fished his cell phone from his pocket, "you can call them right now. Take the phone."

"I don't want it."

"But you want to get home, don't you?"

"Yes."

Darren heaved a big sigh, getting more frustrated. "Well, don't count on a magic carpet, just because my father is the Karpet King!"

"You're getting *fassi*, Darren."

"What's *fassi*?"

"Upset."

"I'm not upset. Don't tell me I'm upset when I'm not upset and you haven't even known me for more than ten minutes in a Jeep!" He pushed up his sunglasses. "And don't talk crazy words. Scottie said you guys were talking in code." He looked over to Sita. "I'm being very patient, considering I'm talking to some runaway chick, or whatever you are, who claims she lives in a cave and doesn't even know the name of the ocean." He wagged his hand. "Okay, I'm sorry I called you a chick. I know that's not cool. You're a teenager and I'm a stranger and your mom probably told you not to take rides from strangers." He jerked his head. "Now I'm apologizing to someone I don't know and I'm giving a ride and breaking a date with my girl-friend! What's that about?" He threw open his hands as the Jeep stalled in traffic. "Don't you see just how weird this is?"

"Weird?"

"Do I look like a dictionary?"

"Everything is good, Darren."

"Right." He glanced into the rearview mirror. "Are you guys okay back there?"

"Okay, okay." Voices from the rear echoed back his own word. Shum was wagging his head like a broken train signal.

Sita peeked through the seats again. "Tell Darren we're cave schooled."

"What's that?" Ty asked.

"I don't know. Just say it." She shot a look to Ko and Shum. "You too."

Their staggered voices filled the Jeep. "Cave schooled!"

Darren wasn't listening. He was thinking about how soon his editor, Marc, could put together the commercial when his cell chimed. He glanced at the phone number. "Yo... Went great. I'm in the Jeep, on my way back. We'll talk later, huh? ... Okay, good-bye." He slipped the phone back in his pocket. "That was my father." Darren sounded annoyed and relieved at the same time.

"Does your mother call you too?"

"My mother died when I was fifteen."

"Many winters ago."

"Yes, if you like counting in winters." Darren seemed anxious to change the subject. "Maybe we'll have pizza tonight if your parents don't pick you up, which, whether you like it or not, I'm going to make sure they do." Traffic was moving again. He gave a shout toward the back. "Do you guys like pizza?"

He thought he heard a grunt. He looked over to Sita. "Do they like salad?"

"Salad?"

"Damn it, Sita, do I have to explain everything? You can't tell me you don't have salad in the cave. It's at the top of the food pyramid." He edged the Jeep to the far right lane.

"What's he saying?" Ty asked, banging on the back of her seat. His breath-relaxing exercise was fading fast.

Sita whispered between the seats. "He's talking about pizza and salad."

"What's pizza salad?" Ko growled. "Like the donut?"

Darren swung onto the Overland Avenue off-ramp. He was thinking more about hanging out with the kids and involving them in one of his dad's commercials. In high school, his mom's secret drinking and her erratic behavior had kept him from inviting over the few friends he did have. He had his own house now. He felt comfortable bringing these kids back to his pad.

"I just want your parents to pick you up before ten," he said.

He drove down Overland Avenue, thinking about the current craze for teenage-driven movies. "Have any of you guys ever acted? Videos, cave-school plays," he laughed, "stuff like that?"

"Acted?" Sita answered with a question, but something the shaman had said about acting out rituals and ceremonies stuck in her brain. "We act," she said.

"Damn, I knew it!" A victory smile rose on Darren's lips. *Caveland Comes to Compton!*" he shouted. "What kind of instruments do you guys play?"

The question disappeared in silence wrapped in a series of turns. "My crib's on the next block."

Lights glowed in the residential windows of neatly gardened one-story re-do's and Spanish-style duplexes.

"Houses," Sita said. "I dream of houses before." She turned to the boys in back. "These are houses."

Darren turned in to an alley and pressed a button on his remote device. A white and brown-trimmed garage door rose with no hands touching it.

The eyes behind him stared in awe. Even Sita rushed a hand to her lips. "It's a magic cave," she gasped.

Darren pulled into the garage. "Everyone out, this is it." He climbed out of the Jeep and opened the rear cargo gate. "Grab your sleeping bags." He caught Ty's apprehensive look.

"We go now?"

"We go," Sita answered, with a reassuring glance.

Darren watched the boys sling their sleeping bags over their backs. He couldn't get the idea of a video out of his mind. *Wow, maybe I caught a break on a mountaintop. This could change the direction of my life... Or maybe theirs too.*

CHAPTER 12

They walked through a large garden area, past a glass patio table surrounded by woven chairs, to the rear of the house.

"Darren's crib!" Shum shouted.

Ko hugged the food *chikup* to his chest. He nudged Shum with a sly smile. "We keep the donuts, Shummy."

The sky glowed with a soft purple twilight. Ty looked up at the rising moon, full and milky white, just like the moon his father had pointed to with the burning stick.

"It's the same moon," he whispered to Sita.

Darren opened a white door, taller than the Jeep. He raised his arm to the wall. Suddenly light filled the room.

"This is the kitchen." Darren smiled broadly. "*Mi casa es su casa.*"

The boys stared at the "moonlight" streaming from glowing things above their heads.

"Moon in the crib," Shum shouted.

"Moon in the Crib!" Darren punched the air. "Great movie title. Come on, check out the rest of the *casa*. You guys are on it!"

Ty, Sita, and the *wings* tagged behind him. "Dining room," he announced in the semi-darkness. "We'll eat in here." Then he called out, "Living room!"

He touched something on a tall, thin pole. Again, with the same suddenness, light filled the room. The *wings'* eyes widened even more when they saw all the animal hides stretched across wood and shiny silver sticks. Their fathers had built *lopsies*, low chairs woven from branches and tied with leather bands to sit on around the fire pit, but these *lopsies* were high off the ground, and one was very long.

Ty smoothed his hand across the back of the long brown hide. "Animal skin. Very nice, soft." He looked down at the table. He could see the short gray fur he was standing on through the crystal top.

"Check out the carpet," Darren said. "You're looking at Berber and it's stainproof, but try not to muck it up. My dad put it in when he bought the house."

"Carpet," Ty repeated, staring at his boots from above the crystal table.

"Can we sit?" Shum asked, in perfect English.

"Go ahead."

Shum and Ko darted for the smaller *lopsie* that spun and rolled under their weight.

"I guess you guys like swivel chairs," Darren observed.

The boys sat together, nodding, twirling, and giggling.

Darren pointed to the wide flat-screen TV to the left of the fake fireplace.

"LCD or plasma? You tell me."

The eyes of the *wings* shifted to a dark smoky gray crystal.

"Window," Sita said.

"Window to the world." Darren laughed. "You got that right. Take a guess. That plasma TV cost me close to a paycheck." He pointed to the fireplace. "Fake or real?"

None of the *wings* understood what he was getting at, but the cement logs looked real enough to them.

"Fire," Ty said, decisively.

"Fake, dude. Bzzzz...you lose." Darren looked over to the four chrome-framed movie posters that decorated the living room walls: *The Godfather, Star Wars, Indiana Jones* and *Pulp Fiction.* He started to ask Ty which movie star was featured on each poster, hoping to catch the kids in their elaborate prank, but Sita jumped in first.

"Is every casa like this?"

"No, Sita. There're all kinds of house sizes, from Beverly Hills to Hollywood. Of course, I'm not an expert on caves," he added with a smirk. "Do any of you want to call your parents now?"

The cozy room fell silent.

"I take that as a 'no.' Well, okay, just hang out and watch TV, but trust me, you're going to call them after dinner. Ten the latest." He looked over to Shum and Ko. Shum was still clutching his spear in his right hand. "Put the spear to sleep, and I'll heat up the pizzas and make the salad."

Ty quickly took a seat on the leather couch and tapped on the clear crystal table.

"Fragile," Darren warned. "Glass. Be *muy* careful." Darren looked over to Sita. "Let's do the salad." He grabbed the TV remote off the fireplace mantel and clicked the "on" button. "You boys can check out the shows," he said, flipping the remote to Ty.

Darren motioned Sita to follow him, but her eyes along with everyone else's in the room were fixed on the crystal hanging on the wall that Darren called TV. A man was talking and suddenly soldiers were firing weapons. Huge *chikups* were rolling through streets filled with smoke and rubble.

The boys gasped. Their mouths dropped open again.

"Sita," Darren repeated.

She walked backward from the room, her eyes still riveted on the fiery images. The last thing she heard was Ty's voice: "Smoke, Ko. Smoke people inside!"

* * *

Darren rummaged through the freezer with a rubber glove on his hand. He removed four boxes of frozen pizzas.

"Smoke people? What's he been smokin'? That's real war, Sita. Those insurgents are messin' up their own country."

"Darren."

"I've got four." He held up one of the pizza boxes. "They're small but we'll cut 'em up and that should do it, along with the salad."

"Darren!" Sita's voice rose nervously.

His twitchy eyebrows shot up. "Four isn't enough?"

"Four is good." Sita paused. "You don't know who we are."

"Who are you?" He dropped the pizza box. "This isn't some kind of murderous cult, is it?" Suddenly, the rosy notion of teenage actors crashing at his pad dissembled into a cloud of real terror. "Some kind of teenage Freddy Krueger clan?" He moved toward the white phone on the counter. His voice spiked hysterically. "Should I be calling the cops?"

"I don't know cops." She shook her head.

"Sita!" Ty, alerted by Darren's half-crazed voice, burst into the kitchen, his bone knife drawn. His eyes, anxious and threatening, shifted between Sita and Darren.

Sita raised her hand. "It's good," she said. "Go back, watch the smoke people."

Ty cast a chilling gaze at the tall white man with a blue rubber glove on one hand and a pizza cutter in the other. "Sita is my friend. You don't touch her."

"Hey, dude, I'm just talking pizza with her," Darren answered, nervously picking up the Trader Joe's box. "Just pizza. Tell him, Sita."

"It's food, Ty," Sita explained. "Frozen. Like big ice sticks in winter."

"Well, we're not going to eat them frozen," Darren jumped in, seizing an opportunity to lighten the mood. "We'll heat them up first."

Sita gave Ty a reassuring look. "Tell Ko and Shum the smoke people are insurgents. They're messin' up the country."

Ty shifted his eyes back to Darren. "No *hoison.*"

"No *hoison*, never," Sita said.

"No *hoison*," Darren added, dropping the pizza cutter.

Ty backed up a few steps "Ty! Ty!" He could hear Shum's voice beckoning him back to the TV. "More boom and sky fire!"

"Go." Sita spoke softly. She watched Ty leave the kitchen. "Ty is my *wing*, my friend." She turned to Darren and smiled, with a hint of apology in her voice. "He protects me. He—"

"What's *hoison*?"

"Kissing. He—"

Darren, more offended than amused, didn't let her finish. "Just to be clear, I'm more scared of you than you should be of me. I never ran around with a sleeping bag and a spear and a knife. That was a knife he threatened me with, Sita. Did he think—"

Sita pressed a finger to her lips. "Shhh. Man Who Stands Alone tells me words jump from my lips like a hand on a hot stone, but you've got your whole mouth on the stone, Darren. Now you just listen."

"Mouth on a hot stone?" Darren couldn't believe she was ripping him. "You haven't been in this house fifteen minutes. And who's Man on the Lone, anyway?"

"Man Who Stands Alone." She enunciated each word. "The Kishoki shaman."

"Oh, really. A shaman. And I'm Obi-Wan Kenobi."

"Listen!" She threw up her hands. "Everything is new here. Everything we see, we hear. I told you we live in caves. In a forest by the River Gan. Nothing we see or hear is like where you live. We call each other *wings*. A girl is a *kanta-wing.*"

Darren cleared his throat. "You mentioned something like that."

"Yes. One time I dreamed we are here. Now we are here."

"Something you saw on TV? News about LA?"

"No! We never see your TV before. There is no smoky crystal in caves. But words and things I see come back to me now."

Darren stared absently at the kitchen sink. "Cave people," he mumbled. "Sort of National Geographic stuff?"

"We are all cave people. Mother, father, *wings*. Ty, Shum, Ko, my family, we live in caves. We never go far or see more. That is our life."

"You've really never eaten TJ pizza?"

She shook her head.

He picked up the receiver from the cordless phone on the counter. "So you really can't call your parents. Is that what you're saying?"

"Yes." Her voice cracked above a whisper.

"Or email them?"

She shook her head. "What's email?"

"Sure, Sita." Darren smiled, dismissing her naiveté. "Like what's a hot dog?" He placed the receiver back on its stand. "You're the first teenager I've met who didn't do email or text." He fell back against the counter. "Am I hallucinating this? I haven't taken drugs since I started shooting commercials for my father. Honestly, I haven't."

Sita smiled. "I don't know what hallucrinsing means. We just are who we are, and we don't know who you are or why we're here."

"Not a clue?"

She shook her head, even though Ty's vision quest rattled through her mind. "No clue."

"How did you get here?"

Again, she stopped short of telling him how she believed her powders and the emmydactyl's blood had vaulted them into the future. "We just climbed the hill," she said, with a shrug. Then, with a look to calm his fears, she added, "I think you are a nice man."

"Thank you. You kids seem pretty good too. I think." A nervous laugh bubbled from his lips. "A little weird but…nice. We'll just see how dinner goes."

* * *

Sita washed the vegetables and Darren sliced them. He was beginning to feel an easier rapport with Sita, even though he had no reason to believe in the *wings'* strange tale. He slipped a Nora Jones CD into the player.

"A cast member turned me on to her," he said. "The music relaxes me."

She pointed to the CD player. "That's like the thing in your car."

"CD player," he said. "I guess that's one more thing the caves don't have."

"But we sing," she said, perking up. "And we have music. Drums, horns, and we tie shells to little hand drums and shake them to make sounds like the rain. Listen, I will hum for you." She hummed along to the tune from the CD. "My mother and I sing when we wash clothes and berries at the river."

"Oh, you live by a river. Well, that's a clue. What's the name of the river?"

"The River Gan. I told you. But you talk so much, you don't listen."

"Lighten up. You didn't remember some things I told you, either." Darren stared at her. *She's reprimanding me in my own house, in my kitchen. The little runt is giving me lip.* He slid a tray of small pizzas into the oven. "Hot, don't touch," he cautioned. "Oven." He broke the word into two distinct syllables.

"We make small ov-ens." Sita mimicked Darren. She made the shape of a tiny round hut with her hands. "With stones in the fire pit. We put food inside."

"That's great." His tone betrayed his lack of interest. He was still bummed over Sita reproaching him for his constant talking.

Loud voices from the living room grabbed his attention. "I'd better see what that's about."

He walked into a wrestling match. Ty and Ko were rolling across the couch, fighting over control of the TV remote. Ko wrested it from Ty, but when he flung his arm back, Shum grabbed it.

"Give me it!" Ko yelled, lunging at Shum, knocking the swivel chair into the standing lamp.

"Knock it off!" Darren yelled, just as the *Godfather* poster slipped sideways.

Ty shouted in Kishoki for everyone to calm down.

Darren glanced over to the TV. A PBS garden show with the smiling face of Jamie Durie and a basket of bright green zucchini filled the screen.

"Garwin is good," Ty gasped.

"I think you mean garden," Darren corrected him.

"Food comes from the garden." Ty repeated the mispronounced word slowly, pointing at the TV.

Darren flipped the remote to Ty. He wanted Ty to understand that there were no ill feelings between them and that he knew Ty was the leader. "You give each boy a chance." He walked over to the lopsided *Godfather* poster and straightened it. "How's that look?" He took a few steps back, admiring the poster. "We eat in five. And give Sita props for helping me." But, instead of returning to the kitchen, he disappeared into a hallway off the living room.

The boys folded their hands on their laps. Together, as if they had practiced the move a thousand times, they turned back to the garden show.

Still breathing hard from the battle, Ko snuffled up a heavy breath.

"I can't hear the man!" Ty cried. "Don't do that."

"He always does that."

"Shut up, Shummy! I don't always do that. My nose is full."

"It's always full."

"Only when I walk by some trees. Not every tree or bush. And I'm going to throw you out of the *casa* if you say that again."

"Maybe it's from this." Ty pointed the toe of his boot into the carpet. "We never have this in the caves."

"Never." Shum nodded. "It's Berber."

Ko slammed the arms of his chair. "Why does he say things like that? He doesn't know Berber from the shaman's beard!"

"Ko, settle down, or you're not getting your turn with the remote." Ty clicked the mute button. "We're going to make a garden."

"Garden?" Shum squinted his eyes in disbelief. "Where?"

"Where we live."

"When?"

"When we get back."

Ko leaned forward in his chair. "How are we going to get back? In the Jeep?"

Ty didn't have an answer. As much as he wanted to be the leader and willed himself to be it, he knew he was lost. He stared at the small black *chikup* in his hand. "That is the greatest question, isn't it?"

"We don't even know where we are," Shum chirped.

"Shummy's right. All we know is one tall white man in a *casa* with a magic crystal. This is a bigger problem than Sita." Ko narrowed his eyes and growled. "Bigger than the moon."

* * *

Sita wandered about the kitchen, waiting for Darren to return. She didn't mind being alone, as long as she knew Ty was in the room close by and she could hear voices from the smoky window, what the *wings* were starting to call the magic crystal. She caught her reflection in the curve of a shiny *chikup*, a silver box

Darren had told her was a toaster. Her face looked rounder. Her mouth waved like a vine when she smiled. *I'm in a different world.*

She touched shiny silver and white objects on what Darren had called a counter. She opened cabinets and drawers. No bird flew out from any door she opened. No lizard or bug scampered across a counter or the floor. Everything felt smooth, angular, and hard. Nothing rough, uneven, unexpected, or mystical like she felt in the caves, along the river, and in the summer forest. A dream, a song, a message could rise out of the mist that veiled the Kishoki cliffs. No dream, she thought, would creep out of the toaster.

Darren stared at her from the kitchen doorway.

"How old are you?"

She turned, not at all surprised by his voice. "I have fourteen summers."

"You look younger."

Sita shrugged with a smile.

"Do you have any idea when you were born?"

"In the cold season when the sun hid behind the moon." She beamed. "It's very special."

"Cool." He held up his hand. "I got this from the closet." A pink summer dress hung at his fingertips. "It's gonna be big. Dorsey's pretty slim, but she's not fourteen. And she's kind of big where girls are big, if you know what I mean." He smiled and brought the dress forward. "I thought you might be getting warm in that cape. Try it on."

"Me? I wear it?"

"Why not?" He pointed to an alcove to the right of the back door. "There's a powder room past the washer, dryer." He raised his hands and drew a square figure in the air. "Big white squares. Squares." He pointed again toward the alcove. "Go ahead."

Darren watched her leave. He walked over to a phone and tapped out a number. "Sweetie, the kids I told you about are at my house. They are so into this cave thing. They've got it locked down.

They've got a language they made up, and they've even got me talking with my hands. They play dumb about everything. Everything," he repeated emphatically. "You've got to see this. They're either the best kid actors I've ever seen or they're on mind-bending drugs. I don't know who or what to believe. Catch you later." He banged the receiver down. "I'm stuck with zoned-out teenagers! Where the hell is my Dorsey?"

* * *

Sita raised her thin brown fingers and touched the face in the bathroom mirror. The glass reminded her of the brilliant glare off the river and sunlit ice that hung from the mouths of caves. She had seen her reflection before, but unlike the water, the surface of the mirror didn't ripple or wash her face away in a wave, nor was it twisted like the face in the toaster. The pink dress hung off her delicate shoulders. The waistline fell to her hips. It didn't matter. The look was feminine in a way she had never seen herself. The neckline scooped down, showing the small rise of her breasts.

"Oh, mama," she kept saying. "Oh, mama, is this what a lady shaman looks like?"

She rolled up the short sleeves and tucked the waistline under itself, pulling up the hem and showing off her calves. She loved the color against her dark skin. She made half turns to her left and right. She turned the silver knob on the sink, just as Darren had shown her when she was washing the vegetables. She brushed her face with the cold water and patted it dry with a blue towel. Then she ran her tongue across her upper lip, blinked, and again she smiled. *This is who I am.*

The dress felt warm and soft against her skin, so different from the leather she was used to. Her face glowed with a smile she had never seen before. She raised her hands above her head, twined her fingers in a prayerful clasp, and whispered: "I am Sita the shaman, and I have a feeling the reason we are here has something to do with Darren."

CHAPTER 13

The *wings* stared at a platter of pizza slices. They were gathered around the dining room table, standing behind the backs of heavy Spanish banquet chairs, part of old display furniture Darren's father had sent over from one of his carpet stores.

Darren put the last plate in front of Shum just as Sita walked in, carrying a wooden salad bowl. He saw the boys' eyes spring toward her. Sita had tied a purple sash around her waist, adding a bit of flare and hiding the double fold of Dorsey's pink dress.

"Where did your cape go?"

Darren noticed Ty's perplexed look, but before he could say anything, Sita cut him off.

"I changed in the powder room."

"Powder room?"

Anxious to get into the conversation, Darren jumped in. "It's a small bathroom next to the washer—"

Sita was quick to stop him. "I can tell him myself. The powder room is a little room with water and a big glass you look in and see yourself."

"Mirror." Darren snuck in the word with a triumphant fist-pump.

"Now I know what Sita looks like." Sita's dark eyes pitched with delight. "I see what you see when you look at me."

"You guys can use the room at night if you need to." Darren took the salad bowl—and the conversation—from Sita. "Don't get uptight about the dress. It's my girlfriend Dorsey's. All the girls wear them in America."

"America." Ty repeated the word softly. "Is that where we are?"

"Really, Ty." Darren shook his head. Actors or not, the parade of naïve questions was trying his patience. "America is a country. To the north of us is Canada. On the south is Mexico. We're in a state called California. In a city called Los Angeles." He rattled off the names, enjoying a mounting pleasure in showing off his schoolbook geography. Like icing on a cake was the knowledge that his father wasn't there to criticize his elementary recitation. "I'll Google you a map tomorrow." He sat down at the head of the table. "Let's eat."

"Google?" Ty raised a brow and grabbed the back of his chair.

No one moved. Darren's eyes shifted to Sita.

"Google what?" she said, in a hushed voice.

"A map. That's what I just said."

"In Kishoki, *google* means cut antelope neck."

"Kishoki?"

"That's what we speak."

"Oh, that's right. Sorry, but they didn't offer that at Bev Hills High." Darren couldn't help it. He was close to twice their age, but he was answering the *wings* like a snotty teenager. He was starting to feel like a foreigner in his own dining room. "I suppose everyone speaks Kokoki but me."

"Kishoki."

"Okay, Kishoki. Your made-up cave talk. I know some Spanish and that's a real language," he answered, acting even more juvenile. "Let's *comida*."

The boys took this as a cue to plunk themselves down in their chairs. Sita took a seat in the empty chair that Ty had saved for her.

Darren took a slice of pizza from the platter, dipped a pair of plastic tongs into the wooden bowl, and set a clump of salad, dripping with blue cheese dressing, on his plate.

He noticed Sita watching him, and then she did the same.

The salad greens reminded the boys of reeds and plants their mothers served. Ty and Ko picked up the leaves with their fingers.

Sita held up a fork. "Fork!"

Instantly, Shum and Ko grabbed their forks and raised them shoulder high. "Fork!" they chorused and stabbed at the salad. Ko smeared slices of cucumber in a pool of dressing and gulped down the forkful of slices.

They sniffed the pizza and tapped their fingers on the gooey cheese and red circles of pepperoni. Shum grinned. "Like little fish."

Darren smiled. At the same time, he felt slightly annoyed that the boys were putting him on. "It's nothing like fish, Shum."

Ko tore into a slice with his teeth. "Fish pizza good!" he declared, chomping on the huge bite.

"It's not fish. It's pepperoni! Pepperoni!" Darren stammered.

Like young wolves, the *wings* devoured slice after slice. They gulped the fizzy liquid that rushed to their lips from the cola cans. "River water with fire," Ty exclaimed.

Darren was already convinced that Ty was the leader of this crew, but Sita, hands down, had the chops to talk. And despite their petty squabbles, he sensed the strong, shared camaraderie of the *wings*. Gradually, their warmth made him forget his own petty irritations.

"I'll get more fire water." He chuckled and ran back and forth to and from the kitchen, refilling the water pitcher and resupplying the Cokes. He watched the *wings* slurp the sweet, fizzy liquid from the bright red cans.

Shum hiccupped. Ko belched. "Fire pit smoke." They all giggled.

"I can't believe you guys don't have a Coke machine. I'll bet if you walked five miles in any direction you'd find one."

Ty reached for another slice of pizza. "We drink from the river."

"Sure, river's good, but Coke's all over the world. Do you guys tag?" Darren searched the four blank faces. "I get it. You don't want to be shouting out something you can get busted for. It's just that it would come in really handy if we were making a rap movie."

Sita tapped two fingers on the tablecloth. Ty immediately picked up on the rhythm, with Ko and Shum flailing their fingers in unison.

"Rap." Darren grinned, bobbing his head. "That's it."

"This is the Kishoki thank you," Sita explained. "We beat our fingers against a stone or wood and chant *Omegu*—thank you. Thank you for the food, Darren."

Darren kept wagging his head, snapping his fingers, not quite able to keep up with the fast-paced rhythms. "Wow, you guys are good. I should have skipped piano lessons and gone to cave school." He laughed and jumped out of his chair. "How about dancing?" Tall as he was, jerking his bony hips, he looked ridiculous to the *wings*.

"*Mishugo*," Ko muttered.

Ty stopped tapping. Sita lowered her embarrassed gaze to the tablecloth.

"Okay, spike the dance idea." Darren pushed back the lop of his hair and glanced at his bare wrist. "Any of you guys see my watch?"

Silence.

"Look, it's no big deal if you took it. Just...like put it on the kitchen counter if you've got it. No harm, no foul. No repercussions." Their mute response triggered a mild wave of anxiety, a tingling in Darren's hands. Again, he brushed back the lop of his wavy black hair. "Okay, it's gotta be past eight o'clock. You guys can watch TV for an hour. Then you've got to take showers and hit the sack." He turned to Sita. "I think they should help clear the table first." She gave him a look he was beginning to recognize as a need for more clarification. "Help take the dishes, glasses to the kitchen."

Sita stood up with her plate and glass and pointed the boys toward the kitchen door. "Take the plates and glasses to the kitchen."

"That's the doorbell!" A trill of chimes sent Darren racing to the front door. "It's probably Dorsey. You'll love her!"

Ty quickly reached for Sita's arm. "Remember, we are together. You are my *kanta-wing*."

"You got it, big boy," she said, and turned her head to the announced arrival of the girl called Dorsey whose dress she was wearing.

The archway was empty.

Darren stood at the front door, surprised to see his production manager. Scottie handed him a stack of papers on a clipboard, designated for the film editor.

"You seem out of breath."

Darren shrugged. "I was just dancing." He could tell by Scottie's blank stare that his answer wasn't taken seriously.

"Oh, you left this in the van." The production manager held up Darren's missing Rolex.

"Wow, thanks. I was just looking for it." He slipped it on his wrist.

Scottie peeked in the doorway. "Those kids still with you?"

"Shh." Darren hushed his voice. "We just finished dinner."

"You said you were dancing."

"Right. After-dinner dance. It's a…" Darren cleared his throat. "A Kishoki custom. They're holding to the same story. They were born in caves and still live there."

"They're not sleeping over, are they?"

Darren didn't want to say "yes," but it wasn't in his nature to outright lie. "We're still trying to reach their parents."

"All I'm saying is, if they sleep over, lock your bedroom door and put a chair or the dresser in front of it."

"Good idea, Scottie."

"If they're still riffin' on caves in the morning, take 'em to a mall." Scottie winked. "You'll find out real quick how close those caves are to a credit card."

Darren held the bronze knob a moment longer after he closed the door. *What a cool idea. That'll be a quick giveaway.*

* * *

Ty stood in the kitchen doorway watching his *wings* scuttling like children from one magic thing to the next. Ko was opening and closing the freezer door, amazed at the cool air he was generating.

"Ko, look at this." Shum was parked at the stove, turning the burner knob, watching a blue flame pop on and off.

Lodged deep in Ty's psyche, in far less time than it took to whisper his name, Ty glimpsed a door to the distant future open and shut. The kitchen and the cave blurred into a whirl of tumbling images before his eyes. The kitchen was in the cave. The cave was in the kitchen. Raising his hand to steady himself, Ty felt the edge of timelessness on the white frame of the kitchen doorway.

He dropped his hand to the golden shell hanging from his neck. It was warmer than his skin or the surrounding air. *Time is in the shell*, he thought. *Man Who Stands Alone put time and words in the shell.*

"Someday we will be here," he announced.

Sita and the *wings* were too busy to hear what Ty had said, but he knew that, even though many winters might pass, more than all the stones scattered along the length of the River Gan, someday his spirit and those of his *wings* would live in a world like this.

"Someday this will be our home," he repeated.

Shum looked up and snapped his fingers. "I like this *casa*. Let's watch the magic crystal."

* * *

Moments later they were all back in the living room, sitting in front of the magic crystal.

"Kick it!" Ko yelled at the men charging up and down the field. "Kick it!"

The soccer game between Mexico and Brazil reminded the *wings* of the scraps of leather wound tightly into balls that they kicked in the clearing. The dark skin tones of the players were shades of their own complexion.

Darren was oblivious to the extraordinary leap in time these ragged teenagers had made, but he was happy they were peacefully engaged in watching the soccer game. He drew the drapes across the front window. "Time for showers, guys. We can catch the score of the game *mañana*."

* * *

"That's the mirror," Darren said, pointing to the sheet of glass above the double sinks. The master bathroom directly off his bedroom gleamed with salmon pink tiles and brown counters.

The *wings* didn't need an explanation. They were waving at their reflections, making faces and baring rows of ivory white teeth. The director heard Ty whisper into the mirror: "Wherever we are, I am still the leader."

Darren stared at the reflections of these three teenage kids, calling themselves *wings*, claiming they were from caves, with their own language, totally unfamiliar with TV, a cell phone, even pizza, as well as the mirror they were looking into. He felt a spike of guilt for thinking any one of them might have taken his watch. Some crazy part of him wanted to believe their story. Scottie's idea flamed through his head. "We're definitely going to the mall tomorrow," he announced. No one was listening.

"Wings! Wings!" He finally got their attention and gathered them around the walk-in shower. He took Ko's reluctant hand and placed it under the showerhead. "This won't hurt. The water is cold," he said, turning the faucet.

"Cold like the river. I swim in the river, Darren. I'm faster than any *wing*."

"That's great. Now, it's going to feel warm." Darren turned the faucet handle clockwise. "Warmer, warmer…"

Ko jerked his hand out from under the water. "Hot, hot!" He jumped up and down, knocking over the shower caddy, sending bottles of shampoo and hair conditioner skittering across the floor. "You tricked me!"

"It wasn't a trick. I'm showing you how to adjust the water temperature." Darren gathered up the bottles off the floor. He held up a bar of lavender soap. "This is for washing, and these," he said, pointing to a stack of bath-size white towels on the counter, "are to dry off."

He stood up, hovering over the boys like a pale, gawky bird. He cleared his throat and rapped his hand against the white ceramic toilet tank. "Pee pee," he said, pointing to the bowl.

"Tunga," Ko growled.

"Sure." Darren nodded, making an effort to appear like a homey. He waved his finger. "No pee pee, poo poo outside." He tore off a few sheets of toilet paper. "Use the poo-poo paper. Got it?"

He studied the dark, silent faces of the boys. *Am I falling into their trap*, he wondered, *explaining things any two-year-old in this world knows? Is that the little rascals' game? Goofing on a white guy.*

He shook off the thoughts. "Take your showers," he said. "I'll get your bed clothes."

* * *

Sita was striking various poses in front of the mirrored closet doors when Darren walked back into the bedroom.

"Don't fall in love with yourself. That's one of the things I'm working on with Dr. Greenberg. Be confident, assertive, but be open." He pumped his fists. "Greenberg's five steps to self-actualization."

Sita shook her head. "Who's Dr. Greenberg?"

"My shrink. I told you in the car. Don't you listen? He's helping me with my relationships with Dorsey and my dad. Short as a dynamite stick, but fires off the truth like a volcano." He slid back one of the closet doors, ruffled his hand across several hangers, and tossed a handful of T-shirts on the king-size bed. "You can wear one of these—" He stopped in mid-sentence. Yelling and screaming from behind the bathroom door drew another worried look. "Should I go?"

Sita smiled. "Kishoki boys like to rumble."

"Rumble! Where'd you get that word from?"

She shrugged. "It just came from the top of my head."

"Well, from the top of your head, tell me the truth: Are you guys from Compton? South Central, East LA? I mean, I'm not trying to stereotype you. You could be from Beverly Hills."

"I don't know any of those places." Sita shook her head. "Stop being a detective."

"Detective? Okay, that's it! You don't have detectives in caves!"

"Darren, the words just jump from my lips. I can't help it. I can't stop them. The more I'm here the more I hear them. I'm a shaman, not exactly but close."

She blinked and turned to the handful of T-shirts he'd tossed on the bed. "My mama knows lots of stories. We sit at the fire pit at night and she tells us beautiful, magical stories." She looked at Darren. "Does your mother tell you stories?"

"I told you, she died."

"But from where she is, she can still tell you stories…if you listen." She smiled and picked up a T-shirt with roses on the front. "But you must believe our story too. Do you think I should wear this one?"

Darren nodded *yes*, and left the bedroom. *What would my mom think?* he wondered. *She loved stories about witches, fairies, and magical worlds, but this is far-out unbelievable.*

* * *

Less than an hour later, the three wet-haired *wings* were standing in the living room, wearing T-shirts that fell to their knees. Scrolled across the front of Ty's black shirt was a band photo and the script: "Red Hot Chili Peppers." Ko wore a purple shirt with "Los Angeles Lakers" lettered in gold across a basketball.

Darren pointed to Shum's white T-shirt with bright blue script across the front: *KARPET KING - We Pull The Rug From Under High Prices.* "That's my dad. He owns five carpet stores in the LA area." He held up a hand of spread fingers. "Count 'em. *Cinco.*"

From the boys' drifting looks, Darren got the idea they weren't impressed. He kept two fingers up. "Roll out your sleeping sacks. Two boys can sleep on the couch."

Ty tossed his bedroll onto the leather couch. Shum did the same, shouting, "Mine!"

Ko dropped to his knees and started to untie his bedroll. "Ko always sleeps with Ko," he growled. "Until my *kanta-wing* arrives."

"She couldn't find the River Gan." Shum yawned. "How's she going to find Darren's *casa*?"

"Go to sleep, Shummy."

Sita walked through the hall doorway. Her damp hair streamed across her shoulders. Dorsey's old T-shirt, with a motor-cycle and roses across the front, drooped to her knees. She was barefoot.

Darren took note of the self-conscious smile that lighted her face.

"I like the soap," she said. "It smells good." She held her wrist to her nose and breathed the fragrance.

"I buy it for Dorsey. Lavender's her thing."

Ty raised his voice. "Where's Dorsey?"

"She never called me back. She's very busy. Actresses get busy."

"What's an actress?" Ko asked, laid out in his bedroll.

"Don't tell me you don't know what an actress is." Darren swung a look to Sita. "What's an actress, Sita?"

Sita paused a moment. Then her eyes lit up. "Scottie said a *blonde prima donna*."

"No." Darren winced. "Actors and actresses are the people I use when I make my films. They play parts, just like you might be playing the part of cave kids when you're really just runaway kids from some part of LA." A sneaky smile lit his eyes. His gaze darted from one face to the next, searching for a telling look. "Am I right?"

"Darren, that's getting old. We've heard you. You heard us. What's wrong with the word *believe*?" Sita wiggled her pretty head. "Call it *trust* if that makes you more comfortable."

"Trust," Shum echoed.

"Okay, I'm sorry." Darren threw up his hand. "I was out of line, although I'm not sure why the hell I'm supposed to trust you. Your parents have probably called the police and I could be charged with kidnapping. That's on my head." In a more reasonable, softer voice, he added, "Let's all get some sleep." He took a step, stopped, and cleared his throat. "Just one more thing. I've already discussed this with Sita. I'm responsible for all of you since you're in my house. Not my house, really, my father owns it, but I'm living in it. That doesn't concern you." His voice wobbled slightly and he breathed deeply. He looked over to Ty. "I can't have you and Sita sleeping together. Understand?"

"Where will Sita sleep?"

"I've got a second bedroom, Ty. It's my guest room. And I've got a small office too. This isn't just a tiny bungalow." Darren wanted to make sure there were no misunderstandings. He pointed to the hallway left. "That's bedroom two."

"They were sleeping together in the bedroll," Ko reported. His moonface glowed with the trace of a sly smile he couldn't resist.

"Maybe so, but they can't do that here, Ko." Darren tapped on his watch. "By the way, I found my watch. Now, if you need to go to the bathroom, there's the powder room in the alcove in back of the kitchen. I'm going to watch TV in my bedroom. If you need anything, just knock on my door." He turned to Sita. "You go to the guest bedroom." When he looked over to Ty, the cave boy had his eyes on Sita disappearing through the hall doorway. "I'm sorry, Ty. That's the way it's got to be."

Darren walked over to the standing lamp. "I'm turning off the lights now. Good night, guys."

"That's the way it's got to be," Shum repeated softly. "On the other side of the sun."

For a few minutes Ty and his *wings* rested in silence.

Ko snorted.

"Don't do that," Shum whispered, from one end of the couch.

"I can't breathe. There's no air!"

"Breathe through your mouth."

"Shhh!" Ty said.

"We're lost," Ko mumbled in the darkness. "We're lost like an ant floating on a stick in the middle of the Big River."

Ty clasped his hands under his head and leaned back. He knew they were lost. Ko didn't have to remind him. Was it from this world, he wondered, that he was supposed to bring back a way to help his people? "It's different. More different than I ever thought a tribe would be."

"Different," Shum whispered.

"Shhh, Shummy," Ko grumbled. "Sleep, before your head falls off."

"One more thing," the spear boy whispered. "We killed the emmydactyl."

"Under the same full moon," Ty mused. "Time jumped, but the moon didn't move."

* * *

It was past midnight when Sita appeared in the doorway and approached the end of the couch where Ty was sleeping. She brushed her fingers across his cheek. Without a word she awakened him, put her finger to her lips, and led him back to the guest bedroom.

Moments later, he held her in his arms under the blue blanket, bordered with a pattern of golden leaves.

"You worry about me," she said. "Sometimes you look at Darren with knives in your eyes. I am your *kanta-wing*. Kiss me in America." She tilted her lips to his, and he kissed her.

"Are we lost?" he asked.

"Not in each other's arms," she answered, and she kissed him.

* * * *

In his bedroom, Darren clicked off the TV. *No Amber Alert or kids reported missing. Just murders and heists. I shouldn't have watched the local news.* He turned toward his bedroom door and closed his eyes. "Please don't steal anything or kill me," he whispered under his breath. Darren pulled the quilt close to his chin. *Maybe I should roll the dresser in front of the door, like Scottie said.*

A tree branch banged against the house. The wind rattled the blinds. Darren got out of bed, dragged an old suitcase from the closet, and set it in front of the bedroom door.

CHAPTER 14

S till dressed in droopy T's, Ko and Shum sat in front of the TV watching morning cartoons, eating bowls of cereal, and giggling. The *wings* didn't look up when Ty came into the room and sat down on the couch. Within seconds, he, too, was laughing at the antics in the *Curious George* show.

"I can do that," Shum yelled. "I can do that!"

The little brown TV monkey jumped around and dodged the adults, much like the *wings'* own childhood cave play.

"Okay, *wings*, the pancakes are almost done." Darren stepped into the living room in his frayed green robe. Nobody looked up. His voice rose along with his smile. "I'm putting syrup and butter on the dining room table." He turned his attention to Ty. "I didn't see you on the couch when I got up this morning. Where did you sleep?" Ty saw a friendly smile, but he heard his father's voice. "Where did you sleep?"

"With Sita."

"In the guest bedroom?"

Ty nodded. He was beginning to feel uneasy.

"Do you always sleep with her?"

"We are strangers here."

"I thought you were my friend."

"You have been good to us."

"Then, when I tell you something, in my own house, why don't you follow that?"

"I don't want a father here," Ty answered, fighting to keep an even tone. "My father has rough hands from the forest and scars on his chest from fighting the emmydactyl. I listen to him."

"Then get him! Call him! Don't give me that phony cave story."

The cross-room questions rang with a parental tone the cave boys understood. Ko and Shum scooched to the edge of their chairs.

Ty didn't like being scolded by a man as white as a river ghost, nor did he like any dark thoughts cast on Sita. He started to get to his feet when Shum came to Ty's defense.

"Sita came with us. Ty didn't want her to come."

"She's a big problem," Ko added.

Ty's cheeks got hot, his breath short and heavy. His sweaty hands clenched into fists. "Sita's my *kanta-wing*. No more talk!"

"Damn it, I'm responsible for you! Hit the mute button!" Darren yelled at Shum. "Enough of this!" He yanked the belt on his green robe tighter. "Maybe I can't find your parents, but a social service agency will!"

Shum jumped to his knees on the swivel chair. Like a rabbit or a wolf, he sniffed the air. "Fire!"

"The pancakes!" Darren's eyes popped. He dropped the subject like a dead rat, whirled, and dashed toward the kitchen.

Darren's swift exit didn't abate Ty's fury. "We are going! We take our bedrolls and we go!"

"Go where?" Shum's eyes lit up with fear. He pointed at the TV. "*George* is a good show."

"Pizza was very good," Ko added. He raised his dark crinkly brows. "Maybe pancakes are better."

"Go where?"

Another voice had entered the room. Ty turned to Sita. She was walking toward him, wearing Dorsey's pink dress, tied at the waist with the purple sash.

"Where are we going?"

Ty answered with a blank, clueless expression. All he knew was he wanted to charge out of Darren's house, distance himself from the white man's language and his sharp-edged tone.

"Where?" she repeated, drawing up to him.

He saw in Sita's questioning eyes the futility of his outrage. She raised her straight, thin brows. "We don't even know what's in front of Darren's house."

Ty took a deep, angry breath. "We'll stay one more moon," he said, tamping down his pride. "Then we go."

"Where's Darren?"

"There's a fire in the kitchen," Shum noted in his soft voice.

"Fire? Why didn't you say something?" Sita charged past the boys, nearly snagging the tail of her purple sash on an end table lamp.

"She's mad." Ko chuckled. "Like river-mad when her booties got wet."

"Enough about Sita," Ty commanded. "Shum, make the TV voices louder. We're not going anywhere yet!"

They had no place to go. As Sita had pointed out, they hadn't even passed through the front door of Darren's house.

* * *

In the kitchen, Darren was mulling a similar problem: "Where are you going to go?" He glanced at Sita as he moved between the counter and stove, waving the last wisps of smoke past his face. "We've got to come up with some answers and make some decisions. I could call some kind of social service organization or a county agency, but, personally, I think we should keep the government out of this. I've got enough problems getting location permits." He poured dollops of yellow batter onto a skillet. "Cops always make me nervous, and that's not good for my eczema. I've thought this over. I think we should go to the mall."

"What's a mall?"

Darren leaned back. He was getting used to her naïve questions, whether they were genuine or not. "A mall is a building with many stores inside it. You know what stores are."

"Stores?"

"Where they sell things, and the mall I'm thinking of is filled with a zillion stores. You'll like it because," his expression brightened, "they have racks and racks, tons of girls' clothes. We can get you a dress that really fits you."

Sita smiled. "I like clothes."

"Of course you do. So does Dorsey. That's why, young as I am, I've had *mucho* experience at this particular mall."

Sita thought for a moment. "You keep talking about Dorsey. Where is she?"

Darren threw some chopped walnuts onto the pancakes. "Like I told you, she's busy. She's very ambitious. You've got to be ambitious to succeed in this town."

"Too busy to call you? It looks really quick when you do it on the cellie."

"Cellie? I don't think I ever called it a cellie. Where did you hear that?"

"I thought that's what you called it."

"Really?" He looked at her with mild suspicion. "I'm making a note of that."

"I'm sure that means something, Darren, but you were telling me about Dorsey. Has she called you back on the cellie?"

Darren smirked. He lowered his voice and glanced over to the doorway, remembering how Ty had raced back into the kitchen with a knife in his hand last night. "No, she hasn't called me back."

"What's up with that?"

"I'm saying…" Darren lowered the flame under the pancakes and turned back to Sita. "I'm saying you're really a smarty, aren't you? But I've already got a shrink."

"Greenberg."

Darren stared at Sita. *These cave kids don't miss a beat.* "I'm beginning to feel like I invited the enemy into my home." He couldn't believe this pint-sized teenager, in a dress that made her look like a wedding cake, was making him feel defensive in his own house. "I really think you should stop asking questions and we should just drop the subject."

"Dropped." Sita didn't say anything more. Darren noticed her gaze stray above his head. "What are you looking at?"

"Nothing."

He brushed his hair back. "Pillow hair?"

"Nothing, Darren. Just looking."

Darren pointed his finger above his head. "Well, you won't find Dorsey up there." The phone rang. "Speak of the devil!"

He grabbed the receiver on the counter. "Hi... The shoot went great. We got all the footage, and Marc's setting up to edit it now. You should have your new commercial with sound and music by the beginning of next week... No thanks, I'll probably just stay home and rest tonight." His voice had lost its spark. Darren went back to the stove and flipped the pancakes over. "I'll try... I said, I'll try. Talk to you *mañana*."

He set the receiver back on its base, took a deep breath, and mindlessly tapped the counter with his spatula. "That was my father. He wants me to go to my stepmother's birthday party at his country club, and I really don't want to go."

"Why not?"

"Sita, I can't leave you here by yourselves and I can't take you with me, and you don't seem to have any immediate plans for getting out of here. Besides, I feel..."

"Feel what?"

"You really wouldn't understand."

"I'm a shaman-in-waiting, Darren. Don't be fooled by my size."

"How about your age?" Darren leaned back on his slipper heels, wondering whether he really wanted her to get deeper into any part of his life.

"What's a stepmother?" Sita asked.

Darren was tired of explaining. "Let's just say she's the woman my father married but she's really not like my mother. I never lived with her, not even one day." He paused. His voice took on a precise beat. "She thinks I'm just living off my father, grabbing what I can."

"Oh, is that true?"

"I work for him, Sita. I think that's different." He went back to flipping pancakes. "First, it was in the carpet business. Then, when I decided to become a film director, he put me through film school and set me up to shoot his TV commercials. They run on Channel 11 just about every day. Very successful." He looked around to see if Sita was still listening. "Why am I telling you all this?" He wanted to look anywhere but at the little girl, and yet the little girl was keeping him from looking anywhere else. "Why am I talking to you when I don't even know you, when I don't even know if you know what I'm talking about? And you're just a kid."

Sita looked above his head again. "You have *nagya*."

"*Nagya*?"

"The Kishoki word for unhappiness. I see it around you."

"Oh, please. I'm not unhappy." Darren turned off the burner. His brow narrowed in a trace of leftover agitation. "You've got to drop this Cave Psychology 101 rap."

Sunlight streamed through the kitchen window, creating a golden path between him and Sita, as if the rays had formed a bright line of understanding that had yet to be fully traversed.

He tilted the skillet over a flat metal tray and let the pancakes drop onto it. "This isn't your problem. It just bugs me that he follows every step I take. Don't you think he could skip one day without calling me?" Darren slipped the tray into the oven and poured more batter onto the skillet. "I shouldn't be talking to you about this anyway."

"You said that."

"I said it because I don't need cave advice from someone who doesn't even know what a stoplight is." He looked over to Sita. "Do I sound like I'm ungrateful, like I'm whining?"

Sita nodded. "Like my little brother."

"Well, I'm going on twenty-five fucking summers and I'm still on my father's leash. Pardon my language. I didn't mean to use that word in front of you." He leaned forward, crossing the golden line of sunlight. "Is your father always on you? How would you like it if he was?"

"My father is good, Darren, but he's not your problem."

"Why doesn't he call if he's so good?" Darren hissed. "What kind of good is that?" He turned sharply back to the stove. "Oh, that's right. He lives in a cave. Ha!"

"We like the cave."

"Because that's all you know!" His voice flew up again. "Have you ever stepped into a house until now? I mean really, if you're telling me the truth, if there's one speck of truth in what you're saying… Isn't this nice? A stove, a fridge?" He pointed the blue spatula around the kitchen, his voice growing more hysterical. "A toaster, microwave over there, cordless phone, dishwasher with a pot-scrubber feature and an energy-saver star? These are real twenty-first century conveniences!"

Sita stepped away from the flailing spatula.

"I'm sorry. I'm not going to hit you." He tossed the spatula into the sink. "I don't want my eczema to come back. Over what?" He raised his watery eyes to Sita.

"The eczema is in your father's voice, not in you."

"Over a goddamn stupid phone call, that's what. I'm sorry. I'm sorry again for using that word. I don't always use bad language around kids. I watch myself."

"Did you hear what I said?"

Darren didn't answer. He saw Ty standing in the kitchen doorway glaring at him.

"He's sad," Sita said. "Darren has problems."

"He has a big problem with me." Ty had his hands open, ready to attack.

Darren shook his head. "No, we're cool." He looked at Ty with remorse in his eyes. "I'm really sorry for what happened in the living room."

Ty shifted his look between Sita and Darren. "Okay."

"Sita's the bomb."

Sita turned to Ty. "I'm the bomb," she said with a smile. "We're going to the mall."

* * *

Darren was amazed at the speed with which the *wings* wolfed down the pancakes. He looked over to Sita, who hadn't yet finished her second pancake. "Don't you like them?"

"Pancakes are good," she said. "The syrup tastes like sap my mother and I find in the forest trees."

Her answer somehow settled Darren. He had talked more to Sita, revealed more of himself to her than to any of the *wings* or, for that matter, to any teenage kid. Maybe Scottie was right about a bogus cave story, but he wasn't right about Sita, Darren thought. *Shaman or not, she's definitely a different kind of kid.*

He leaned back, looked across the table, and smiled. An unaccountable, warm feeling rose within him. Somehow, the kids, despite all their bickering and horsing around, relaxed him more than any prescribed or street drug he'd ever taken. He was in charge of something, a world as small as a dining room table, inhabited with no more than four runaway runts, but it was something he had helped create and was free of his father's meddling hand. He glanced at his watch and tapped his coffee cup.

"Mall time."

* * *

Star gazed at the rain clouds moving across the summer sky. He looked at Sita's father, Pau, a short, stocky man with black hair braided and wound tightly over the crown of his head. A thick mustache and beard darkened his moon-shaped face. Both men turned grimly to the dead emmydactyl they had dragged from the river. They kneeled on the rocks and cut open its belly. A powerful stench arose as they dug into its guts and pawed through the waste. There were no human remnants. No telltale locks of wings' hair, body parts, or the flaming red stone that had hung from a leather string on Ty's neck.

The river rushed past them, but neither man imagined that it flowed into a body of water that touched the shores of a land tracked with the footprints of their son and daughter ten thousand miles and ten thousand years away._

CHAPTER 15

Ty, Sita, and Shum crammed into the backseat of the green Jeep.

"Safety belts!" Darren shouted.

"Safety belts," Shum echoed.

Darren glanced over to Ko, sitting next to him in the front seat. The grumpy teen had his arms folded across his chest.

"You're kind of quiet, Ko. Any of these streets familiar to you?"

"Nothing looks familiar," Ko answered in his growling monotone. "I am a stranger here."

"A stranger in a strange land, is that it?" Darren was still fishing for some clue that would expose the kids' cave concocted story.

"You got that right, boy scout."

Darren did a double-take. "Where'd you get that from?"

"TV. It's a mind-blowing experience."

"I suppose that's from TV too?"

"The elders think I'm dumb because I'm strong, but I'm a locked-in Houdini," he growled again. "I remember everything I hear. Sticks in my ear like Oprah Winfrey." Ko winked. "This language game is a snap."

"You're not making any sense. Do you even know who Oprah Winfrey is?"

Ko rubbed the stubble on his chin. "No clue, Mr. Who. I've got TV knockin' at my brain."

Darren blinked. He didn't know whether to laugh or to turn the car around and drive them to a Greyhound bus station.

"How far is it?" Shum shouted from the back.

"Any minute now." Darren sped through the intersection. *I'm unhappy. She said I was unhappy. She doesn't know a damn thing about me.* He rubbed the red mark on his chin. *She knows as much about me as Ko knows about Oprah Winfrey.*

* * *

Darren made a right turn into the Westside Pavilion parking. The Jeep spiraled up the huge concrete structure, turning through shafts of light and shaded tunnels.

"It's like a giant cave," Ty whispered to Sita. "We're going back in time."

"No, Ty. The shadows are playing a trick." She patted his knee. "We're still in the future."

Darren drove up to the rooftop landing. "Remember, you don't touch anything in the stores. You can look all you want, but don't touch. If you drop anything, break anything, I've got to pay for it."

Darren parked. The boys and Sita piled out. They hadn't taken two steps when they stopped, mesmerized by what they saw.

From their view above the city, through a crosshatch of willowy palms, leafy trees, and summer haze, the streets, traffic, houses, and buildings spread out like a fantastic puzzle of jumbled, colored shapes and moving parts.

"Ty, where're you going?" Darren shouted. "Don't go near the ledge!"

Ty's gaze fixed on high-rise windows flaring with sunlight. Waves of heat rose from red tile roofs. He felt the staggering height of the cliffs beneath his feet. He breathed in the smoggy LA air and reached for the golden shell on his chest to center himself. But what he felt running through his heart was the red stone he had buried for Sita in his father's cave. The bright colors of red tile and stone merged in his mind. Through a curtain of scarlet light swaying in the winds of time, he saw the closeness of caves and tile roofs, the beginning and end of his journey.

Then he felt Sita's hand couple his.

"Are you afraid?"

"No."

"You feel warm." She rubbed her forehead against his arm.

"I will live here," he said. "I don't know how, I don't know when, but someday, I swear, I will live here."

"You don't want the cave anymore?"

He turned and looked down, taking in the sweet beauty of a face he had loved since childhood. "The cave is my home now, but some day, in another time—"

"Ty, Sita! Let's go!" Darren was flapping his long white arms as if he were preparing for lift-off. "This is madness!"

* * *

The escalator descent to the third-floor Pavilion shops was even more eye-popping than the car ride down the Topanga Canyon mountain. The *wings* looked into the faces of shoppers, less than an arm's length away, passing them on the ascending steps, clutching all sizes of bags and boxes.

Ko tugged at Shum's shoulder. "Big cave, Shummy! The sun is in the cave."

"The sun is in the cave!" Shum roared back.

Ko bopped him on the head. "You don't have to say everything I say. I'm a Houdini."

"Who am I?"

Ko squinted his eyes. "This is the question everyone asks, Mr. Shum. You're probably my assistant."

Before them, laid out in shimmering glass and glittering light, they saw little caves filled with unknown treasure. They nudged each other, pointed, grunted, and laughed. Shum let out another sharp howl, which drew a pumped fist from a boy wearing a cap with a beak.

Sita squeezed Ty's hand.

"It isn't as bright as the shaman's cave," he said, "but it's so much bigger! A thousand caves!"

As Darren got off the escalator, he took each *wing*'s hand, guiding them over the final step. Ko and Shum watched the metal stairs disappear into the floor.

"Where'd they go?"

"They die after you step on them, Shummy. Like spiders." Ko looked up at the escalator. "I'm beginning to understand everything."

Darren waved his hand across the mezzanine. "This is what we call an American mall."

"American mall," Shum repeated, looking directly at Ko.

"I can hear, Shummy. I told you, don't repeat."

Walking along in their ragged leather jerkins and long, gnarled hair, the boys were beginning to draw quick glances and double takes. They tugged at Darren, insisting on stopping at every window display, gawking at tall, silent dolls that looked like people clothed in colorful patterns. "Mannequins," Darren called them. They stared at trays of gold, silver, and sparkling jewelry and watches like the one Darren wore.

Ko tapped the window in front of a gold watch. "That's something I could use."

A few steps ahead, Sita and Ty stopped at a window. "Look!" She pointed Ty to a white girl with curly blonde hair seated in a tall chair. The woman standing behind her was twisting locks of the white girl's hair. "That's something I'd like to try."

"That's not why we came to America." Ty pulled Sita along like an impatient father. "We don't need hair tools."

"Well, we didn't know we were coming to America. There are a lot of futures. Time is a bundle, and stop pulling my arm."

"I'm pulling the bundle." Ty laughed. "We're here, Sita. We've got to find something that will help keep our people from dying. Not hair tools. We can't stay here forever."

"Then get us back, sweetie."

In a few steps, he and Sita had caught up to Darren. "What do people do with all this stuff?"

"They need these things to live, Ty. Nothing is simple in America. We're not cave-simple. We really boogie and we need stuff to do it."

"Boogie," Sita repeated, under her breath.

"We are boogers," Shum cried out.

"No, not boogers!" Darren threw up his hands. "Boogers are what's in your nose. Boogie means 'Let's go, let's move on.'"

Ko nodded. "Good idea. Let's boogie, Mr. Who."

Darren turned sharply. "And stop calling me that!" He shot a look to Sita. "What's wrong with him? Why does he say things like that?"

"He was born on a moonless night."

"Oh, of course." Darren nodded with a dollop of sarcasm. "That must be another lesson from Cave Psychology 101."

By the time they reached the Disney Store, Darren had lost most of his patience. "Keep your hands in your pockets," he warned the *wings* again. "Don't touch anything."

Ty watched Ko blink his eyes and bounce up and down in front of the display window. The burly *wing* was staring at piles of toys and furry animals. Then Ty heard Ko growl.

"Watch this, Shummy."

"No!" Ty's hands flew up like goal posts.

"Ko!" Darren's voice rang across the mezzanine as Ko rumbled into the store.

"You can't take that!" a shocked salesgirl screamed, seeing Ko grab a plush Winnie the Pooh. "It's just for display!"

Darren bounded into the store. "Ko, stop it!"

The cave boy zigzagged through a maze of aisles, dodging the hysterical salesgirl, the store manager waving his arms, and Darren, still shouting a barrage of useless orders.

"Stop your son!" the store manager yelled.

"He's not my—"

Darren lunged across a counter of Princess dolls, spinning them into orbit. His hands clamped down on Ko's shoulders. He looked up into the eyes of the angry store manager.

"He's not my son," Darren sputtered. "Check out the skin tones." He shifted his gaze to his white hand against Ko's mahogany brown skin. He apologized for the melee, yanked Winnie from under Ko's arm, and hustled the insubordinate *wing* out by the scruff of his jerkin.

"That boy needs medication!" Darren could hear the store manager yelling.

"I told you, no touching!" Darren was red-faced, gasping for air. He steadied himself on the mezzanine rail and went over the rules again, riveting his icy gaze on Ko. "We're going to a big store now. A big store. Behave yourselves!"

"Behave yourselves," Shum repeated.

"And don't mock me!" Darren turned his snarl on Shum. "You've never been in a mall before."

"We tried to tell you that!" Ty snapped.

* * *

Sita followed Darren and the boys into a gigantic cave Darren called Macy's department store.

She straggled behind, enchanted by the beautiful sculpted bottles that smelled of flowers, incense, and herbs. Her eyes surveyed the rainbow display of colors in tiny pots of powder and what looked to her like pointed red shoots wrapped in small golden stalks.

"Everything looks so beautiful," she sighed. *Even Man Who Stands Alone doesn't have this many powders.*

"I know just the colors for your complexion." A young woman leaned her slender frame across the glass counter. She moved aside the small counter invitation: *Free Three-Minute Makeover with Shawna.* "You need desert shades. Muted. Nothing too tacky or harsh. Have you got three minutes?"

Sita sorted for *minutes* in her mind. "Like time?"

"Like hop on the stool. You won't be disappointed. You've got a beautiful brown coloring. You don't want to fight your skin tone."

Sita climbed aboard the stool quicker than she could say the *River Gan.* "I don't want to fight anything."

The clerk laughed. "I know I said muted, but let's try this blue eye shadow."

"Eye shadow?"

"Don't worry. It's hypoallergenic. Your pretty eyes should have some glitter. Close your eyes, honey, and welcome aqua blue. It's free." Sita followed the cosmetician's instructions. "What's your name?"

"Sita."

"Sita. That's unusual. Sounds Indian. My name's Shawna, sounds a little Indian too. But different Indians. East, West." Shawna applied the blue eye shadow. "You're Gandhi, I'm Geronimo. Know what I mean?"

Sita laughed politely.

"Next, we're going to put some color on those sweet lips. This is called Sedona Red."

Sita closed her eyes again and felt the soft brush across her lips. "Do all girls put on Sedona Red like this?"

"A lot of girls use the brush. Some use the tube."

"Can I open my eyes?"

"Sure." Sita could see a wary look on Shawna's face. "I hope makeup isn't against your religion?"

Sita shook her head. "It's not against anything. I love colors."

"Good, you're looking like a princess. If you've got a boyfriend, he's going to be blown away."

"Sita! Sita!"

The name rang across the cavernous showroom. Sita heard the familiar screech of Darren's voice. She hopped off the stool. "I've got to go."

"Is that your boyfriend?"

"It's a long story, but definitely not. I'm Ty's love handle." Sita turned toward Darren's voice. "I'm coming!" She stopped just long enough to catch her reflection in the counter mirror. "Blown away. Wow, Shawna, I thank you."

"Sita!" She could hear Darren's voice getting closer.

"I will come back," she said, moving down the aisle. "Definitely. With Ty, in another lifetime!" She ran over to Darren and grabbed his hand. "This is a great store!"

"I don't want you ever to leave me!"

"Your hand is shaking."

"I'm not shaking. You can't just walk off by yourself." He glared down. "What did you do to your lips?"

"Sedona Red." Sita blinked her eyes. "Aqua blue."

"How did you have money to pay for that?"

Sita was almost airborne at Darren's side, having trouble keeping up with his long strides. "It's free, Darren. Shawna's the bomb."

"Stop saying that."

"You said it first. You told Ty I was the bomb. He's going to be blown away. Wait'll he sees me."

* * *

"Ty, stop looking at Sita. All that stuff washes off." Darren had gathered the *wings* in front of the Junior Miss department. He was starting to sweat with impatience. "Just pay attention to what I tell you. Ko and Sita, I'm talking especially to you."

But the boys couldn't keep their eyes off Sita's face.

"Sedona Red," she whispered.

"Pay attention, Sita. You can't keep walking around in Dorsey's dress. And you guys can't look like a bunch of sheepherders."

"What's a sheepherder?" Shum looked confused.

"This is no time for questions, Shum. We're going into different parts of the store. Keep together right behind me."

"Together behind me," Shum repeated.

"No, Shum." Darren pointed to himself. "Behind me."

Ko poked Shum. "Didn't I tell you to stop repeating? If you don't know something, put your money on Houdini."

Darren recognized a store assistant and waved her over.

Lakita had almond brown skin and cornrowed hair streaked with purple and gold highlights. Darren lowered his voice, jerking his head back to the *wings*. "This is for a movie. Pick out some outfits for the young girl, nothing too expensive. Don't go over three hundred dollars for the whole shebang." He smiled confidently, handing Lakita his Macy's credit card. "You did great the last time. Dorsey loves that dress."

"I'll do my best." Lakita looked over to Sita, slowly sinking into a sea of pink. "She's darling, just needs the right size."

"She's fourteen summers," Darren added. "With a mouth that shoots bullets."

The director hurried the *wings* to the Boys' Department.

* * *

An hour later, Darren stood, in a fatigue of spent nerves, at the register counter. The cashier clerk chewed gum and scanned the apparel price tags.

The boys, huddled around him, were dressed in black and khaki cargo shorts and designer T-shirts. Each boy clutched a large Macy's bag.

Ty poked Darren's elbow. "Sita's here."

Lakita walked over with Sita at her side, cradling her own Macy's bag. "We got along really well and got lucky." Lakita handed Darren his Macy's credit card and a very long receipt. "Total damage was three hundred and seventy dollars."

"What's lucky about this?" He stared at the receipt. "I told you not to go over three hundred."

"Mr. Davies, the girl needed shoes. She can't be running around in those buckskin booties."

Darren looked past the sequined camisole Sita was wearing, past her new low-waist jeans embroidered with flowers, to the peasant sandals on Sita's little brown feet. "Those were seventy dollars?"

"She fell in love with a pair of wedgies. On sale, by the way. I'm sure you're very proud of her. She's such a lovely, polite girl."

Sita smiled.

The boys stared at her. A single word dropped from Ty's lips. "Bomb."

Sita and the *wings* followed Darren to Foot Locker and walked out thirty minutes later, the boys sporting fancy white sneakers.

"Great day! Shoes fit!" Ko exclaimed. "Let's *comida*!"

At the mezzanine Food Court, Darren ordered teriyaki chicken, burgers, and fries for everyone. Sita pushed aside her peach smoothie and leaned across the table. "I love shopping. Thank you, Darren."

Her feelings of gratitude caught him by surprise. *They've never been in a mall before.* Darren was stone-cold certain.

* * *

The boys sat in the Jeep's backseat, fussing with their bags of new clothes and trading back and forth their windfall of T-shirts.

Ko and Shum were pulling at a pair of Jockey briefs, seeing how far the elastic would stretch.

Darren shouted at the boys, "Keep it down!" as he crept through traffic.

If these teenage kids really are from caves, where are the caves, Darren wondered, *and why did I, Darren Michael Davies, out of all the millions of people drinking coffee in Los Angeles, meet them on a mountaintop? Was it just to spark a movie idea in my head?*

He glanced over to Sita in the front seat beside him. "Another brilliant idea just hit me."

"As long as it's not about your father, I'm here to listen," she said, hugging her Macy's bag.

* * *

The *wings* crammed in Darren's small office. They clustered around the director as he sat at his computer. "This is what 'Google' means." He clicked on the Internet, sounded out the word "Kishoki," and typed it in. All that came up was a series of Japanese names on Myspace and some Japanese cartoon animation.

"Bummer. I thought I had it." Before the last word had skipped from his lips, he snapped his fingers. "I've got it! The eagle on the backs of your jerkins. You guys could be part of some gang, the Eagles!"

The *wings* stared in silence as images and text jumped on the screen: The Fraternal Order of Eagles, the Eagles' Croatian Soccer club.

He pushed back from his desk. "Gee, I thought we had it." Then his eyes popped wide open again. "Hang on! This time I've really got it!" He slid the chair back. His fingers flew across the keyboard. In seconds, shades of green, yellow, and orange, surrounded by huge dollops of pale blue, spread across the monitor.

"Okay, *wings*, this is a world map. Do you recognize any of these countries? I mean continents." He wiggled his cursor, finally landing it on Southern California. "We're right about here. Los Angeles. Do you recognize any of the other places?"

Ko pointed to the mouse. "Move it." The burly boy smiled as the cursor zigzagged across the screen. "It looks like *moca*," he said.

"Is that a country or a town?"

"It's the Kishoki word for bug," Sita answered.

Ty's voice shot out of the darkness. "This is all places!"

Darren swirled the cursor around the map. "Exactly! These are all the countries of the world. The blue is water. Your caves have to be somewhere on one of these colored parts. What looks most familiar: green, orange, or yellow?"

"Green," Ty said.

"Why?"

"We hunt in forests."

"Okay, now we're getting somewhere." Darren leaned into the screen, reading off the green area script: "North European Plain, the Appalachian Mountains, or the Amazon. Do any of these ring a bell?" No one answered. "Well, you've got to be somewhere. There's phone service all over the friggin' world!"

"River Gan," Ty blurted out.

Darren sat up. "Is that a river near your home?"

Sita was growing impatient. "I told you that in the kitchen. My idea, Darren."

Darren typed in River Gan. "The River Ganges in India," he mumbled, reading off the search result. He slumped back in his chair again. "It might take Dr. Greenberg to figure this out."

"More pictures," Ko and Shum said, nudging the back of Darren's chair.

The office was beginning to feel like a sauna. Darren got up to open the window. "This is a magnitude ten conundrum."

Ty grabbed Sita's hand and pulled her out of the room. "I've got it!"

* * *

Ty closed the guest bedroom door. "I've got the conundrum!" He swung his arms into an air circle. "We, Kishoki, live in a giant place! With many lands. Darren called them countries."

107

Sita jumped up on the bed. "Continents."

"Okay, continents. Don't waste your time correcting me because I've got a brilliant idea just like Darren said, and I'm getting the language just as good as you." He paused, readying himself for his grand statement. Then, in a steady, clear voice he announced: "The Kishoki live somewhere in this whole world."

"That's not a great idea, Mr. Conundrum," Sita answered flatly. She folded her arms and crossed her legs, covered in her classy new jeans. "I told you before there are many worlds. This is just one future world."

"Future is time, Sita." Ty took a step to the foot of the bed. "Time is in the shell."

"So?"

"Man Who Stands Alone gave me the golden shell in Kishoki land. Don't you see? Kishoki land and where we are now are the same." He pulled the golden shell from beneath his T-shirt and held it before her eyes. "Look! The shell is here, now."

Ty watched his idea light Sita's eyes, and words slipped from the smile on her lips. "Place is time!"

"Yes! That's what I'm saying!"

"But how do we get back if we're already in this world?"

"How do we get back to where we are?" Ty's voice dropped. He stared at Sita's new brown sandals. "That's the real conundrum."

The front door bell chimed.

"I'll get it!" Darren's voice and footsteps clopped down the hall.

Ty and Sita looked at each other. "Who's that?"

Sita slid off the bed. "Darren threatened to call some kind of agency for lost kids."

"But we're not lost," Ty exclaimed. "I've broken the code. We're in the world!"

CHAPTER 16

"This is Dorsey." Darren turned to the tall young woman in dark eyeglasses at his side.

Sita and the *wings* smiled politely.

"Darren tells me you hang out in caves. That's a hoot. I never lived in a cave, too many spiders." Dorsey wrinkled up her nose, but Sita could tell she was making an effort to be friendly. "I used to love weenie roasts and grillin' burgers outdoors. Is that mostly how your parents cook?"

Sita glanced over to Ko and Shum. The *wings* stood silent, rigidly erect. They had heard white girls talk at Macy's and on the magic crystal, but never standing in the same small room, less than the length of Shum's spear away from them.

Sita had no trouble understanding Dorsey, but she wasn't sure she trusted her smile, a "topical smile" or *garripa*, the Kishoki called it, that never went deeper than the lips. Now, Sita was too busy making a mental sketch of the blond prima donna in her black blouse open to the rise of her breasts, and the black tight-fitting jeans, as black as an emmydactyl's fur, that showed off her long legs. "We cook in caves," Sita finally answered, looking up from the splashes of red that covered Dorsey's toenails.

"Doesn't it get smoky?" Dorsey wrinkled up her nose again. She turned to Darren. "Do you believe they cook in a cave?"

"They have their own system," he said, clearing his throat. "Speaking of which, we ought to do some grillin' of our own."

"You didn't invite me over for burgers, did you?" Dorsey's jaw dropped. Her high, tingling voice swept across the room. "Let's order in from Ling's. Right, guys? You like Chinese, don't you?"

Sita raised her head, certain that half the sparkling charms from the Macy's counter dangled on Dorsey's wrists, fingers, and ears. She noticed Dorsey's lips were darker than Sedona Red and her eye shadow was light blue like her eyes. Sita looked for an aura above the pile of the actress's blonde curls. She saw nothing but motes of dust through the fading light. "We'll eat what you want to eat," Sita answered.

"Well, shrimp in lobster sauce is one of my faves, but you don't have to eat that." Dorsey pointed at the boys, circling her finger, which ended in a bright red talon. "I've got a feeling you would love barbeque spareribs, sweet and sour chicken, and lots of fried rice."

Wow, Sita thought, beginning to feel the back of her neck heating up, *she's dangerous. I'll bet she's a baby emmydactyl.*

* * *

"I love spareribs," Ko jawed, biting chunks of meat off the bone.

Chinese take-out was a hit. Everyone had heaping plates of food on their laps. Shum cracked open his fortune cookie and tossed away the little white slip of paper inside.

"That's your fortune you're throwing away," Dorsey chastised sweetly. She looked over to Darren. "Can't they even read? It's not Chinese, Darren. It's in English." She turned to Ty. "Are you guys Mexican? Or from Africa? You can tell me. I'm not going to deport you."

"We're from the world," Sita said proudly.

"From the green world," Ty added, giving Sita's answer more weight. "What's a fortune?"

"Like Bill Gates's money." Dorsey voiced a loud "Ha!" and clapped her jeweled hands. "But on these little slips of paper, *fortune* means future. What's going to be in your futures."

"Like the world," Ko mumbled.

"Exactly. Like the world is our future if we give it time." She looked over to Darren. "What's our future, big guy?"

Sita saw a big, loopy smile cross Darren's lips, but, with a mouthful of food, he just waved his chopsticks.

Ty cracked open his cookie and handed Dorsey the slip of paper. "Read it, please."

Dorsey wiggled her butt in the chair and lit a cigarette. "I feel like I'm playing Miss Librarian in a kiddie show." She blew a stream of smoke to the side and read the fortune. "'You go beyond your father's dream.'" She handed the fortune back to Ty. "Of course, if your father's dream was just a cave, all you gotta do is rent a room with a bed and a john to get beyond that, honey."

Ty frowned. "Nothing about the River Gan?"

Sita jumped on the question. "Like how we get back to the River Gan?"

Ko and Shum stopped eating to listen.

"Gan... Gandhi... India!" Dorsey snapped her fingers. She shot a look to Darren. "I think I'm busting the mystery."

"It might be an off-shoot of the Ganges. It's in India and they have *mucho* caves." Darren lowered his voice to a whisper. "I ordered *Caves of Ajanta,* on Amazon."

Sita was less interested in Darren and Dorsey's guessing game than what was on her slip of paper. "Will you read my fortune?"

"Sure, honey." Dorsey took the fortune. "Oh, this is interesting: 'You have the gift of learning. Light will always surround you.' Put that in your voodoo box," she said, handing the fortune back to Sita. "You probably could learn to read real fast. And you won't even need a lamp! You're walking around in a cloud of light. Ha!"

Darren had heard enough. He felt restless and vaguely uneasy about Dorsey's comments. He wasn't sure if she was being condescending to Sita or simply cute. Still, he had experienced enough exchanges with Sita to know that, despite her cave-schooling and only fourteen summers, she could hold her own in just about any conversation. Darren felt confused, in a way he hadn't experienced before, over where his allegiance belonged.

He got up from the swivel chair and walked over to the wall of DVDs beside the fake fireplace. "Well, guys, your fortune for tonight is a special treat. Dorsey and I are going to go to my bedroom to work on a screenplay, but you dudes are gonna see one of the greatest movies of all time. It's kind of old, but it's a classic." He pulled a DVD from a shelf of films and slipped the disc into a player. "*Star Wars!* Anybody see it before?"

Sita looked over to Ty. "He's still trying to trick us."

Darren clicked a few buttons on the remote and watched the stream of images fill the screen. He smiled and paused the DVD. "The story takes place far, far away. Even past cave land. Somewhere in the—"

"They don't care, Darren." Dorsey cut him off. "They just want to see a movie." She stubbed out her cigarette in her leftover lobster sauce and got to her feet. "Right, kids? Cave people spend a lot of time looking at the sky. Don'tcha?"

"We read the stars," Ko piped up unexpectedly.

"Bingo." Dorsey raised a thumb. "Cave people are the original primitives. I read my horoscope every day. I'm a Sagittarius, Leo rising. Moon in…" She tilted her head back, tapping her foot. "Moon in Virgo? I think that's it."

Darren released the pause button. "They really don't care, Dorsey." *Star Wars* music roared through the speakers.

* * *

Ty squeezed Sita's hand, as much enthralled by the fantastic images as he was delighted that she was witnessing this special event beside him.

He forgot about Darren and Dorsey, about his lifesaving quest, the caves and River Gan. Ty was Luke Skywalker. Then he was Han Solo. His heart jumped back and forth between his heroes.

Sita drew her feet up under her and leaned her head on Ty's shoulder. "I am your Princess Leia."

"Beast, beast!" Shum shouted at the sight of Chewbacca.

Ty laughed with Ko and Shum at the sight of C-3PO. The Stone Age boy let his imagination take flight in the cockpit of a zooming thing he'd never seen before battling the TIE fighters.

In the pixels of an invention that hadn't been created until ten thousand years after their deaths, the *wings* found a sense of solace, rootedness, and comfort. They were transported by someone else's mind, by someone else's quest.

Ko pounded the arm of his chair. "This is better than the mall!"

They stared at the end credit roll and the silent blue screen. No one said a word. Ty noticed Shum's eyes were wet with tears.

Sita saw it too. "What's wrong, Shum?"

"It's beautiful," he whispered. "But it ended."

Ko leaned back in the leather armchair and crossed his legs. "Shummy thinks it's beautiful. It's in his DNA."

Shum smiled through his tears. "TV talk."

The hallway door opened. Darren stepped out. "Bedtime."

No one objected. Ty knew that the movie would play again in the *wings'* minds and carry them into their dreams.

Still teary-eyed, Shum clicked the off-button on the remote. "We are Kishoki. But we are star-fighters too."

The *wings* crawled into their bedrolls. Hand in hand, Ty and Sita returned to the guest bedroom.

She blew out the candle on the bedside table and snuggled with Ty.

He felt a cool night breeze drift through the open window. The blinds made a tingly sound like the ripple in Dorsey's voice.

"You like Dorsey?"

"Maybe." Sita pulled the blanket up and turned on her other side. "Maybe not. I will see."

"Did you like the mall?"

"I'd love to go back with my mother."

"But do you think that's what we're looking for? All these amazing things we saw have no place at the River Gan. It's like someone is tempting us with a beautiful stone or with food we could live on forever, but we can't touch it. I mean, we can't take it back to our caves. That's why we went on this journey. To bring something back that will save our people." He thought some more, staring into the darkness. "If we can't take anything back, why are we in Darren's house?"

"Maybe when we find out why, we will find our way back to the River Gan."

"Maybe we'll go home in a *Star Wars'* ship."

Sita giggled. "I'll fly with Luke Skywalker."

Ty hugged her closer. "You will fly with me, or you're not on the ship."

CHAPTER 17

Sita stood in the kitchen doorway, sparkling in a sequined blue camisole. Her hands were propped at the sides of her new jeans, like a model in a teen magazine.

"I like the sandals, but I like these better," she said, looking down at her chunky black slip-ons, with jeweled straps and soles two inches thick. "Do I look taller?"

"Yeah," Darren answered as he mixed up some pancake batter. "But I still don't see why you needed two pairs of shoes."

"Lakita said, if it's for your movie, let's go for it."

"I said that to *her*," Darren replied, making a clear distinction. "We, you and I, never talked about a movie."

"I really think we did, Darren. Besides, the wedgies were on sale."

"Well, you're not in any movie yet, and it's my father's credit card. And you probably never had a cave sale."

"Sorreee."

"And don't say it like that."

"That's the way I heard it on the TV. I think you're mad because Miss Dorsey left early to meet someone. Am I right?"

Darren was moving back and forth between the counter and the stove. It seemed to Sita that he was almost as restless and irritated, *helepsa* in Kishoki, talking about Dorsey as he was when it came to his father.

"No," he finally said. "She's on her way to a breakfast meeting with a television producer."

Sita didn't think his "no" was very convincing. "Are you in love with her?"

"You bet! She's my honey."

"Is she in love with you?"

Darren's voice grew quiet. He shifted his gaze to the kitchen window. "Of course, love is a big thing, isn't it?"

"In Kishoki, we know when we love someone. Here, people live more winters and summers than we do. Our time is shorter, so we know who we love."

"So what you're saying is, because the clock is ticking faster for you, you've got to make the right decision the first time."

"Our heart knows that. It's not ticking, like you said. It's not what we hear in our head or between our ears."

"You always go too deep, Sita. Pass me that bowl." She took a blue bowl from the counter. "You're fourteen and I'm twenty-four. I think we should be talking about something else."

"Like your father's credit card?"

He grabbed the bowl from her hand. "That's none of your business!" He went back to pouring batter into the skillet. "You've really got a mouth, don't you?"

"You told me, Darren. I'm not the one who screamed about being on my father's leash. Twenty-four fucking summers."

"Don't talk like that!" Darren snapped.

"You're getting upset."

"Because you're a kid, and you challenge whatever I say." He wiped his hands on a dish towel. "Where are your *wing* buddies?"

"They went out the front door."

"The front door? They've never done that!" Darren flew past Sita, through the dining room, stopping with his hands on the living room window.

"I guess it's okay." He was watching Ty and a skinny kid with spiky hair. "They're skateboarding."

Sita came up beside him. "Skateboarding?"

"The board with wheels. That's a skateboard."

They watched Ty balance one foot on the board. Shum and Ko took a step back, giving their leader room.

"In those shorts and T's, they look just like the neighbor kids." Darren looked down at Sita. "Cave boy goes X-Games."

"Ty never falls." Her gaze stayed on the *wing* she loved as he took off down the sidewalk. "But your pancakes are burning again."

"Damn!" Darren whirled like a dervish in his sea-green robe and raced back to the kitchen.

Sita smiled and turned to the window. Ty's ability on the board didn't surprise her. "Go, Ty, go," she whispered. She watched him glide up the street until she could no longer see him.

* * *

"He goes far," Ko observed, proudly. "*Star Wars* far."

"Yeah," the kid said, with a worried, slightly annoyed look. "But he's got my skateboard. That's three hundred bucks." He folded his arms and waited. "Where do you guys live? Watts? Compton?"

Ko raised a brow. "With our friend, Darren." Ko was a few inches shorter than the kid, but he knew his broad chest and thick, muscled arms had an intimidating effect.

"Look, dude, I don't want to cause trouble, but that's my skateboard. How do I know he's coming back? I was just being friendly."

"We are friends," Ko said with a smile. "Ko and Shummy."

"My name's Jason."

Shum nodded. "Hello, Jason. Greetings from the River Gan."

"Where's that?"

"In the green world." Ko folded his arms. "You can Google it."

"Well, it's nice to meet you guys. But friends don't run off with a dude's skateboard. He could be in Westwood now."

"Ty sees through fog," Ko boasted, feeling a need to defend his *wing* and the Kishoki clan. "He is never lost."

"Never lost." Shum punched the air. "In a city called Los Angeles."

Ko grinned. "Bagels."

Shum smiled back. "Donuts."

They slapped each other's hand with a low-five.

Jason shifted an uneasy look from one *wing* to the other. "Look, dudes, like I said, I don't want to cause problems, but if your bro isn't back here in the next couple of minutes, I've got a cell and I'm gonna call someone." Jason swallowed hard and took a step back. "I just want my skateboard."

"*Wings*! The pancakes are getting cold!" Darren was standing at the open front door. "Where's Ty?"

"Do you know these dudes?" Jason yelled back.

"They're houseguests. Where's Ty?"

"That's a fuckin'-A good question!"

"Hey, watch your language!" Darren stormed down the pathway, still in his robe.

"He's got my skateboard." Jason's face was turning red. "And if he's your houseguest, you're paying for it if he doesn't come back. My old man will come over here and whack your ass!"

"Take it easy." Darren turned to Ko. "Where's Ty?"

"He's coming. I hear him."

Darren and Jason both looked up the empty street. "I don't see him."

"Kishoki hear far," Shum piped up. "We listen to the wind. If two leaves rub their tails, we can hear them."

"Leaves don't have tails," Jason snapped. He pulled a cell phone from his pocket. "I'm gonna file a police report."

Darren threw up a hand. "Keep the cops out of this. These kids have traveled a long way to get here."

"Well, maybe they should go back."

"Watch yourself, kid. These are my friends."

"Jason," Ko butted in. "His name is Jason."

"That's Ty!" Shum shouted, excitedly.

Ty zoomed into view, bending around the street corner with his left foot toeing the front of the board, his right foot slashing the concrete.

"Wow," Jason yelped, in spite of his anger. "He really busted that turn."

The sound of wheels grew louder. Ty was swinging his arms, slapping his right foot against the ground, speeding in a blur toward Darren and the *wings*. His ginger braid was flying behind him. He spun the skateboard sharply into the grass and jumped off.

"What a ride!" Ty's grin was broader than the board he handed back to Jason. "Thank you, dude."

"There, you see," Darren said, grinning with relief. "You've got your skateboard and nothing bad happened. End of story."

"He told me he never skateboarded before. I don't believe it." Jason dropped the board. "You dudes better learn something about property." He jammed his cell back in his pocket and took off.

Darren shot a look to Ty. "This isn't cave land. You just can't take people's stuff."

"I didn't take it, Darren. Who has the skateboard?"

"Jason."

"Exactly."

"Exactly," Shum repeated, pumping his fists. "Jason's got the board."

"Remember the word *wheels*," Ty cried out as they walked back to the house. "I think I know why we came here!"

Ko looked at the make-believe watch on his wrist. "Duly noted."

* * *

Darren gathered a bat, a softball, and a glove from the alcove closet. In a demanding voice he told the *wings* that, unless they got his permission, the front door was a security gate. No exit. "You've got a big backyard to play in. And I've got a game for you that you're really going to like and nobody gets hurt." He held up the wooden bat. "This is called America's pastime. Baseball!" He handed the fat ball to Ty. "I wasn't a super ballplayer, but my dad always had Dodger season tickets, so I got to see a bunch of games with my friends."

"You don't have to tell us what you weren't good at," Sita pointed out. "We're all *not* good at something or other. And we don't care what your father said or did."

"I just bought you a new wardrobe! I showed you *Star Wars!*" Darren couldn't believe he was hearing smack again from Sita. "And we're in my father's house!"

"Don't yell at Sita!" Ty shouted, which only encouraged Sita.

"That's a problem, isn't it? In your father's house." She nodded slowly, as if the wisdom of the world were in her words and she was wrapping up a noteworthy legal point. "You said so, yourself." She stared at his striped pajamas. "Tie your bathrobe."

"Okay, that's it." Darren yanked his bathrobe belt. "Wait'll you have kids. Then you'll see exactly what 'talking back' feels like! This isn't cave town. This is the biggest town on the West Coast. Bigger than Coco Land or Kashumi Land or whatever you call it! We're playing baseball!"

He stumbled across the threshold as he hustled the kids out the back kitchen door.

"Put the paper plates where I point." Darren ordered the *wings* around the makeshift diamond, explaining that each plate was called a "base," with the batter and catcher positioned at "home plate."

"Ladies first!" he said, preempting any arguments amongst the *wings*.

Sita swung wildly at the first pitch Darren lobbed. Ten pitches later she was still waving at the summer air. Shum, playing catcher, ducked his head with the swing of her bat and chased each ball that bounced behind him.

Ty stood in the outfield, near the flower bed that bordered the garage. His mind drifted, waiting for Sita to hit the ball. He spun around to the sound of a car speeding past in the alley behind him. *Wheels! That's it. Wheels and gardens. That's why we came here!* He ran to the alley gate.

"Ty!" Darren yelled. "Get back to your position! Keep focused on the game!" Then he looked over to Ko, who was grinning and biting his lip. "What's so funny?"

"Sita's going to hit Shummy before she hits the ball. Roll it to her!"

"*Shag loc faca!*" Sita yelled back, roughly translated from Kishoki as *Shut your face!*

With the next pitch, she hit a weak ground ball directly at Ko. He fielded it cleanly with Darren's only glove and raced over to tag her, slapping the ball against her back. "Out!" he yelled. "Out! My turn. I hit!"

"Okay, you've got the idea. I'm going inside to put on some clo—" Darren stopped. His eyes froze on a stocky man in an olive green suit standing in the kitchen doorway. "Hi, Dad." The words shot from his throat more like a missile than a greeting.

"What are you doing in a bathrobe, Darren? It's almost noon."

"Baseball. I was just teaching some kids the game."

"You never played baseball in your life. What's happening with the commercial?" He turned a sharp look to Sita and pulled the cigar from between his lips. "Let's talk inside, Darren."

The man's gruff voice reached every corner of the yard. Ty forgot about wheels and watched the two white men, taking note of Darren's bent head and slumped shoulders as he entered the house.

"Emmydactyl attack," Ko muttered.

"You guys keep playing," Darren shouted from the kitchen window. "I'll be back in a few minutes."

Ko picked up the bat. "Throw the ball," he shouted to Sita.

"You laughed at me and tagged my back hard, on purpose! Throw it yourself!" She dropped the ball at her feet. "I'm going in the house."

* * *

Sita slammed the screen door. She hadn't taken two steps into the kitchen when she stopped. The same gruff voice she had heard outside was now flying against the living room walls.

"I don't care what problems they've got getting home, you can't keep them here! It doesn't look good. You're a grown man, for God's sake. You can't have a bunch of colored kids in your house shouting and screaming—"

"They don't shout and scream."

"Let me finish! What about the girl? She looks like she stepped out of one of those MTV videos. Do you have any idea the trouble you could get into for harboring a runaway teenage girl, if she's even that?"

"Dad, take it easy. She's a teenager, and she's not a runaway."

"Then where's her home?"

"In a cave. Something like—"

"In a cave? Are you nuts? Just because you're in the movie business doesn't mean you've got to fall for every crazy story. That's why they call it make-believe, Darren!"

"I believe them."

"You believe them? You don't know even know how to get in touch with their friggin' parents! Or their last names! Your job is to make commercials for me! That's what I'm paying you for. That's why you're living in this house! That's what I put you through film school for. That's what I want to see."

"You'll see the new commercial soon enough. Marc called me and I'm stopping off at the editing room tomorrow."

"Good. By tomorrow I want those kids out of here."

Sita heard the front door slam. Then she heard Darren's bedroom door close, not with as much force as his father's anger, but with a click she felt had the sound of frustration or *choyoa*, the Kishoki word for despair.

She looked out the kitchen window. *We're causing Darren too much trouble.* The backyard sparkled with sunlight despite her gloomy thoughts. Ko was running from one paper plate to the next. Shum was chasing him with the ball. Ty was screaming, "Tag him! Tag the tank!"

Place is time. We're in a crazy place at the wrong time. Sita went to the fridge and pulled out a six-pack of Coca-Cola. *They're my wings,* she told herself. *Darren's father doesn't want us here. Dorsey thinks we're dumb because we can't read. Maybe no one wants us, but Ty brought us here for a reason.* She glanced back at the empty kitchen doorway. "This is his vision," she said. "But my mother is going to go crazy worrying about me, and she's never seen a stove or a baseball game and she's never gone shopping at Macy's." She rested the six-pack on the counter and looked out the window. *My father would love to build houses like Darren's house. He built our beds off the ground in the cave so we wouldn't sleep on the ground, and he wove reeds and branches and bound them with leather straps to make* chikups *for my mother to put clothes in and vessels.* "My sisters and brother," she whispered to the side of the cabinet, "could play in the backyard, Darren called it, and wouldn't have to worry about snakes biting them or beasts biting their necks and dragging them away."

She turned back to the open window. Ko was jumping twice on the paper home plate. "Safe!" he shouted, throwing out his arms. "I'm safe!"

"Safe," she murmured. "Just not home."

* * *

Darren stayed in his office most of the day, making phone calls, ensuring that his father's carpet commercial was on schedule and setting up a date with Dorsey. He let the *wings* come in for half an hour, showing them Web videos of skateboarders doing tricks.

"Dorsey and I are going out for dinner tonight. You won't have to hear more questions from her. She's coming over here, but we're not staying." He leaned back in his chair. "I could get you guys pizza or burgers."

"I like pizza with pepachoni," the spear-thrower said.

Ko gave Shum an elbow nudge. "Pepperoni." He made a circle with his lips. "Roni, roni, peppa-roni."

"Looks like pizza wins." Darren pointed a finger at Ty. "What's Sita doing?"

"She's in the bedroom, resting."

"She's tired," Ko smirked. "From all those swings missing the ball."

"She's a shaman," Ty snapped. "They need rest."

"Right, anything you say." Darren picked up the phone and tapped a number. "She's a shaman and I'm the pizza man. And my father is out of his mind upset."

"*Fassi* in Kishoki."

Darren raised a glance to Ty. "Big-time *fassi*."

* * *

Sita was sitting on the bed, resting against a pillow. The door opened and Ty walked in.

"Dorsey is coming over, but they're going out. Darren is ordering us pizza."

Aside from a little smile that seemed as sad as it was sweet, Sita didn't say anything.

"What's wrong?"

"What's wrong?" She took several quick breaths. "We are lost, Ty, and nobody wants us here."

"Maybe we're not lost. Maybe this is why we're here."

"So you can learn how to play baseball or skateboard?"

"Skateboards have wheels, Sita."

"So? We don't have wheels," she fired back. "We live in caves. We hunt with spears and sing by fires. Darren laughs at us because we can't call our fathers or mothers, but what would happen if we tried to call them? Would they pick up a stick or a bone and say hello?"

She pushed her head against the pillow and bit her lip to hold the tears back.

Ty sat down on the bed beside her. "You like your beautiful clothes, don't you?"

She sniffled up a "yes."

He brushed his hand across her hair. "And I love my beautiful Sita." He kissed her lips. "That is why we're here. To show us that wherever we are, our love will keep us strong. Our love is not a place. Our love is time itself."

She had never heard him talk like this. She hugged him harder, feeling his warmth against her. She always knew Ty was different than the other *wings*. Now she knew why.

"We will get back," he said.

"How?"

"The answer will come to me. And our people will be proud of us."

CHAPTER 18

D orsey shifted her weight impatiently from one foot to the other. "Are we ready?"

"We're just waiting for the pizza man." Darren had changed to black jeans and a white shirt.

She turned to Ty and Sita sitting on the couch and blinked a "Hi" smile.

Sita didn't say anything, but she noted the red dress Dorsey was wearing, with thin straps that went over her bare shoulders and ended above her knees. A pink flower peeked out from her golden curls.

"The kids learned to play baseball today," Darren said, managing an upbeat smile.

"Oh, how neat." Dorsey pointed her gold, beaded purse at Ko and Shum. "How long are you going to stay?"

"They're going to stay as long as they want." The words flew out of Darren's mouth before he knew what he was saying.

"Well, they can't stay here for*ever*." Dorsey stretched *ever*, as if it was the downbeat on a song. "I mean, they have school and family. Even cave kids have some kind of routine." She turned to Ty and Sita. "Don't you?"

"We have things we do," Sita answered.

"Of course. When I was your age, I was very busy. I had schoolwork. I babysat, I took piano lessons and voice."

"Pizza man should be here any minute," Darren said.

Dorsey kept on talking. "You kids can't mooch off Darren for-*ever*."

"Dorsey, they're not mooching."

"Don't be so sensitive, D. What do you call living at some-one's house, eating his food, getting new clothes? Macy's clothes, I might add. Wow, that's taking advan-*tage*." Again, she stretched the last syllable of the word. She glanced over to Ko and Shum. "I don't mean to insult you guys, but we've got to be emotionally honest. That's coming from inside," she said, tapping her crimson nails against her chest. "From actor's depth."

"They're my friends, my buds! Don't talk to them like that."

"Jesus, Darren, don't get worked up. I don't want to see that eczema." Dorsey folded her arms. "Where's the pizza guy, any-way?"

"Pizza man is here."

"Oh, you're hiding him, is that it?" Dorsey looked over to Ko with something between a smile and a smirk.

"Ko hears distance," Darren explained.

"Two leaves rubbing tails," Shum added.

The doorbell chimed.

"See! What did I tell you?" Darren leaped from his chair and charged for the front door. He came back with two large flat boxes. "One's with pepperoni and one's veggie, just mushrooms, onions, and bell pepper." He set the boxes on the coffee table and opened them. "I'm going to be gone a couple of hours. That's two." He waved two fingers in front of Ty and Sita.

"They know *two*," Dorsey said, growing more impatient. "Let's go. We've got reservations."

Darren wasn't listening. He took a deep breath and spoke to each of the *wings*. "Don't open the door for anybody. Nobody," he said firmly. "My father has a key, but I don't think he's going to stop by tonight. He's got a poker game." Then he took Dorsey's hand. "Eat pizza, watch TV. Don't go outside."

"Bye, bye." Dorsey gave a little wave with her beaded gold purse.

* * *

"I love pizza," Ko howled, jamming half a pepperoni slice into his mouth.

"We all like pizza," Ty countered. "We like skateboard, we like baseball, we like TV, pancakes, and Coca-Cola."

"And burgers," Shum added smartly.

Ko looked up, surprised at Ty's harsh tone.

"But no one likes us." Sita jumped into the conversation, as if Ty had set her up to hammer down the truth.

Ko grumbled between bites. "Darren says we're his buds. He just said it."

"Yes," Sita answered. "But Darren isn't really in charge of himself. His father tells him what to do, that guy he called Greenberg tells him things, and Dorsey tells him what she wants him to do. You just saw that. Everyone tells him something. He doesn't fight for himself. Dorsey says to us, 'When are you leaving?' When you invite someone over to your cave, do you say to them, 'When are you leaving?' Huh?" She looked at the downcast faces of her *wings*. "Maybe I can't hit a baseball, but I'm a *kanta-wing*. I know how girls talk, what they mean. I'm fourteen summers and Darren told me Dorsey is twenty-three, but my fourteen summers are like her twenty-three. Maybe thirty." She took a bite of pizza. "Definitely thirty."

Ty nodded. "Sita's right."

"We die young," she went on, still munching on her bite of pizza, "so everything we do, what we are, is pushed together in a circle like the pizza."

Ty jumped on Sita's point. "Both pizzas are the same size. But look at the veggie. Many things are on the veggie. We are like the veggie. Many toppings in the same size."

Ko and Shum stared at their leader.

Shum raised a finger. "Does my mother know this?"

"No, of course not, Shum. She's never even seen a pizza. It's a comparison."

Sita had the urge to step in, but she could see that Ty was making her point perfectly. She knew they would listen to him before her.

Ty shifted his look between the *wings*. "Which one do you eat faster?"

"Pepperoni," they answered together.

"Because it's only pepperoni. It goes faster. Right?" He pointed to the pizza. "You don't have to spend time chewing all those veggies."

Shum wiggled his head.

"Don't do that," Ko said. "It's disgusting."

"So is when you snort."

"Listen!" Ty rapped the glass coffee table. "Maybe we don't live as many winters as Darren-people. He's almost twenty-five winters and look how young he looks."

"He told me his father is fifty-six winters," Sita added. "No Kishoki is fifty-six winters except Man Who Stands Alone."

"Exactly. But we have many toppings packed into our short life. And time is in the toppings."

"Time is in the toppings." Shum snapped his fingers.

Ko shot a look his way and burped. "You have no idea what he is talking about."

"Ko, enough!" Ty was trying to get his point across. "Our mothers have children before these people do. We have to fight to stay alive every day. When our fathers come home with a ram or bear from the forest or a fish from the river, it's a celebration because that's one more day we are here to look at the sun standing up over the mountains or the moon running with the clouds. The people in LA, what Darren calls a city, know that time will always be here because the lights from the cars glow and move through the night into the morning, never stopping, but we have only the flames of the fire pit in our caves that we have to keep burning through the night so we know that morning will be with us out of our dreams. Nothing is spread over in our lives. Each day is vital to our survival, and we feel these things through our bodies and our minds, like when the River Gan is rushing fast. Everything comes to us in a day and a night because death lives with us like the nails on our fingers."

Sita had never heard Ty speak with such passion or with the white man language, as if it was his. Ko and Shum had folded their arms, listening with the respect they gave to a clan elder, afraid to look at either the pizzas or their nails.

"That's why all of this, on one small veggie pizza," Ty continued, looking down at the cardboard boxes, "is more like our lives than the pepperoni on that one. Like the golden shell." He pulled the necklace from beneath his T-shirt. "The golden shell is small, but all time is inside it."

"Ty's right," Sita said, almost breathless from Ty's explosion of words. "But let's not get caught up in pizza comparisons. The point is, Dorsey wants us gone and so does Darren's father." She turned to Ty, who shot back a supportive look. "We can't stay here because we're not wanted here. In our clan everyone is together. Right?"

"No Kishoki goes out of the circle." Ko burped again. "Here it is different."

Ty folded his arms. "We must go."

"Go where?" The smile slipped from Shum's face. He put down his third slice of pizza.

"We will find the Antelope People."

Ko looked up. "Antelope People died long ago."

"That's what our fathers told us. They wanted us to believe that they made the right decision to stay behind, that nothing good came of the elders' journey to find a better life than the caves.

But no one ever dies, Ko." Ty told his *wings* that the Antelope People had children, and *they* had children, and *they* had children too. "The Kishoki stayed behind, but they are here."

Shum munched his last bite slowly. "If Antelope People have children, have children, have children, isn't Darren an Antelope People?"

Ko looked up in disbelief. "What has gotten into him?"

"Darren is an Antelope man," Ty answered. "But he is filled with the shadow of his father. No light comes in."

Sita swallowed her last bite. "You got it, big boy."

Ty got to his feet. "Take your bedrolls. If we wear our new clothes, nobody will look at us. We will look like mall people."

Ko raised his eyes to the front window, shaded with nightfall. "Where are we going to sleep?"

Sita looked at Ty for the same answer.

"We will find a place to sleep. That is what the golden shell will tell us. Man Who Stands Alone speaks to the golden shell."

Ko and Shum turned with frowns to each other. "Before, you said bad things about Man," Ko reminded Ty.

"That was before. Then I told him I would trust him. I will keep my word."

Ko raised his chest and his fist. "We fought the emmydactyl together. We watched *Star Wars* together. You took us on this journey, and we followed you." His eyes lit up and he punched the air. "And we will again! Into the night!"

Shum raised his fist. "Into the night!"

"Okay! Put your knives inside your bedrolls." Ty turned to Shum. "Leave the spear here."

"No!" Shum took a step back. His eyes filled with fear.

"Shum, if people see you with a spear, they'll take it away. Maybe even worse, they will take you away!"

"Sita is right," Ty added in support. "They will think you want to kill. The moon is already over us. We must go now."

"But Darren won't know anything," Shum said, with a trace of sadness in his voice.

Ko bit his lip. For one of the few times in his life, he looked stumped. Ty turned to Sita.

"We don't know how to write," she answered. "Besides, they'll all be happy we're gone."

When Ty closed the front door, Sita told him to knock on it three times. "Man Who Stands Alone told me, one is to put love where you live." And when Ty knocked again, she said, "Two is to put light where you live. Three is—"

"Three is what, Sita?" he asked impatiently, his fist poised at the door.

"Three is for our spirit to return."

Ty knocked a third time and Sita smiled. She had no idea where they were going.

Ko shouted, "Let's move!" He was standing on the sidewalk, bedroll on his back, waving his arm. Shum was next to him, holding a branch for his spear. Ko yelled again, "Let's blow this popcorn stand!"

CHAPTER 19

"Do you know where you're going?" Sita asked. She had never walked on a sidewalk or crossed a street before.

"Towards the biggest light," Ty answered. He glanced back. Ko and Shum were looking into living room windows and racing through front yard sprinklers. Ty watched them stop to pet a small white dog that a middle-aged woman held on a leash.

"He won't bite," he heard the woman say.

"It's like a *yakshi*," Shum answered in Kishoki.

"It's a Yorkshire Terrier," the woman gently corrected him.

"Come on!" Ty yelled.

He turned right onto the first busy street. A soft aura of light arced the night sky. The *wings* caught up and stopped again and again at the brightly lit shop windows. Nothing appeared to their eyes as amazing as the glittering collection of mall stores, but even Ty was enchanted by the vibrant window displays of surfboard, scuba diving, and soccer gear, decked out with the bold, striking patterns of their respective athletic attire.

"Sita?" Ty looked behind him. "Where's Sita?"

Shum shrugged. "Maybe back. Lots of stores with girl shoes."

"I told you to stay together!"

Ko protested that they had stayed together. "Shummy and me."

Ty's heart was pounding as he retraced his steps, dodging through the summer night shoppers and students from nearby

UCLA. Then he saw her. Sita was standing in front of a big window. Behind the glass were the fake people Ty had seen in the mall windows. The lights shining on the red and brown manikins dwarfed Sita. She hugged her arms against her chest as if the warmth of the lights and the summer night had fled her body. Her dark eyes swam with the unsteady motion of fear.

"Sita!"

She looked up. At the same time, two rough-looking men dressed in black T-shirts and black jeans spun around. They had no hair on their heads, and pictures ran up their muscled arms.

"Who's the shrimp?" The one wearing a thick, silver-studded bracelet grinned.

Ty walked toward them. He saw the upturned curl of their lips and hostility in their eyes, the same leer he'd seen on rodents running from the river caves.

Ignoring their threatening looks, Ty addressed his *kanta-wing.* "Let's go, Sita."

The hairless men stepped in front of Sita. "She ain't going nowhere," one of them said. "Take that blankie on your back and go back to your momma."

Sita tried to step around the two bullies. "Ty is my brother—" Before she could get another word out, Ty watched the hairless man with a skull picture on his forehead thrust out his arm, blocking her.

"She's ours," the hairless man sneered. "And we don't like colored dudes hanging out up here."

Ty wished his knife were not lodged in his bedroll. "I'm taking Sita with me," he said. His voice was cool, smooth, showing no sign of fear.

"We like her, butt-face. You're not taking nobody nowhere." Then the skinhead's small rodent-brown eyes flashed on the two boys with bedrolls on their backs approaching behind Ty. "Looks like some of your homo bros come up to get you before they see your bloody head bashed in."

Ty didn't have to look. He felt the presence of Ko and Shum. Sidewalk shoppers made their way between them and the skinheads. A few slowed down to witness the confrontation.

"Go home, go back to your caves," the man with the silver bracelet snarled.

The irony of the taunt drew a thin smile to Ty's lips. "We will when Man tells us to." His jaw hardened. He took a step closer. In his mind he knew that these bullies, each more than a head taller than he, had never fought an emmydactyl. "We are Kishoki," he said. "She is with us."

"What's Kishoki? A dance for dwarfs?" The hairless men burst into another roll of mocking laughter.

Ty saw Sita press her back against the store window. "I'm okay," she said in one trembling breath.

He shook his head. The image of Princess Leia flashed through his mind. In that moment Ty knew who he was. The cave boy turned Luke Skywalker took another step closer. Shum and Ko marched at his side.

The skinhead stared back. "One more step and they can scrape you off the sidewalk in the morning."

Ty took the next step. He reached out with his hand. "Now I will take her."

The guy with the skull picture on his forehead grabbed fast, twisted Ty's arm, and slammed him to the ground. Sita screamed. Ko shouted, "Veggie power!" He and Shum raced forward and flung their bodies, fists flying, at the skinheads. Ty was under the crush of boots and sneakers. The hairless men cackled, warding off the short, dark boys, batting them away like summer pests. Then, through the forest of legs, Ty saw Ko's punches land solidly against the ribs of the guy with the bracelet.

The skinhead's face clenched up in pain. "He's got rocks for hands!" he shouted.

Before his partner could turn on Ko, Shum jumped on his back and yanked his head back. Ty scrambled to his feet and started pummeling the hairless man.

In his mind he was battling the emmydactyl. In his heart he was saving his princess.

More people stopped to watch. A woman holding a teacup poodle screamed, "Someone call the police!"

The skinhead backed up, slamming Shum against the storefront window. The spear thrower slid to the ground. The thug leered and kicked him with his black studded boot. "Go back to your hole," he muttered.

But Ty's relentless attack and the fury and power of Ko's punches were too much for the white boys. "They're animals!" one of the hairless men yelled. They both staggered back. Blood was running down the jaw of the guy with the skull tattoo. "Okay, get the fuck out of here! You can take the dumb bitch." He was leaning against the storefront with his arms wrapped around his stomach.

Ty helped Shum to his feet. The three *wings* gasped as sweat rolled down their foreheads and cheeks. Their fists stayed clenched.

"We are Kishoki." Ty's lips barely moved as he uttered each word. "You don't laugh anymore."

Then he shot a look to the street, alerted by a loud cry, like the piercing scream of a night bird. A blue and white car stopped. The violent sound stopped too. Everyone stepped back. A man in a dark blue suit jumped out of the car and pushed through the ring of people.

"TV cops," Ko whispered to Ty. "Excellent show."

"What's going on here?" The cop's look shifted from the *wings* to the skinheads leaning against the glass storefront.

"Those guys started talking to me and they wouldn't let me go." Sita pointed to the skinheads.

The thug with the tattooed forehead spit blood on the sidewalk.

The officer turned to the *wings*. The dark sunglasses that shaded his eyes made it more difficult to tell to which *wing* he was talking. "What's your relationship to the girl?"

Ty shook his head, still trying to catch his breath. "Relationship?"

"We're friends," Sita answered.

"Do you live around here?"

"Yes." Ty nodded. Like Ko, he, too, had seen, at the mall and on TV, tall men dressed like the cop-man.

"Yes, where?" The cop repeated the question. "Where do you kids live?"

Ty rubbed the back of his hand across his chin. "With Darren."

"Darren who?"

"Darren Davies. His father is the Karpet King." Feeling protected, Sita answered, moving away from the skinheads.

"Five stores. *Cinco*. He has five stores," Ko growled, nudging his way into the conversation. "It's on Shummy's T-shirt."

"*Cinco*?" Cop-man raised a brow. "*Habla español*? Do you speak Spanish?"

"We speak Kishoki." Ty looked up at the cop's face, almost as dark as his own skin. "It's close to Spanish."

A guy near the front of the circle, still in his restaurant gear, called out: "Didn't you ever see those cheesy carpet commercials: 'I'm Glen C. Davies. I wear a rug, so I know what a good rug means!'" A few people in the crowd laughed at the burger boy's mimicry.

"Oh yeah." Cop-man smiled. "I've seen those commercials." He looked over to Sita. "Come over here." He pointed to the skinheads. "You guys stay up against the window, or I'll bust you for fleeing arrest on top of sexual assault." He turned back to Sita. "So are you guys in the carpet commercials?"

"Movies," Sita answered.

"*Star Wars*," Ko added. "It's an old classic."

Ty shot a "shut up" look to Ko before turning back to the cop. "We didn't start the fight. We were just walking."

"They wouldn't let me go," Sita added. Her voice was growing stronger.

"I saw it," the woman cuddling the teacup poodle said. "All those boys did was try to defend her against the skinheads."

A kid wearing a black headband jumped in, supporting the woman's account. "They had the girl up against the window. She was trying to get away."

Cop-man turned to Ty. "So what's with you guys lugging the sleeping bags?"

Before Ty could get a word out, Sita answered. "Those are for the commercials. They're practicing."

"I thought you said you guys were doing movies?"

"We are," Ty jumped in. "But Darren wants us to start with small—"

"Small stuff." Sita clasped her hands and raised her shoulders.

"Okay, you kids get your butts back to Mr. Davies' house. I'm Captain Martinez." He warned them that he might call Davies to make sure their story was legit and they were in his house.

Ty was beginning to feel a little uneasy about getting Darren involved. "He's very busy."

"LA is a busy town. Get going. You've got a curfew anyway," Martinez cautioned. "I'll take care of these guys."

Finding his way back to Darren's house was no different for Ty than his solitary forays into the Kishoki forest.

Sita walked at his side. "You saved me."

"Nobody messes with my princess." Ty smiled and grabbed Sita's hand. His heart was still beating hard, and the misty fog settling over the rooftops and through the trees brought a chill to the sweat on his back and chest.

Shum tried to keep up, but was limping badly.

"His foot hurts," Ko cried out.

Shum wagged his head "No," and rubbed the side of his chest. "It's here."

"Ribs." Sita turned to Ty. "Maybe walk slower. The man kicked Shum's ribs."

"I know what happened." Ty slowed his pace, but Shum was faltering badly.

"I'll carry him." Ko adjusted his bedroll. "He carried the spear. I carry the spear carrier. No problem for Ko." The relentless fighter tilted his body forward. "One Kishoki night, one emmy-dactyl. One LA night, two skinheads. It's a wash."

Shum climbed up on Ko's back. They walked that way, Shum's arms draped over Ko's bedroll, his legs cradled under Ko's arms, until they reached Darren's house.

Sita wasn't sure what to do.

The *wings'* victory over the skinheads bolstered Ty's confidence. "I'll think of something," he said. He looked toward the house. Lights blazed in the living room window. "Darren is home. We turned all the lights off when we left."

Sita peered into the window. "I don't see him."

"Maybe he's in his bedroom with Dorsey."

Sita glanced at the empty street. "Her car isn't here." She raised her eyes. "I've got a plan."

"What?"

"We go together to the front door and push the doorbell. Darren showed me how."

"That's not a plan. We have no place else to go."

"Okay, Mr. Let's-Find-the-Antelope-People." Sita set her hands on her hips. Any trauma she had suffered on the Westwood streets was history. Her lip was back. "What idea have you got that's a real plan?"

"Captain Martinez told us to go back. If he catches us again, he'll put us in the blue and white car with the red stoplight on top. We've got to hide in Darren's house."

"Oh, that's really different than my plan," she said, sarcastically.

"Stop fighting!" Ko cried out again. "Shummy's going to get sick on my head!"

"Stop yelling!" a neighbor shouted from an open window.

Ty looked over to his wounded *wing* on Ko's back. Shum was groaning and his eyes were red. "We've got to get him in the house."

Sita rang the doorbell.

"I hear his footsteps," she whispered. "We'll see if he's really our friend."

* * *

The front door whooshed open at the same time Darren's mouth flew open. He glared down at his missing wards. "Where have you been? Get in here!" The *wings* scrambled in, under a non-stop, withering explosion of words. "What do you think you were doing? Do you have any idea how worried I was? How could you do this to me? I gave you explicit orders!"

"We didn't let anyone in," Ty mumbled.

"Don't talk to me. Do you realize you left the kitchen door unlocked?" Darren paced in front of them like a drill sergeant. "You didn't even leave me a note!"

"We don't know how to write," Sita answered tersely.

"Did I say you could talk?"

"You sound just like your father," she shot back.

"You don't know what my father sounds like." Darren jerked his head toward Shum, draped over the back of Ko. "Why is he on Ko's head?"

Ty answered in a loud voice. "He got hurt!"

"Don't shout. That's what happens when you leave home." Darren looked into the eyes of the bedraggled runts. He said again he was worried and his voice faltered. "I just didn't know what happened to you." The drill sergeant façade crumbled in the swirl of his emotions. He took two deep breaths and clenched his fists, as if he was pushing back all the tears and feelings raging inside of him.

"You should sit down," Sita said. "You probably had a very hard night with Dorsey."

Darren walked over to the corner, next to the DVD shelves, and slumped down. Sita and Ty retreated to the couch. Ko gently slipped Shum's bedroll off the spear boy's back and rested him on the swivel chair.

Darren looked from one face to the next. "Why did you do this? Look at you. You look like you've been in a fight." Before anyone could answer, the phone rang. "It's Dorsey or my father." Darren looked toward the kitchen, but he didn't move. "I don't want to talk to either of them."

A deep voice drifted back to the living room from the answering machine. "Mr. Davies, this is Captain Martinez of the Westwood Division. I'd like you to call me back at—"

"The police!" Darren leaped to his feet and raced for the kitchen phone. His voice ricocheted through the house. "Officer, Officer, I'm here!" He hugged the receiver to his ear. "This is Darren Davies! … Of course." His voice dropped. "Yes, houseguests," he continued, marching back into the living room. "They seem to be okay." His eye caught Shum's glum look. "Well, sort of… Fight? … Westwood? … Skinheads? … Oh, wow… Aha…. Well, we haven't started yet, we're making the commercial first…" He looked over to Ty and Sita as his voice started to fade. "Soon… That's right, that's my father… Oh, that's a great idea. The sleeping bags roll out into room-size carpets. I'll definitely keep that in mind… No, I understand the curfew. Thank you, Captain." He clicked the phone off and turned to the *wings*. A look of disbelief crossed his face. "You were in a fight?"

"Skinheads against the Kishoki warriors," Ko growled. "We were banging dudes."

Shum's sputtering laugh sank into a painful groan.

"Are you okay?" Darren's head swiveled from side to side. "Is he okay? What's wrong with him?"

"He hurt his chest, Darren," Ty answered for Shum. "One of the guys threw him on the ground and kicked him."

"Maybe a rib's broken!" In one swooping stride, Darren was at Shum's chair, kneeling beside him. He raised the *wing*'s T-shirt and examined the crimson welt on his chest. "I'm going to get an ice pack."

Sita got off the couch and hurried after Darren into the kitchen.

"Why didn't you tell me any of this?" Darren frantically pulled an ice cube tray from the freezer compartment.

"Because we couldn't talk," Sita answered. "You said 'no talking.' You were yelling at us and we were scared."

"More scared of me than of the skinheads?"

"We don't care about the stupid skinheads, Darren. Don't you get it?" She walked over to the sink and half filled a water glass.

"What are you doing?"

"I'm making a potion for Shum's hurt."

"A potion?" His voice shot up again. "What's a potion?"

He watched her empty some powder from one of her pouches into the water and mix it with a spoon.

"I made this for Ty when the emmydactyl cut his arm." Sita tore off several sheets of paper towels.

"Emmydactyl? What's an emmydactyl?" Darren threw his hands out, totally at a loss. "What are you talking about?"

"A beast, Darren. Like the guys who tried to hurt me." She spooned some of the mustard-colored mixture onto the paper towel. "You probably wouldn't understand this, but in our world there are terrible beasts in the forest."

"Sure, I understand beasts. You probably didn't see *Jurassic Park*." He pointed his finger at her. "Scary movie."

"But we don't live in a movie. And you don't either. Get real." She looked at the ice cube tray in his hand. "Put that back in the fridge."

"I don't believe this is happening to me." His glance shifted from one kitchen appliance to the next, as if they were the friends that were supposed to be answering him. "I was on a mountain, making a carpet commercial for my father." He jammed the tray back in the freezer. "And all of a sudden I'm listening to an elf in wedgies tell me about potions and emmydactyls!"

"How do you think we feel? We're lost in the biggest, craziest world we could ever imagine." Her voice dropped to a low flame. "And we don't have a daddy to buy us a house."

Darren pointed toward the doorway. "If Shum wasn't a step from death right now, I'd tell you a thing or two, young lady. You Kishoki have smart mouths. No wonder you live in caves and no one wants to find you."

"Shut the freezer door," she said.

They marched back to the living room. Darren and Ty gently guided Shum to the couch.

Sita applied the mustardy yellow compress to his swollen ribs. Darren turned down the light.

"It's going to rain," Ty said.

"It Never Rains in Southern California," Darren mused. "That's an old song, but it's pretty true, except for a couple of nights ago." He sat back down. Sita could see he was upset over the phone call or maybe something she said. He looked up. "Which reminds me—"

"About what?" Sita raised her eyes.

"Why did you leave my house?"

Ty didn't hesitate. "Because no one wants us here."

"Your father says we should go, and Dorsey talks to us like that too," Sita added in support. The room quieted. They sat on the floor only a foot away from their host.

Ko growled, "We're not stupid, Darren."

"I never said that, Ko. And just between us, Dorsey is not a part of this discussion. She has problems. She's an actress. She's very temperamental, and she's under a lot of stress."

"What's stress?" Shum's voice rose from the dark corner of the couch.

"It's when you have pressures, you worry a lot."

"*Shimata*," Sita said in Kishoki. "Do you think living in a cave is easy, Darren? Do you think we don't have worries and fears and sickness? You think we aren't afraid that a beast will tear us apart, or a flood will wash away our food, or we'll never even find food, or freeze to death looking for it?"

"You're raising your voice, Sita, just like you did in the kitchen."

"I'm sorry, but those are pressures too. We can't get take-out when we're starving. No Chinese, no pizza." Her voice started to tremble with a desperation she wasn't used to feeling. She took a breath and exhaled in a harsh whisper. "That's why we're here."

Ty put his hand on Sita's. "We're looking for a new way, a better way to live."

"Well, I don't think you're going to find it in Westwood." Sita watched Darren rub his hands, as if he were hoping an answer would rise from the heat. "I'm alone too," he said. "You don't have to live in a cave to feel lonely."

"Everything is about you," Sita snapped.

"I'm just sharing my feelings." Darren blew out a puff of air. He looked over to the picture window. Thick drops of rain splattered against the ghostly pane.

"It's raining," Shum reported from the couch.

"You were right, Ty. The rain's here. I was wrong." Darren listened to the rain a few moments longer. "Can I tell you something? It's about me, okay, but I've never told anyone this, not even Dr. Greenberg." He waited for a sign of approval, but he only got blank faces in return. "Ever since my mother died, I've felt alone. Even when I'm with Dorsey, some part of me is watching: *What am I doing*, it's saying. I don't know if it's my mother's voice or from somewhere else. But I don't know the answers either."

"The answers will come," Ty said. His eyes opened spooky-wide. "Maybe it's our voice you are hearing from far away?"

The rain hit the window harder and beat across the roof.

"We live so you can be here. No us, no you." Sita pointed to herself and Ty. "No us, no fridge, no TV, no *Star Wars*!" Her voice was hardly audible, spattering words between the beating rain. "You think you are alone, but you are only alone in your mind. We Kishoki are alone in a world."

"We need you, Darren. And you need us."

Darren leaned back against the wall and looked at Ty. "We have wars. You saw it on TV when you first got here. People are starving, homeless. People tear each other apart in the name of some stupid idea." Darren had heard his mother say these words and himself say these words in his mind many times, but he had never voiced them before. "Our beasts are bombs, bullets, maniacs who want to rule the world."

"What are you doing about it?" Ty asked.

Thunder raged through the clouds. The living room lights flickered.

Darren glanced up at the ceiling. He would have expected this kind of bluntness coming from Sita but not from Ty. "You're saying there's a reason we're together?"

Ko swayed his dangling legs back and forth. "That's what they're saying, Einstein. It's the pizza topping theory."

Darren shot a look over to his nemesis. "How do you put up with him?"

Ty smiled. "He beat the crap out of two skinheads and carried Shum on his back all the way home. That's how."

"I guess that makes up for a lot." Darren nodded and got to his feet. "I've got a big day tomorrow. Appointment with Dr. Greenberg, then I've got to stop by the editing room." He looked over to Shum's bedroll on the floor. "Why doesn't he stay on the couch and we put this over him?"

Ty cave-hopped over to the bedroll, laid it out, and helped Darren cover Shum.

Like a concerned father, the young director leaned down and ruffled the boy's hair. "How's them ribs?"

"He kicked me, Darren, or I would have put him in the trees."

"Don't worry. You're home now."

* * *

Sita listened to the rain and imagined it washing away the last remnants of terror the skinheads had forced on her. She imagined dark scraps of fear riding the current of a storm-swollen River Gan until they disappeared in the waves.

Ty lay next to her in the darkness.

"Can you hear the rain?" she asked.

"Yes."

"It sounds just like it does when I stand under trees along the river path."

She felt his hand take hers. "I thought everyone we met would be good and want to help us," he said. "That's how my vision looked. But there are beasts in the city, too, just like the beasts in the forest."

Sita nuzzled her face against his chest. "How can we ever get back to Gan," she asked, "when we can't even go to the big street with lights without fighting and turning back?"

"We're not ready to leave," he answered. "The reason we're here is becoming clearer."

* * *

Star stood at the entrance to the cave, watching the rain pour down through the moonless black sky. He wondered how his son would find shelter in the raging storm. He knew there were caves along the river cliffs, but without a fire to see what kind of danger crawled through the dark interior, it was a treacherous place to seek refuge.

Star felt a hand on his shoulder. Su leaned her head against his arm and together they looked into the watery eyes of the rampaging storm and wondered what was happening to their only child.

CHAPTER 20

Ty had a fistful of reservations about accompanying Darren to his morning meeting with Dr. Greenberg. Sita encouraged him to go. "You will see more of the world you came to see. Like you said, maybe it's not time to go back. Maybe the reason will become clearer."

He told her that he dreamed he had skateboarded back to the caves. "I went up and down the mountains and it was easy. I just pushed with my foot and the wheels never stopped."

"First, you tell me a *Star Wars* ship will take us back, now you skateboard. Big difference, sweetie." She smiled and held his arms. "I'll stay here and put more potions on Shum's chest."

"Sita."

She looked over to Darren, standing in his office doorway. She gave Ty a quick kiss and walked back to the office.

"This is it," he said, bringing up the Macy's website on his computer. Darren wrote "shoes," "dresses," "jeans," and "sweaters" on a piece of paper with crude replicas beside each word. "Then you click the mouse on the word or picture you want to look at." He swooshed the mouse over to the shopping cart icon. "Don't ever click the mouse on the shopping cart. Big trouble for me."

"Chill, Darren." Sita moved the cursor to shoes. "I don't know your credit card number. Besides, believe it or not, they don't ship to the River Gan."

Darren shook his head and walked out of the room.

* * *

He backed the Jeep out of the garage, made a left turn at the end of the alley, and headed toward the boulevard. "Like I told you, Greenberg's the man who helps me understand my relationship to my father and Dorsey."

Ty sat quietly, observing the corner strip malls, boys flying by on skateboards, and buildings that jutted like cold, faceless cliffs into the sky.

"He's called a therapist, Ty. A 'shrink,' most people say in Los Angeles. That's because he can charge you for a full hour and shrink it into forty-five minutes." Darren glanced to see if Ty got the joke. "Whatcha thinking?"

"It's bigger than anything I thought the world could be." Ty leaned back and looked over to Darren. "Do you think Dr. Greenberg is anything like Man Who Stands Alone?"

"What's the Man like?"

"He's got one eye covered with feathers and a long white beard. And he sits in front of a fire pit with animal skulls next to him."

Darren smiled. "I don't really think they're riding the same horse."

"Man Who Stands Alone doesn't ride."

"It's just an expression, Skater." Darren reached over and smacked Ty's knee. "Sounds like your thing is more like voodoo, and Greenberg is more into modern theories, Freud, Jung, Adler, that kind of stuff. Does this Man charge any kind of money?"

"No."

"Big difference number two, Skater. It costs *mucho* bucks to sit in someone's office and vomit up your problems." Darren turned right on to Santa Monica Boulevard. "Does this voodoo Man help you see things?"

"Man sees everything. I made fun of him, but I really believe he's helping me now. Big time."

"Maybe he'll help you get home. You should try to get in touch with him. Of course, he probably doesn't have email, either." Darren looked over to Ty with a big, earnest smile. "Skater, you make me feel good. I don't know what it is, morning after a rain, ions in the air, or what, but we're hanging together, first time, and I'm feeling the energy, the *chi*, the Chinese call it."

"Isn't that what's on the pizza?"

"That's cheese. Don't be nutty."

He turned into a parking structure under a three-story red-brick building. "Dr. Greenberg could be a big help. Once he identifies who you are, he'll pinpoint where you come from. He did fieldwork with the pygmies."

They got out of the Jeep and walked over to the elevator.

Then a smile beamed across Darren's face as if he'd just keyed in on the mystery of the *wings*. "You know what I've never asked you guys?" He slapped the side of his head. "Your last names! Ty what?"

Ty stared back with a mystified air. "Ty what?"

"Look." Darren opened his hands, as if the answer was written on his palms. "My name is Darren Michael Davies. Darren first name. Michael middle name. Davies last name. That's my father's name. *Comprende*?"

"My father's name is Star."

"Star what?"

"Star is all I know."

Ty stared at the light above the elevator doors.

The light blinked. The steel doors opened. The search for a last name was over.

"Here we go," Darren said. "Super mystery revealed in forty-five minutes, max."

* * *

Ty shook the therapist's hand. Aside from children, Dr. Greenberg was the shortest white man Ty had ever seen. The shrink's bald head was on an even plane with Ty's forehead.

Ty took a seat close to the right corner of Greenberg's desk. It was a long, shiny wood table piled with books and papers. Darren sat in an armchair next to the window.

"So, what are we here to discuss: your father, Dorsey, or your hesitancy to strike out on your own, which is it?" The doctor looked at Darren through clear glasses with gold stems.

Darren gave a quick account of his dinner date the night before with Dorsey. It was at an expensive restaurant. "She wanted to go there because a lot of important show biz people frequent the place. We talked mostly about her career and—"

"What?"

Ty folded his arms, glad the talk was between Darren and the doctor. Then he saw Darren look toward him.

"Well, she's not really into the kids."

Greenberg shot up with a surprised smile. "You weren't planning on having a child with her?"

"No."

The shrink nodded in Ty's direction. "You mean this boy?"

"And his friends." Darren explained that altogether there were four, including one girl, and they had been with him for three days.

"How long are they planning on staying?"

"Well, that's the thing. That's the puzzle. We don't know how to get them back."

Greenberg looked over to Ty, who was beginning to feel uncomfortable. He was afraid the man in the brown suit would start asking him questions in the same quick voice with which he was questioning Darren.

"They have families, and they really don't want to stay here," Darren went on. "Last night, they tried to run away."

"Obviously, if this boy is here, they didn't succeed. Why not?" Greenberg gave Ty a glance, but turned to Darren for the answer.

"They got in a fight in Westwood. The cops broke it up and sent the kids back to my house."

"Violence, huh? Gang fighting?" Greenberg swiveled to Ty. "You don't know where you live, or you don't know how to get to where you live?" The question hung as he narrowed his eyes. "Or you're making up some kind of story? You can tell me the truth. These walls are like steel. Your answers won't leave this room."

Ty didn't like the look in Greenberg's eyes. No one questioned a Kishoki's truthfulness. "I know where I live. Along the River Gan."

"How do you get there? How did you get here?"

"We tasted emmydactyl blood and Sita's powder."

"What's emmydactyl blood?" The shrink wrinkled up his eyes. "Who's Sita?"

"That's the girl I mentioned on the phone this morning," Darren jumped in. "She and Ty are a couple. Teenage love stuff. Very sweet."

"Darren, you're butting in. This has to be a natural colloquy if I'm going to get anywhere." Greenberg tugged at the knot in his emerald tie and turned back to the visitor. "What is emmydactyl blood, young man?"

Ty didn't know if he should mention forest beasts. He was feeling sweat on his back.

"It's a terrible beast, Dr. Greenberg. Like *Jurassic Park*. These kids—"

The shrink's right hand flew up, cutting Darren off. "You're butting in again. I'm doing just fine and have for thirty years, including four field trips to New Guinea, without your help!" He glared through his glasses at Ty. "Emmydactyl. Is it some street name for a drug? Like horse, shrooms, or keefer?"

Ty shook his head slowly.

"Yet, you said you ingested some powder. Do you take that orally or snort the emmydactyl?"

"You don't snort the emmydactyl." Darren plunged in again. "Sita has powders. She calls them potions. Man Who Stands Alone taught her."

Turning his back on Darren, Greenberg sniffed up twice and thrust his finger between his lips several times. "You know what I mean, Ty. Which one?"

Ty stared at the man behind the desk. He could feel a knot forming in his stomach.

"Is Man Who Stands Alone your dealer, the Big Ace?"

"No! He's not a druggie!" Darren cried out. "You're going the wrong way!"

Ty could see Greenberg's body stiffen. "No one, especially in front of another patient, tells me I'm going the wrong way. It may be, Mr. Davies, that you should be going another way with another therapist. I find your behavior unacceptable. Now…" He swung back to Ty and pushed a stack of folders to the side. "I was asking you, young man, if, in fact, this person you call Man Who Stands Alone is your drug contact or dealer?"

"Man Who Stands Alone is a shaman."

"A shaman." The shrink was getting restless. "You mean someone who chants, uses herb concoctions, magic stones?"

Ty swore to himself that this was the last question he would answer. "A shell," he said. He was getting more upset by the fighting between Darren and Greenberg. He knew, at least he felt, that he was the cause. His whole body was heating up.

"Okay, shells. And did he tell you to go to Darren's house?"

Darren jumped up. "I told you. We met on a mountaintop in Topanga!"

"I'm warning you, Darren. Stop butting in. You're wrecking the flow." Greenberg swiveled back to Ty. "So, you kids were on a mountain. How come? Were you just out traipsing around, camping, what brought you there?" His eyes narrowed. "A secret patch of marijuana?"

Ty rubbed his hands. His head felt squeezed by the flurry of questions. Again, he promised to himself that this would be his final answer. "The future," he said in a voice so low it sounded like a whisper.

"The future. What future? Whose future? Dystopia? Is that what you're saying?"

Darren screamed out, "He doesn't know anything about dystopia!"

Greenberg leaped to his feet. His chair hit the back wall. "I am so fed up with you, Darren. I'm doing this as a personal favor to you. You asked me to talk to this boy. Let me talk to him! This new generation is all about dystopia. You, a fledgling filmmaker, ought to know about this. Seventy percent of my clients are in show business. These kids see before them a bankrupt, catastrophic world. A world of desperate survival. Fighting for food, living off the land, clawing to survive in the fury of dysfunction! Am I right?"

Ty saw the doctor's eyes, like bright yellow bug eyes, glaring at him.

"Was that what this is all about? Preparing for a terrifying, vicious, dysfunctional world? What grade are you in?"

"He went to cave school!" Darren blurted out.

Greenberg yanked his emerald tie again, nearly pulling it off. "That's it, Darren. Turn your chair around or leave the office."

Darren leaned back and gulped air. "I'm sorry, Dr. Greenberg, but I know these kids. They never went to school."

Greenberg narrowed his eyes at Ty. "Is that true? You're illiterate. You can't read or write? Your parents can't read or write either?" Ty didn't answer. "So how do you live?" Greenberg flung his arms forward, leaning across his desk. "According to Darren, you came with sleeping bags, bone knives, and spears."

"One spear." Darren held up a finger. "Shummy's spear."

"You must have bought them at some store. You're asking me to believe you move through society without money, without any kind of transportation, and you can't find your parents, and the only street address you have is the River Gan?" Greenberg threw his fists in the air and brought them crashing down on his desk. "You're lying, young man! You're making a big joke at my expense!"

"I'm paying for it!"

Greenberg whirled to Darren. "Your father's paying for it!" He fired another question at Ty. "Why don't you want to go home?"

Ty felt like a rope was tightening around his neck. He got up from his chair. "I want to go home," he said, backing toward the door.

"Wait for me!" Darren leapt out of his chair.

Greenberg scrambled to the corner of his desk as the office door flew open. "You wanted the truth, you got it! I just needed the facts. In all my field research, I've never heard of emmydactyl. Morphine, methamphetamine, yes!"

Darren was heading for the open door.

"He's from a rough-and-tumble world, Mr. Davies! Drugs, street fights! Quack shamans! That's not the Berber carpet world," he stammered. "That boy dyed his hair ginger!"

The door slammed shut on "ginger!"

Ty looked down the hallway. Darren was racing toward him at the bank of elevators. "I'm sorry," he said, gasping for breath. His face was red, his eyes crimped with sadness, and his voice was weighted with a feeling that Ty had never heard before. "I'm really sorry."

Ty pushed the button with the arrow pointing down.

"He had no idea who I was, Darren."

"No."

"Or where I'm from."

Darren shook his head again.

When the ding sounded and the silent doors opened, Darren took Ty's hand. They walked together into the elevator. The *wing* felt the white man's hand surround his fingers. That was another thing Ty had never felt before.

* * *

Darren drove out of the McDonald's parking lot, past the golden arches, into city traffic.

"How you feelin'?"

"A lot better. Burgers are great."

Darren watched Ty dip his last French fry into a pool of catsup, hoping the food would settle him.

"When we fought those guys in Westwood, I knew what was going to happen. They throw fists, we throw fists. But in Dr. Greenberg's office, I didn't know what he was going to say or even if I was going to understand it. He kept pounding questions on me."

"You did great, Ty. I know how you hate when people start grillin' you. He's never been that way with me. Maybe because my old man pays the bill."

Ty didn't respond. He powered down his window.

"Maybe it's true about short guys having a Napoleon complex. I studied him in my European history class. Not Greenberg. Napoleon." Darren jogged the Jeep around a double-parked car and bobbed his head. "'I'm an educated fool with money on my mind/Got my ten in my hand and a gleam in my eye.'" A sly grin crossed his lips. "Know who that is?"

"Do you really think I care?" Ty closed the burger box on his lap. "I have no f'n idea."

"I suppose you learned that from TV too."

"From Ko, Darren. And don't say anything bad about him again because I love Ko."

"Love him, but he's got a smart mouth and he's disrespectful."

"Maybe so. But he'll die for you. You need *wings* like that on a journey."

Darren wheeled around a corner onto the boulevard. "How about Shum?"

"His heart is bigger than your *casa*."

"You Kishoki are really tight. I get it." He wanted to say more, something about guys in foxholes or undercover cops, but Ty interrupted him.

"Don't you have someone who'd fight for you? Darren?"

Darren kept his gaze straight ahead. His voice sank to a whisper. "No, not really."

"You do now." A smile followed Ty's words.

Darren adjusted his sunglasses. He tapped the steering wheel. His voice died again by the end of the second word. "Thank you."

Ty didn't add anything, but he didn't move his eyes away, either.

Oh, sure, just what I need. I'm gonna start bawling in front of a cave kid. Darren straightened himself up and cleared his throat. "I know sometimes I talk too much. I always get nervous before I see one of the commercials I shot for my dad." He slowed down to a red light.

"Look!" Ty was pointing past Darren's eye line to something on the driver's left.

Darren shot a look across the street. "The record store on the corner? What?" He raised his eyes. "The billboard?"

On the record store roof, a giant billboard jutted into the sky. A trio of animals—an elephant, an ape, and an antelope—loomed life-size in brightly colored panels. "Go South This Summer – The San Diego Safari Park" was scrolled across the top.

"Is that what you're looking at, Ty? The billboard?" Darren glanced back. The passenger seat was empty. The car door was open. "Ty?"

157

He turned back to the street. Ty was dodging cross-street traffic against a crescendo of blaring horns.

"Ty! Ty!" Darren screamed. The light turned green. Cars behind him were honking. He accelerated through the intersection and swooped into a red zone, nearly peeling off a fire hydrant.

When he looked back, he saw Ty shimming up a crosshatch of iron pipes and wooden slats. Partially dismantled billboard scaffolding leaned against the side of the building. Ty hung onto the ledge of a second-floor window. Darren couldn't believe his eyes. *He's going to kill himself or get us both arrested.* "Get down!" he shouted.

By the time Darren edged the Jeep forward, Ty had swung his leg up to an adjoining window ledge and was balancing himself upright. Darren watched the Kishoki boy raise his hands to the edge of the flat roof, pull his body up, and disappear.

Then he saw the slim brown figure, in his baggy black shorts and black T, racing across the rooftop toward the billboard. He knew it was Ty. The sunlight struck his amber skin, and the filmmaker imagined a golden butterfly fluttering across the roof. When Ty reached the sign, he stood beneath it and raised his hand, jumping up and down, pointing to the panel directly above his head. "Antelope," he shouted. "Antelope People!"

"Antelope people! It's an animal! Get down!" Darren jumped out of the Jeep and pressed his body against the driver's side door. "Get your ass down here!" he screamed above the din of passing cars. "And be careful!"

Ty waved back, which only brought another hoarse cry from Darren. "Get down, you little rock head!"

People on the sidewalk stopped to see what Darren was shouting about. "Get the tagger off the roof!" a lady holding a sun umbrella yelled.

But another feeling was rising in Darren. The feeling was new, or a reinforcement of what he had felt when he apologized to Ty and took his hand in the elevator. He watched the cave boy clamber down the side of the building and swoop like a monkey through the scaffold piping to the sidewalk. The feeling caught in Darren's throat again. He realized it was pride in and concern for a boy whose story he hardly believed, for a teenager who claimed to have emerged from the mist of time. Darren shook his head. *This is something I could never do.*

Dodging cars, he raced into the middle of the street and grabbed Ty's hand. They scooted through traffic to the Jeep. Darren shuffled Ty across the driver's seat, got in, and joined the parade of cars.

"What was that all about?" Darren was trying to relax, but he was gulping air.

"The Antelope People," Ty answered proudly. "My people."

"Ty, that's a zoo park. Those are animals up there. Those aren't people."

"Yes, but it's a sign."

"Yeah, a zoo sign."

"You understand one way. I know another. You read the letters on the sign. I listen to what the sign is telling me."

"It's not that simple. Not everything is voodoo." Darren nodded to himself, trying to justify his own thoughts. "That was a very busy street you crossed. You could have gotten killed. You'd have been a dead antelope." As the minutes and miles passed, his irritation gradually succumbed to the boy's safe presence beside him. He fished a package of spearmint gum from the console and offered Ty a stick. "Go ahead, take off the wrapper and chew it."

Ty stared at the silver foil. "What is it?"

"Gum." Darren unwrapped his stick of gum and put it in his mouth. "Go ahead. It's mint. Good for the nerves." Ty followed Darren's instructions. "Don't swallow it, just chew." He told Ty to save the wrapper and, when the flavor was gone, put the gum in the paper. "We got it from the Indians." Darren took a deep breath.

"You guys are sort of like the Indians. Politically correct, Native Americans. The buffalo, the antelope, shamans."

"I never mentioned buffalo, Darren."

"I'm just sayin'."

Ty explained that the Kishoki were part of the Antelope Tribe. The Antelope People left, but the Kishoki stayed behind in caves. "My clan thought the Antelope People died in winter storms."

Darren looked over to the cave boy, chomping away on his gum and smiling. All the vestiges of the Greenberg nightmare seemed to have vanished in the swirl of Ty's rooftop flight.

"We came from far in the past. It's like a dream, Darren. The Antelope People went through many dreams. Now they are here. And someday I will be here too."

"You're here. You've just got to talk like a homeboy and watch you don't get hit by traffic." Darren chuckled, slapping Ty's knee. "Skater, we're gum chewers! You're from a stone-cold cave and I'm from the crib of luxury, but we're getting along. Who woulda thunk it? Maybe we're on the same road, together."

Darren hung a left on Highland Boulevard, turned right on Sunset, and needled his way through narrow side streets into the depths of Hollywood.

"I'm going to tell you something I've never told anyone, not even Greenberg."

"You've already told us something you never told Greenberg. About your mother. Sometimes it's good to be quiet, Darren."

"Right."

He pulled into a small parking lot alongside a gray three-story building. He cocked his chin toward Ty. "Is my eczema breaking out?"

Ty studied Darren's chin. "It's a little red, but not like it was."

"Good. Let's go."

* * *

Decades of smog and neglect had coated the second-floor windows with grime. The building façade, scarred with cracks and tagged with zigzag script, stood on pitted cornerstones.

"Hollywood's got a lot of glamor up front, Ty, but don't let that fool you. The back rooms are all about knives and mirrors."

They climbed to the second floor and walked down a dimly lit corridor until they reached the sign "2B" on a dark wood door.

Ty followed Darren into a cramped, airless room. The only light came from the glow of two computer monitors sitting side by side on a workbench.

"How's it going, Marc?"

The film editor swung around. Backlit by the glow of computer screens, all Ty could see was a white man with a short, scraggly beard and round glasses covering his eyes.

"It's coming together," he said.

"Let's take a look."

Marc swiveled back and dragged the computer cursor to an icon. The picture of a giant "Karpet World" store popped on, underscored with music. Then a voice boomed: "We carry all the famous brands of carpets and rugs for every room in your house or office! Sink your feet into our carpets, as lush and beautiful as the hills that surround us, and send your heart soaring!" Over this, a shot panned the sunlit Topanga Canyon.

Darren nudged Ty. "That's the mountain where we met. You guys climbed up and Scottie tried to chase you off."

With the mountains behind him, a stocky man in his fifties, wearing an olive green suit, appeared on screen. His slick brown toupee was topped with a gold crown. In a gruff staccato voice, he launched into another carpet spiel:

"I'm Glen C. Davies, owner of Karpet World. I wear a rug, so I know what a good rug means. I guarantee you the lowest prices, the best service, and I'll give everyone who buys two rooms or more of my fabulous carpet free installation!" He threw his stumpy arms to his sides. "Why go to the Middle East when you can buy a Persian rug at any one of our five convenient locations? And we won't make your wallet a hostage!"

Darren leaned to Ty. "That's my dad." He looked back at the monitors. "Looks like we got it all, Marc. Give me a shout when you lay the graphics in."

"Gotcha."

"Oh, by the way, this is my friend Ty."

"Nice to meet you, Ty." Marc raised his hand in the semi-darkness. "Hey, wait up, Darren." The editor ripped a sticky note off the computer table. "Some guy down the hall stopped by. He was on crutches, said he wanted to talk to you. Left a phone number. Room 7B."

"Thanks." Darren shoved the note in his pocket.

As they walked down the hallway, Ty seemed more interested in the note than Darren, who was more eager to hear Ty's reaction to the commercial.

Ty smiled. "I liked it. The mountain looks just like the mountain we climbed."

"That's what filming is all about. You point the camera at something, record it on film or digital, and then you can play it back."

"If we could take a camera back to the caves, we could record my people and then send it back to you." He looked up. "Except it would have to jump over the sun."

Darren nodded, as if he understood the concept. He looked down at the sticky note and stopped in front of door #7B. *Walsheim Productions* was lettered on a piece of white paper taped to the front. "Walsheim Productions. Never heard of it."

Darren knocked. No one answered.

Ty set his hand against the door panel and closed his eyes. "I've got a good feeling about this."

The young director chuckled. "It's called a door, Ty."

"Yeah. The door of opportunity."

* * *

They drove back in silence. Ty, relieved that Darren had stopped talking, kept thinking about Mr. Davies in the magic crystal on Marc's desk.

"I know people aren't really in the TV," he said. "Like you told us. But, if the people aren't in the box, how do they get there?"

"It's a miracle, sort of. I mean, it's technical too. Something called electronics." Darren wasn't an expert on anything, including technology, but he had a fairly reasonable understanding of how TV worked. "Anyway, in the end," he said, "the tiny little pieces are broken down and sent as electronic impulses through the sky and then put back together on the other end, but it happens faster than you can blink an eye." He looked over to Ty. "Don't hold me to every word, but it's something like that."

Ty leaned back in his seat, wondering if he, Sita, and the *wings* weren't some kind of broken-up picture from the forest caves, sent by the emmydactyl's blood or Sita's potions, and put back together on the mountain. "So, we're here," he finally said. He placed his gum in the silver paper, thinking how jealous Sita would be if she knew about the gum. "Does everyone in America chew gum?"

"Lots of people. Bubble gum's the dope. I mean, not dope dope, not really dope." Darren was too busy making a right turn into the alley to go on. He told Ty to press the garage door opener.

The white door rose smoothly. Ty imagined it was like the animal hide pulled back from the mouth of his cave, but it wasn't the past he was entering.

"The little pieces are coming together in my head, Darren. We're back in Darren-land."

"We never left."

"Maybe not in your mind, but I've got two worlds inside of me. The one I'm coming back to and the one I never left."

CHAPTER 21

Ko jumped off his chair with Darren's first step into the living room. "We weren't watching TV all day, Darren. No way. We were outside."

Darren looked over to Shum. "What about your ribs?"

"Sita made the pain go away." Shum raised the cheese curl bag.

"That's the good news," Ko said. "But we have a problem. Not a big problem."

"A little problem," Shum agreed.

* * *

Darren stared at a broken window set in the back wall of the garage.

"Ko hit it," Shum said.

"With the bat?"

"No, no, Darren. I hit a dinger. The ball went through the window. Like TV talk, I jacked it."

"That's what happened," Sita confirmed. "I pitched and Ko slammed it. He ran around the bases twice."

Darren shook his head. "I didn't even notice it when I drove in." He looked over to Sita. "But my father will notice it. We've got to fix this before he comes over again."

Sita brushed aside Darren's concern. "Did Ty see Dr. Greenberg?"

"I saw him, Sita." Ty nudged into the conversation.

"Dr. Greenberg wasn't helpful. I'm sure Ty will tell you."

"Darren has big news too."

Darren gave Ty a surprised look. "I do? What?"

"The man who left you a phone number."

"That's not news. I don't even know what that's about." Darren shook his head as if to say, *Drop the subject.* "Let's go inside."

Sita wouldn't let it go. "What do you think it's about?"

"I just told you, Sita, I don't know."

"Darren said it was a production company."

"What's a production company, Darren?" Sita persisted.

"A production company is a kind of business that makes films. But this isn't *Star Wars*, count on it."

"*Star Wars*!" Ko and Shum's eyes flipped up at the mention of the film.

Darren dismissed their excitement with a hand wave. "This is just a dinky company, or they wouldn't have an office with a piece of paper taped to the door." Sita's pestering questions were rubbing against his annoyance over the broken window. "This has nothing to do with you and probably nothing to do with me, either. It's getting very hot out here. My skin isn't like yours. It burns easily. I'm going inside."

The *wings* followed Darren back to the house.

"But you should call that number," Sita said.

"Why?"

"Maybe it's good for you. You don't know anything about it, you said so. So maybe you call and you find out. That makes sense."

"That makes sense," Shum echoed, from several feet behind them.

"I had a good feeling," Ty added.

Darren glanced back and opened the kitchen door. "Maybe I don't care." He stopped at the counter and glanced at the phone. The message light wasn't blinking.

"Maybe you should care."

"Sita, I'm twenty-four, you're fourteen. You should be listening to me. I'm not listening to you. You don't know where you live. You don't know how to get home. You didn't even have underwear when you got here. Why should I be listening to you?"

Sita planted her hands on her hips. "You think you hurt my feelings just now? No way. I am a shaman. Do you know what that is?"

"Yes." Darren got right back in her face. "A man who does magic tricks, and you're not a man! You're not even a grown-up!"

Sita backed up against the counter and jammed her hands against it. "I am learning, Darren. That's something you don't understand. A shaman does not just mean potions and chants and sacred fires."

"Oh, really. What does it mean? Shells on your booties?"

"Relax, Darren," Ty intervened. "Just breathe."

"Ty's right." Sita lowered her voice. "It's understanding who you are so you can understand who everyone else is. It's seeing the world as something greater than that little red spot on your chin, something fantastic, a mystery you join, even though you don't know where it will lead or how it will end."

Darren stood silent for a moment, wondering where she came up with all those words. "You don't know what you're talking about."

"Really?"

"Yes, really. And don't you think I know where this phone call will end?"

"No."

"Ha! You don't know Hollywood."

"I know where I am and why I'm here. I even know," she said, looking up into his eyes, hushing her voice, "why we're in this kitchen."

Darren shot a look to Ty. "I hope you don't marry her, because she'll drive you nuts."

"I like nuts," Ko shouted from the living room.

"I've had enough of this." Darren headed for the doorway. "I'm going to my room and lie down."

"Sita is right!" Ty said. "Marc told you to call him."

The director whipped around. "Marc didn't say that! He just said there's a phone number on the note. Telling a person there's a number isn't an order to call. That's English! Besides, he works for me. I don't take orders from him!" Darren's forehead was reddening. He looked from Ty to Sita. "I'm not doing this for either of you. Or for whatever you said!" He marched over to the phone, pulled the sticky note from his pocket, jerked up the receiver, and dialed the number. Seconds later, he spoke into a voice mail, left his name and number, and hung up. His voice cracked with a trace of disappointment. "I left a message."

"Good." Sita paused. "Darren?"

"What?"

"You weren't doing it for us, and that's the best part."

"Sure. Next you're going to tell me I'm doing it for Mr. Walsheim." He left the room, shaking his head.

Ty looked over to Sita. "He can't get us back to the Gan, but maybe we can get him out of his father's house."

She nodded slowly. "Maybe that's why we're here."

* * *

"You know the house rules," Darren cautioned on his way out. "You don't let anyone in. My dad has a key."

"What about Dorsey?"

"No. Just shout through the window, 'He's not here!'"

Ty was happy Ko and Shum were going along with Darren to pick up tacos. The two Stone Age kids listened to the back door close, leaving them for the first time alone in the house. They had never sat in either the swivel chair or the bulky armchair, mostly commandeered by Shum and Ko. They rested their heads against the soft leather backs and closed their eyes. A dusky, golden sunlight filled the living room. Ty started to giggle.

"What's funny?" Sita wondered, but she was giggling too.

"We are here, in America." Ty swiveled the chair toward her. "But maybe we are only here in our dreams."

"What a dream," she sighed. "I love America, don't you?"

"I saw more today, just like you said. I saw Darren's father on TV. And you know what else I saw?" He paused, enjoying his moment of knowing something Sita didn't know.

"What else?"

"The antelope. It was on a billboard. That's a big sign. And it means the Antelope People are here, Sita. And Darren explained to me how TV works. It's little pieces that people send through the air and then they come back together inside the magic crystal."

Sita threw her head back and groaned. "You learned all that while I stayed here playing stupid baseball with Ko and Shummy."

"You told me to go."

"I know," she answered in a wistful tone.

"And you know what else I did?" Ty's smile broadened, watching her jealousy rise again. "Chewing gum."

It was clear that Sita had no idea what chewing gum was, which bothered her almost as much as Ty's experience with it. "What is it?"

"You chew it." Ty moved his jaw up and down. "It feels like *chikaya* but it's sweet."

"Do you swallow it?"

"No, never." He explained how you put it back in a small silver paper once the flavor is gone.

"What a day." Sita shook her head. Ty's adventures chastened her, but soon the sparkle came back to her eyes. "What if we had a house like this and we had babies and a car?"

"Ty and Sita in America."

"Yes! With a kitchen and a shower and a backyard."

"And a skateboard and computer and..."

"A TV!" She clapped her hand. "We'll be just like everyone else at the mall."

Ty turned his head to the magic crystal. His eyes flew open. "Sita, press the sound! It's the Garden Show!"

Sita pushed the mute button on the remote. A white-haired man in his fifties was pulling a green hose along a vegetable garden, watering the plants.

"That thing's called a hose, Ty, just like the one Darren has in the backyard."

Ty waved a dismissive hand.

"Well, Mr. Chewing Gum, you keep talking about a garden, but Kishoki don't have a hose." Sita leaned toward his chair, fired up over all the things he'd done without her. "Just like the zucchini aren't really in Darren's living room. It's just little pieces on TV!"

"Sita, you keep talking and I can't hear the man!"

"So how are you going to get water up the hill from the river? Water doesn't run uphill. If it doesn't rain, say good-bye to the veggies."

"Say good-bye to Sita if you keep talking."

"Man Who Stands Alone knows more about plants."

"Man Who Stands Alone doesn't have a garden. Maybe that's why I'm here!" Ty banged the chair arm. Before he could say another word, the slap of the back door stopped him. "Did you hear that?"

Sita muted the TV sound. Footsteps crossed the kitchen floor. "Only Mr. Davies has a key," she whispered.

The Karpet King strode through the dining room and stopped in the living room archway. He wore a dark blue suit and a red tie. His gray eyes shifted between the two *wings*.

"Where's Darren?"

"Tacos," Ty answered.

"Tacos? What the hell's that mean? Tacos, New Mexico?"

"It means, Mr. Davies," Sita piped up, "that Darren has gone to get dinner for his houseguests."

"You? Is that who you're calling houseguests?" The *wings* watched Davies' twisted smile fade quickly into a tight, grim face. "Weren't you supposed to be leaving?"

"We're helping Darren," Ty answered calmly.

"Helping him fix the garage window?" the Karpet King shot back. "Which one of you did that?"

"It happened in a baseball game," Sita answered. "I was pitching. Ko hit a homer."

"Who's Ko?" Davies barked. "Is he paying for the window?"

"Ko is definitely low on cash and…" Sita flopped one leg over the other and brushed the knee of her new jeans. "We don't have credit cards like Darren."

"We'll see how long he keeps those if this goes on. Tell Darren to call me as soon as he gets back." Davies marched through the living room.

The kids heard the front door slam. They rushed to the picture window and watched a black car pull away from the curb. Ty turned to Sita. "Mr. Davies doesn't want us here."

"We know that, Ty. But Darren does. He thought we were just silly kids doing rap music, but just like that garden needs water, he needs us. You said that in the kitchen."

"Were you always this smart?"

"I do a lot of thinking when I'm online shopping." Sita smiled and took her lover's hand. "I see the pictures of the shoes and clothes, but in my mind I see the light on the River Gan and I see the shadows of trees on the caves when the sun is at the edge of the cliffs where you and I would walk together. I think of Man Who Stands Alone and the silence that surrounds him and lets me be a part of that silence, where everything I feel and have ever felt becomes a moment of what Man calls *kashwei*."

"*Kashwei?*"

"Grace."

"I don't think I know what that means."

"Someday you will, my little feather."

* * *

"Sorry we're so late." Darren handed Ty and Sita white Styrofoam containers. "Got you guys chicken tacos." Darren crashed on the floor, nestling into the corner by the DVD shelves. It was becoming his fixture spot. "What else did we do, Shum?"

"We bought a piece of glass for the broken window."

He turned to Ko. "What else?"

Ko's dour face blossomed unexpectedly with a mountain-size grin. "Bubble gum." He poked his tongue through the wad of gum in his mouth. Instantly, a fluffy pink bubble perched on his lips.

Sita stopped in the middle of biting into her taco. "Bubble gum? No way!"

"I can go bigger!" Shum breathed slowly, expanding the pink bubble on his lips. He jumped up and spread his arms.

"It's bigger than Ko's!" Darren shouted.

Bang! It popped, plastering a pink web of gum across Shum's chin and cheeks.

Ko doubled over, laughing. "Maybe his was bigger," he wheezed, "but I didn't make a mess on my face!"

Darren folded his hands. "Don't worry, Sita. I bought gum for you too. And Ty."

"I'll help you fix the window." Ty stopped eating. "Your father was pretty *nagwana*."

"*Nagwana*? My father?"

"Angry," Sita translated. "Super angry."

"How does my father know? Was my father here?" Darren nearly knocked over a shelf of DVDs, jumping to his feet.

"Your father was here and asked a lot of questions."

Darren looked at Sita. "What did he say about the window?"

"He wanted to know if Ko was going to pay to get it fixed. Then he said something about your credit cards."

Darren felt his jaw tighten. "You shouldn't have said anything. You should have let me handle this."

"You weren't here, and we didn't invite him in."

"I know how to talk to my father, you don't!"

"You know how to agree with your father." Sita set aside her taco. Her voice opened softly. "You always worry about what your father is going to say. 'What will my father say about the commercial? What will my father say about the window?' He never worries about what you're going to say. Why?"

The question confused Darren. He could feel his thoughts stumbling over each other in his mind.

"He doesn't care, Darren."

"You don't even know my father."

Sita spun her head toward Ty. "Do I know his father?"

"Sita's a shaman."

"She's a shaman with a shoe fetish!"

"So what?" Sita plunked the taco box down on the end table and got off the armchair. "Did you ever think your feet are connected to your brain? That's what got us here. You're the one who doesn't move. You're the one with the red spot on his chin. What does your father say about that? He's the reason your chin is red and your chest itches!"

"You don't know what you're talking about." Darren let the words drift from his mouth without any fight left in his voice. "You're fourteen summers."

"You keep saying that, but maybe our summers are longer than yours. Think about it." Sita swung her hips and left the room.

Darren turned to Ty. "Is she really a shaman?"

"Man Who Stands Alone is teaching her."

Darren shook his head. "Man Who Stands Alone, shamans, emmydactyls, and caves. This is all so crazy."

Ty got off the swivel chair. "So is TV, Darren, and fridges and cars and malls and cell phones. But we are here and you were never there."

"Never." Ko blew another bubble.

* * *

Sita was already asleep when Ty crawled into bed. His thoughts drifted to the two of them sitting in the living room, talking about credit cards and living in America. He thought of how Star would laugh at him if he talked about cell phones, magic crystals, cars, and bubble gum. He could hear his father's voice as if he were speaking to him from the bedroom door: "You go in the forest, wander many moons, then you come back and crazy talk about things no one can see." Star would laugh harder, like he did when Ty showed him the net woven of vines for catching fish.

The laughter dissolved into Sita's voice taunting Darren: "What will your father say?" The words swirled in Ty's head: *What will your father say?* The breeze ruffled the blinds and one word rushed through his mind. *Baseball!*

Ty jumped out of bed, raced past Shum on the couch and Ko on the floor, maneuvered through the dark dining room and kitchen lit by the overhead stove light, until he reached the alcove closet. He pulled out the baseball glove and stared at the webbing. *That's what it needs! I weave the net tighter with leather strips, small holes so the water goes through but not the fish.* He tossed the glove back in the closet, closed the door, and the ridicule of all the elders stopped, as if he had trapped their haunting laughter in a dark, hidden tomb.

He rushed into the living room. Ko and Shum were still asleep. Ty walked over to the picture window and pulled back the drapes. The moon, no longer full but still robust, glowed in the midnight sky. *My father's moon. Someday he will not laugh at me.* Beams of silver light showered the chairs and couch. Ko wheezed,

173

snorted, and turned in his bedroll. Ty looked back. Shum raised a drowsy eye.

"What are you doing?"

"I've got a great idea for catching fish," Ty whispered.

"Fish? Is Darren going fishing?"

"No. Go back to sleep. I'll tell you in the morning. But..."

"What?"

"I climbed to the top of a record store. I touched the antelope. That's a sign the Antelope People are here! And I have a plan for getting us to the River Gan!"

"How?"

"On the backs of the antelope."

Shum's head hit the couch pillow. His eyes closed.

CHAPTER 22

"Let's go before the sun gets too hot." Darren had on his Panama hat and work gloves, anxious to fix the garage window before his father returned. "You're going to learn how to replace glass. You never know when you'll be getting windows. Time's faster than you think."

"Everything's faster than Ko," Shum added, tossing his breakfast plate in the sink. "Except when he's eating pizza."

"Shummy, be nice. I brought you back from the dead and carried you on my back."

"That's a little over the top." Darren shut off the coffeemaker. "But Captain Martinez did say neither of those skinheads believed you were fourteen summers."

"They'll never forget the Kishoki Cannonballs."

"You don't even know what a cannonball is."

"So what?" Ko stuffed the last bite of French toast in his mouth. "I'm a Kishoki. I know the first part."

* * *

Sita sat in Darren's office staring at the computer screen. She studied the different Macy's fashions with only half-hearted interest. Her attention wandered to the movie posters tacked to the walls. Like *Star Wars*, she knew that each film was, just as Darren had told her, a gift of someone's imagination. She wondered why no one had imagined her Kishoki world and River Gan.

"Sita."

She turned to the office doorway. Ty was alone, holding a plastic water bottle.

"I'm homesick, Ty."

"Homesick? Talk Kishoki."

"*Galmushky*. Like what hunters feel when they are gone too long."

"I saw the antelope, Sita." His eyes lit up, and he lowered his voice. "I'm working on a plan."

"What kind of a plan? Antelope on skateboards?"

"Not funny." Ty heard Darren calling his name. "I'll tell you later. I've got to fill Darren's water bottle." He stopped. "But, Sita, remember what I say, our world is coming back to us."

She shook her head and returned to the computer. Sita moved the mouse back and forth, sending the little black cursor flying in all directions across the screen. *If I make myself very small with my potions, I could crawl into the computer and Darren could move the mouse and send me back to the River Gan!* "That's a plan too, Ty!" She spoke as if he was in the room. "But then I'd be back at the River Gan without you." She sighed. "Not an option."

She pushed the desk chair over to the corner window, climbed onto it, and looked out. Ko was chasing Shum with the water hose. Darren was yelling at them, "Stop! You're not helping fix the window!" The burly *wing* turned and shot Darren with a stream of water.

"Damn it, Ko! No more bubble gum! Turn it the other way!" Darren waved his hand toward the fence.

"I'm sorry!" Ko yelled. "Soreeeee!"

The phone rang. Sita stopped laughing and looked back to the desk. She heard Dorsey on the voice mail: "Are those kids still there or back in Mississippi? I feel cramped, D. Left out. I checked Missing Children under *America's Most Wanted*. I saw a boy who looked a lot like Shumba, Simba, whatever he calls himself. Call me back, sweetie."

Sita cringed and jumped off the chair. "She's toast."

* * *

Darren threw down his work gloves on the kitchen counter and looked over to Sita. "We did it! I'm going to get some heavy screen mesh to cover the glass." He cocked his chin and smiled as if he had just pulled off a classic handyman move. "You didn't think I could fix a window, did you?"

"I'm proud of you, even though I had no idea what a window was until we drove down the mountain in your Jeep."

Darren ignored what he perceived to be a slightly condescending tone in her voice. "I'm good with that, Sita. The job needed to be done, and I did it." He glanced over to Ko and Shum. "We did it together," he said, correcting himself. "Even though there were a few bumps in the road. Look at me." He opened his arms and pointed a finger at Ko. "I'm sopping wet. Mr. TV Head turned the hose on me."

"I didn't see you, boss man," Ko insisted.

"How could you not see me? I'm the tallest white person in the yard. In fact, aside from the mums and a fence post, I'm the only white thing in the yard!"

"I'm sure Ko didn't do it on purpose," Sita spoke up. "He likes you."

"Oh, sure, when it's time to pony up the bubble gum and pizza."

"That's not fair. We didn't run away because we don't like you. It's your father and Dorsey who don't like us."

Ko stood with his mouth open. Sita could see Ko's surprise that she was defending him. She didn't stop to gloat. She pointed a finger at Darren.

"Do you think we, *kids* you call us, fought a beast the size of this kitchen and went beyond the hunting grounds our fathers had ever tracked for a slice of pizza?"

Shum shook his head. "No way."

Sita took a step closer to Darren. "Did it ever occur to you, Mr. Son of the Karpet King, that we're here for a reason, that we're really not lost, I mean really, really not lost?"

Ko folded his arms. "No way."

"But that's what you keep saying." Darren looked down at Sita. "Why don't you go home if you're not lost?" he countered, with a smirk.

"Maybe we know something you don't, and you know something we don't. The difference is, like I told you before, we are willing to learn."

Under the shade of his Panama hat, she could see Darren's face turning red. "I think it's always good to have discussions like this, but now I've got to get out of these wet clothes." He stopped in the doorway and looked at Sita. "You've got to get off my back."

The *wings* watched Darren leave the kitchen. They shifted their gaze to Sita.

"So we're not lost, Sita." Shum's willowy voice rose out of the silence. "But where are we?"

Ko nudged him. "North of Mexico."

"Okay, enough silliness." Sita commanded their attention like a mother hen. "Wash up and put on dry clothes. And Ko…" She stopped him as he walked out of the kitchen. "Next time, watch where you point the hose."

The boys snickered on their way out.

She walked back to the sink and poured herself a glass of water. She looked over to Ty, leaning against the kitchen counter.

"Are you frightened?" he asked.

"No. Why should I be frightened?"

Ty shrugged. "You really slammed Darren. Your hand was trembling just now when you poured the water."

"I don't think so." She was being defensive, and she knew it. "I'm just tired. It's hard to make Darren listen."

"What makes you think you're supposed to make him listen?"

"Because we decided that he's a part of our family. If you were doing something wrong and I saw it, wouldn't you want me to tell you?"

"Like making fun of Man Who Stands Alone?"

"Yes." She took a sip of water. She knew she shouldn't have let Darren rattle her temper. Man had told her so many times to stay centered on the light inside her. "But I heard a phone message from Dorsey, and she said we're America's-most-wanted-something, and she was making fun of us again."

"No one wants us in America except Darren. Dorsey's no one you should get upset over."

Ty was right. She knew that, and she knew that she had to draw into her own shamanic light and not let Dorsey's ignorance and negativity sap her energy. She bit her lip to keep the tears from falling.

Ty walked over and held her close. "I know you're homesick," he said and volunteered his own comfort and solution. "Maybe we should take your potions again. Maybe they'll take us back to the River Gan."

"What if the potions take us into a different future and there is no Darren? Just monsters like Darth Vader?" She sniffled and wiped the tears from her cheek. "Keep thinking."

* * *

Darren came back from his bedroom and handed out treats. "We're starting over," he said. "We're all friends again."

Shum shoved a handful of cheese curls into his mouth and followed Ko into the living room.

Ty and Sita lingered in the kitchen, helping Darren clean up the breakfast dishes.

Sita filled a skillet with soapy, hot water. "Did you call the man this morning?"

"What man?"

"The man on the piece of paper in your pocket." She wasn't sure if Darren was playing dumb or if he really had forgotten about the phone call.

"I left my number. He hasn't called back. Besides, in case you didn't notice, I was crewing up a window replacement."

"So? That's history. Call him again."

"I don't want to sound desperate because I'm not." Darren slammed the cabinet door. Ten minutes hadn't gone by and they were back in a fight. "I thought you heard me when I told you to get off my back."

"I'm not on your back. I'm on your heart."

"Oh," he smirked. "Just one more of your little cave-baked profundities."

"I don't know what that means." She paused, keeping her temper in check. "Darren?"

"What?"

"Look at this house, at this kitchen. You have everything we don't have. But we have something too."

"Yeah, a nutty story about cave life."

"No." She moved away from the sink. "We have each other. I don't see any of your friends come by. Only Dorsey, who you put up with." She raised her hand, as if to stop him from a smart comeback. "Let me finish. You have never told us, not once, about any friend you have. So maybe it's possible that we are your friends. No matter how we got here, that's why we're here."

Darren answered with a blank stare, as if all the fanciful scaffolding of his life had just crashed in a major heap of dust.

"Yesterday, you hit my knee and called me Skater," Ty added. "You said we'd be together forever."

"Call, Darren. No excuses."

"Why is it so important to you?"

"Because it's for you."

"Maybe it's something good for you," Ty agreed. He looked over to Sita. "The call comes from somewhere, right? Like the man's voice on the Topanga Mountain."

"We didn't know him, but he brought us to you."

Darren shook his head. "This is getting way too mystical for me. I'm not even a vegetarian."

He fished the sticky note from his pocket, walked over to the phone, and tapped out the number. Seconds later he was speaking into the receiver. "Yes, Mr. Walsheim. This is Darren Davies." His voice spiraled higher along with his nerves. "You left a note for me with my editor… Sure, that would be great. What's this about? … Uh-huh." He confirmed the appointment and hung up. "There. Are you happy? I've done it."

Sita smiled. "Not me happy, Darren. Are you happy?"

"Who is he?" Ty asked.

"Mr. Walsheim, that's all I know."

Sita repeated the name slowly three times.

"Ring a bell in cave land?"

"I know that's a joke, Darren, but sometimes the sound of a word makes associations with other planes of thought. My shaman taught me this."

She watched Darren's gaze drift to the golden light shining through the kitchen window. "Okay, sham-girl, let's finish the dishes."

Sita swirled the soapy dishwater suds. She casually mentioned that Dorsey had called while they were fixing the window.

"I know. I'm meeting her for lunch in Santa Monica. That's like a place near the beach where the ocean is."

"We like the ocean," Ty said. "That's the Big River."

Darren chuckled. His dark mood seemed to be lifting. "I remember. Maybe I'll take you guys with me but not to lunch with Dorsey."

"We don't want lunch with Dorsey," Sita replied sharply. "And she definitely doesn't want lunch with us."

"Hey, now it's your turn to lighten up." His plan was, he told them, to drop them off at the Santa Monica Pier.

Sita closed the dishwasher. "What's at the Santa Monica Pier?"

"Rides, sweetie. Rides like you've never seen."

Sita looked over to Ty. "Do you want to go? It's rides."

"The only thing you can do here is watch TV," Darren pointed out. "Baseball is on the jacks until I put some mesh over the window. Besides, it's a beautiful day."

Ty jumped in. "Can we go to the zoo park after we get done?"

"No, Ty. That's at least a two-hour drive. You'll love the Pier."

Sita noted Ty's frown. "Maybe the Pier's better than the park."

"But this is a special park," he moaned. He walked out of the kitchen, shouting to Ko and Shum, "Get off your butts! We're going Big River with Darren!"

CHAPTER 23

D arren parked in a public lot near the ocean and walked with Sita over to the Pier. A few steps behind them, Ty, Shum, and Ko had stopped, huddled on the promenade pathway, their heads tilted up, staring at a huge wheel filled with people, turning in the sky. Alongside the wheel, small yellow cars raced through looping curves. Sita could hear the squealing and terrified, hysterical screams of the occupants as the cars coursed through the ocean air.

"Ferris wheel," Darren said, answering their astonished looks. "The little yellow cars are called a roller coaster. Pretty neat, huh?"

Kids on skateboards and shoe skates flew by, zigzagging between the tourists and locals. Teenage girls, wearing hardly any clothing, strolled past.

"*Zacas*," Ko growled.

"They're called bikinis," Sita said. "Lakita showed me them at Macy's."

Ko couldn't take his eyes off a dark-haired girl in a leopard print bikini. "Beautiful... Amazing... This is why we came to America, Shummy. I want to take her back to the River Gan."

"How are we going to get her back? If she saw you lived in a cave, she would cry for the next ten winters."

"But she would cry on my shoulder, Shummy."

They hadn't yet taken one step onto the Pier.

* * *

Darren felt Sita tug on his arm. She looked up at him like a child asking a favor. "Will you buy me those?" She pointed to a guy standing behind display racks of knock-off designer sunglasses. He was wearing clown shades with little propellers on the sides of each lens.

"Sunglasses?"

She blinked. "But not the ones he's wearing."

Darren walked with her to the racks. "Why not?" he said. "You're the only one who tells me what I should or shouldn't do, which drives me crazy, but you're also the only one who never asks for anything. Except…"

"Macy's. But I really didn't ask, Darren. You told Lakita I needed clothes."

"Okay." He smiled. "You win this round on a technicality."

Sita nodded. "Big technicality."

Darren didn't think, for a minute, she knew what the word meant, but he was also learning never to be surprised by what she did know. He stood by watching Sita try on three, four, then five pairs of sunglasses. He checked his watch. "Come on, Sita, I'm going to be late."

"They've got to fit right, Darren. I've got a small face."

"With a big mouth."

"Don't be mean, we're having fun. I want these." She looked at herself in the table mirror. A pair of bronze sunglasses, with big oval lenses and rhinestone frames, shaded her eyes.

This is what it must be like to have kids, Darren thought. Too caught up in his career ambitions and in his fears and anxieties of wrangling himself free of a father, it had never crossed his mind before what it would be like to be a father. It had never occurred to him that the young girl he was looking at, with the smart, snappy mouth and the wild claims of being a shaman, was somewhat like a daughter he might someday have.

"Thank you, Darren," she said as they walked into the sunlight. "I feel more comfortable now. I feel just like the rest of the girls."

He was happy she was happy. Even when the boys pestered her to try the sunglasses on, she would only say, "Not now, my little ones."

Darren felt Sita tug on his arm again. "Dorsey's over there," she said.

He looked over to the blonde actress in white cowboy boots, red miniskirt, and fringed red halter. A guy in striped swim trunks was talking to her. He looked about forty, with wavy black hair and a surfer's tan. Darren waved his arm. "Dorsey!"

He saw her hand the guy a slip of paper. Then she walked over to him.

"Who was that?"

"Just a friend. Someone from an acting class." Dorsey peered down at the *wings* through her jeweled sunglasses. "I thought we were going to lunch alone?"

"We are. They're going to stay here at the Pier."

"Good. I've got a few things we've got to talk about."

"Wait right here. I'm just going to buy the kids tickets, and I'll be right back. And don't run into any more guys from your acting class." The words slipped out before Darren could catch himself.

Dorsey frowned. "Darren, don't be childish. You've been hanging out with these kids way too long."

* * *

Darren grabbed Sita's hand.

"We're not the kids she thinks we are, Darren."

"I know that."

They wound their way through the crowded Pier. Skin tones of white, brown, black, and yellow mixed together in a collage of people color, all ambling up and down the Pier. Everyone seemed to be holding up a camera or smartphone, grinning, mugging, taking selfies and pictures of each other.

They passed restaurants, arcades, and open-air shops fenced with sale racks of T-shirts, flip-flops, postcards, and beach umbrellas. Boom box music pounded the salty ocean air.

Darren was having a hard time getting the *wings* to move along.

"Look!" Ty pointed to a young black street performer holding a twenty-foot-long white snake. The Chinese girl posing next to him cradled the serpent's belly, giggling and wincing in wide-eyed delight.

"Come on!" Darren yelled, urging them to keep moving.

"Look!" Ty stopped the *wings* again. "The Big River!"

Darren threw up his hands. "That's the ocean!"

Below them, past the Pier, they saw an endless stretch of sand, with sunbathers perched on towels and blankets and lines of children and grown-ups wading into the sunlit water.

"Damn it, guys, come on! This way!" Darren veered to the left, under a great arched sign: *Pacific Park.* "This is where all the rides and game booths are," he shouted. The fusion of music, machines, laughter, and screams banded together with a deafening roar.

"You wait here!" Darren yelled, trying to get the *wings'* attention.

Looking up, less than a hundred feet away, they saw the incredible rides the *wings* had seen from the walkway. Their hearts were giddy with excitement.

Ko's head swiveled and bobbed from one side to the other, unable to focus on any one thing. "Unbelievable."

Darren returned minutes later with a handful of green wristbands. "Listen," he said, "put these on your wrists. You can go on any ride." He quickly explained that they had to show the attendant their wristband. "If one person goes on a ride, you all have to go on the same ride. That's the rule. No leaving each other. Understand?" Shum and Ko were too busy putting on their wristbands to nod or mumble "yes." Darren checked his Rolex. "I'll meet you back here at four thirty. You can ask anyone the time. They'll tell you. Don't forget: four thirty."

Darren pulled out his wallet and handed Ty a ten-dollar bill. "I'm giving each of you ten dollars. You have to pay to play the games. You give the man ten dollars and he'll give you back some money. When you use up all the money, that's it, no more games. *No mas.*"

Shum didn't bother looking up from his new wristband. "*No mas,*" he mumbled.

* * *

Ty watched Darren wade through the crowd until his head, cresting above most of the tourists, disappeared. He felt a tiny pang of sadness for his lonely white friend who had taught him how TV worked and the joy of chewing gum. The surrounding excitement of the Pier pulled Ty back. He turned abruptly and bumped into Sita, nearly knocking her new sunglasses off her nose. "Let's go!" he said.

They sped over to the Ferris wheel and waited in line for the next ride. Sita and Ty climbed into a red carriage. Ko and Shum slipped into the blue one behind them. The big wheel started to turn, rising higher and higher above the earth. The *wings* clung to the safety bars. Their shrieks and laughter melded together with children born ten thousand years after them.

"Kishoki live!" Ko howled.

High above the Pacific, looking out over the sunlit ocean, Ty saw Sita's lips move, but he couldn't hear her.

"What?" he shouted.

"We are here because he is here," she whispered to the wind. "Darren holds us to this time and place just like his father holds him to his carpet world!" Her swirling black hair covered half her face and she yelled, "Without Darren, we are gone from our journey dream!"

Ty turned to Sita with a wild grin. "Are you talking to me?"

She shook her head with a smile to match his. *Only Man Who Stands Alone understands this. Only he knows time.*

Screaming even louder at each dizzying rise, turn, and headlong dip, the *wings* lost any notion of Los Angeles, America, even the longing for their caves. They were caught up in an adventure of speed, wind, cries of terror and joy, hurtling through a timeless world. Their faces took on the forces of machinery and nature, wavy and stretched like masks in a house of mirrors.

They flashed their wristbands and gobbled up the rides: the Pacific Plunge, the Pirate Ship, and the Sea Dragon.

"That's it," Sita said, holding up her hands. "My tummy needs a rest. Let's go to the games."

"No more rides?" Ty looked up in disbelief.

Shum turned his gaze to the colorful game booths. "Sita's right," he said. "My stomach is uneven."

Ko raised his crinkly brows. "Shummy's tummy is jumping."

* * *

Shum's deftness with a spear fueled his marksmanship at heaving beanbags and balls at stacked bottles and rows of ceramic cats. The jitters in his stomach disappeared.

"Yes!" he shouted, as two more cats crashed to the asphalt.

The attendant frowned and threw up his arms. "That's three pandas!" he shouted. "No more!"

"*No mas!*" Shum stomped the ground beside the booth like a Kishoki warrior.

"Amazing," Ko growled, shaking his head. "This is your calling, Shummy, north of Mexico." He stood aside, beaming with pride, with two giant pandas, the trophies of Shum's previous successes, pressed against his barrel chest.

At the booth across from them, Sita and Ty kept arguing and throwing darts at stubborn balloons.

"Take off your sunglasses," he demanded. "That's the problem! You can't see with them on!"

"You aren't wearing sunglasses, and the balloons aren't popping for you either!" Sita snapped back.

"Yo, dudes!"

Shum and Ko walked toward them, grinning like they'd just killed another emmydactyl. The spear thrower was lugging a huge panda under each arm, while Ko nestled the third on his shoulder.

The fact that any of the *wings* had won something brightened Sita's mood.

They pooled the last of their money and headed for the bungee-jumping apparatus.

"We go up in the sky, we bounce down like big dust balls." Ko nudged his pal. "This is why I came to America."

"That's two times." Shum grinned. "Once for a wife and now to jump like a dust ball."

"Don't laugh, Shummy. Maybe I'll jump over the sun, back to the River Gan."

Each *wing* was fastened into a leather harness, raised high above the ground, and then set free.

Sita screamed and giggled in every breath.

"We're big flying birds!" Ko yelled, flapping his powerful arms through the air.

Bouncing up and down on the safety net beneath them, they shouted and hooted, releasing all their fears and concerns of being adrift in a future world, a world and a venue which offered no ticket back to the River Gan.

Standing unnoticed, off to the side, Darren watched as the *wings* laughed and cheered each other on. One after the other they leaped into the blue ocean sky. He felt closer to them than he did to any of the few friends he'd ever had. *I haven't felt trust since my mother died*, but he felt deep within his heart he could trust these unbelievable kids.

When the last of the *wings* had completed their jump, he waved his arm. "Hey, guys, I'm over here!"

"It was amazing!" They nodded like talking bobble-heads as they ran over to Darren.

Sita grabbed his hand. "You made us very happy, Darren." He saw the gleam in her eyes. "We will never forget this."

"Never," Ty added. "Unless time makes us."

* * *

Sita sat in the front seat on the way home. The three giant pandas sat on the laps of each of the boys in the back. They embraced the stuffed toys without a word of chatter, as if, in silence, they were clinging to all the wonderful memories the day had borne.

"Good lunch?"

Darren, lost in thought, looked over. "Lunch? It was all right."

Sita sensed he didn't want to talk. She adjusted her new sunglasses and looked out the window.

"Dorsey thinks it's silly to be spending so much time with you guys." He didn't say the thought recklessly, but he seemed to be directing it more to himself. "And she wants me to ask my father if he'll help raise money for an independent film."

"Do you think we're silly?"

"No. I think you're very special."

"You are too, Darren. What's wrong?"

"I feel dumb. I'm twenty-four, you're fourteen, and I'm listening to four kids who can't tell time on a clock." He didn't say anything more. At the end of the block, he pulled into a Burger King.

"Burgers!" Ko yelled from behind the panda's head.

"Fries and shakes!" Shum added. "North of the border!"

* * *

By the time they got home, everybody's jumpy stomach had settled.

"Okay, guys, listen up." Darren stood in front of the DVD shelves. He explained that his editor, Marc, had left a message, requiring Darren to drive down to the production building in Hollywood. "It's about the graphics. My dad wants to see the commercial tomorrow."

"What's graphics?"

Darren looked over to Ty. "That's all the writing, the words you see on a commercial. Anyway..." He held up a DVD. "I think you're really going to like this movie. It's called *Ice Age*. I'll put it in the player now, but you can't watch it until after you've finished eating and cleaned up the mess." He turned to Sita. "You make sure everything's cleaned up." He handed Shum the remote. "Push *play*, the big middle button, just like we did for *Star Wars*."

By the time Darren was gone, the *wings* had finished eating and cleared all the empty containers and refuse.

Ty sat with Sita on the couch. He leaned back and looked over to Shum. "Click *play*." He took Sita's hand and propped his feet on the coffee table. "Nothing can be better than *Star Wars*," he whispered.

Within seconds, the room had turned into a temple of silence. The only tablet opened was the TV. Once again, the *wings* had fallen in love with someone else's imagination.

Lost in a frightening Ice Age world, a little boy, struggling to find his home, is saved by a wooly mammoth, a saber-toothed tiger, and a sloth. The *wings* watched with joy when the Ice Age boy waddled into his father's arms as the movie ended.

Ty jumped to his feet and flung up his arms. "That's me! I'm going to run back into my father's arms!" He looked over to Shum. "Do you remember what I told you about getting back?" He checked Shum's blank stare. "Last night, Shum, when I opened the window cloth so the moon came in."

"Last night I was in a big sleep, Ty."

"You talked to me."

"Shummy talks all the time," Ko growled. "That doesn't mean he's not sleeping."

No one heard the front door open.

Mr. Davies stood in the entry. His hand rested on a rolled-up, upright rug. "Where's Darren?" His voice roared across the living room.

Four heads spun around.

Ty opened his mouth first. "Hi." He jerked his head back to Shum. "Click *stop*."

Davies' fierce gaze moved like a shadow across their faces. "I'm very disappointed you're still here. Where's my son?"

"He went to the editing room to see Marc," Ty answered coolly.

"Graphics," Ko added, tapping his fingers.

Ty watched Davies' gaze shift to the rolled-up rug. "I thought this would look good in this room."

"It will look beautiful," Sita assured him.

"Yes, it will look beautiful. But not with you here!" Davies hissed and pushed the rug to the floor. "You haven't even seen the rug!"

"I see the future."

"Then why can't you see it's not right for you to be here? Maybe you can't see with those sunglasses on, Miss Runaway. The future is without you here. You're evicted!" He threw his stubby right arm up. "It's almost midnight. My son is a grown man, an adult! He doesn't need your kind to make his life work! He's got me." His eyes, filled with the fire of a rampaging emmydactyl, turned to the three plush pandas lined up on the couch beside Ty and Sita. "What the hell are those for? More houseguests? Hah!" he snorted.

"Santa Monica Pier," Ty said, still maintaining a calm voice.

"I won." Shum raised three fingers. "I threw the ball and knocked down the bottles. Three times, three pandas. I'm amazing."

"Shummy…" Ko flashed a "cool it" sign.

"Oh, that very good," Davies snarled. "Maybe you'd like to go back to the Pier, Mr. Amazing. I'm going to give each one of you twenty dollars. You can go back to the Pier. You can play all the games you want, win all the toys you want." His double chin rose with every puff of his chest. His stony gaze darted from one silent face to the next. He upped the ante. "Forty dollars each. You don't even have to go to the Pier. You can go to a mall and buy all the toys you want. They're even better than the crap at the Pier."

Still, no one said a word.

"Sixty bucks. Help me roll out the rug and it's sixty smackers a piece in your pockets."

"We'll roll out the carpet." Sita leaned forward. "But we don't want your money, Mr. Davies."

"What the hell's wrong?" he barked, stamping his foot. "I'm offering you more dough than your parents ever gave you, ever even thought of giving you! All you've got to do is leave this house!"

The image of the little man waving his arms and shouting in the box on Darren's editing table jumped through Ty's mind. "Mr. Davies, we will leave when Darren tells us to leave."

Sita piped in. "We take our instructions from him. If he is not here, we are not here."

"Well, he's not here, so amskray."

"Amskray," Shum mumbled. "Kishoki word?"

Ko shot him another "cool it" glance.

Ty kept his eyes on the Karpet King. "We don't mean *not here in the house*. We mean, in our lives."

"Well, that's even better, whatever that means. He's not going to be in your life because you are not going to be in his life." The way he bit off each word reminded Ty of his father yanking off the bark of trees. "Do you know whose house this is? This is my house. I own it! If I want you out of here, you'll be out of here. Damn right. That's life, girls and boys. I've been nice. I'm not nice any- more. Do you want me to call the police?"

Ty smiled. "Darren talked to the police."

"He did?" Davies' eyes bulged with sudden interest. "When?"

Ty didn't want to say two moons ago.

"When we had a big gang fight." Ko sat up and knocked his fists together. "Cave boys against the skinheads."

"Turf wars," Shum chimed.

"So the police talked to you?"

The four heads nodded yes.

"Okay. So Darren is finally taking action. Good." A satisfied smile crept onto his lips. "Tell him I was here. This rug is for the liv- ing room. It's a present." He pointed to the floor. "And if he wants to, he can give you the rug. Keep in mind, it's Persian. Plus, I will still give you each sixty dollars if you leave tomorrow. That's a present too."

He huffed out of the room.

The front door slammed. Ko peered out the window. "The white man is a big problem."

"He's the problem, Ko. Color is never the problem. Darren is white, and he's our friend."

Shum nodded, agreeing with Sita.

"Color makes life pretty. Shoes, dresses, all different colors. And flowers. And animals." Now that the Karpet King was gone and Ty had become an observer again, Sita was getting worked up. "Maybe we'd be a different color if we were born here."

The boys paused to think this over. Ty spoke up first. "Sita learns from Man Who Stands Alone."

Bolstered by Ty's remark, Sita didn't stop. "Skin color is only outside. Inside is us. Inside is the living person, eating, breathing, dreaming. We are all the same inside."

"All the same," Shum murmured. "Inside, we're all the same."

Sita rose to her feet. "Inside we're all the same," she sang. "All the same, all the same..."

Once again, the beauty of her voice filled the room, just as it had in the forest. This time Ko did not jump up angrily and scream at her. He, too, was mesmerized by Sita's song.

Ty watched her, in her jeans and sparkling camisole, move from one *wing* to the next, taking the floor just as he had seen girl singers on the magic crystal. *She's amazing*, he thought.

* * *

Darren stood in the living room entry. The blue light of the TV screen fell softly over Shum asleep on the couch and Ko in his bedroll on the floor. Each boy had his arms wrapped around a pastel panda. Darren's gaze slowly turned from the rolled-out Persian carpet on the floor to the half-gallon container of ice cream in his hand. He walked past the boys into the kitchen. Then he retraced his footsteps and opened his bedroom door.

The third plush panda was sitting on his bed, resting its head against the pillows.

Darren walked over to the night table and emptied his pockets. He stared at the yellow sticky note in his hand. *Who is Mr. Walsheim? Another show biz wannabe producer? Why is it so important to Sita that I see him?* He shook his head. *She's a shaman without a Hollywood clue.*

He looked at the closed bedroom door and thought of the suitcase, like a security alarm, he had dragged in front of it the first night the *wings* slept in the house. *Someday they'll be leaving. Who knows? Maybe we'll all be leaving.*

The rattle of shutters drew his gaze to the window. Ty's words floated through his mind: *Do you have someone who'll fight for you? You do now.*

CHAPTER 24

The morning light caught Sita's face as she moved through the kitchen. "If you don't go," she insisted, "Darren isn't going either. He'll probably sit outside at one of those coffee places, and when he gets back, he'll tell us he really saw Mr. Walsheim."

"Why?"

"Because, Ty, he's not like you. He's afraid of what his father will say or maybe do. Look how many times we had to tell him to call Mr. Walsheim." She lifted her shoulders and spread her hands, as if she were explaining why Star hunted. "It's really simple. With you along, he can't back out of the meeting. Got it?"

"Got it."

Sita winked. "We know the lingo, *masuqa*."

* * *

Ty was thinking about what Sita had said as Darren drove past a coffee place. People were sitting outside, talking into their cell phones.

"Why is everyone talking on their phones? Why don't they just lean across the table and talk to each other?"

"Don't be nutty, Skater. They're not talking to each other on the phone. They're talking to people in the distance, far away. Like when I talk to Dorsey or my dad."

"Does it work like TV, except you send little pieces of words instead of little pictures?"

Darren smiled. "You can't ask me to explain the principles of every technology, Ty. I'm not Einstein."

"Ko thinks you are."

"Ko is just being silly and a little annoying. Which reminds me. No cave talk. Don't mention caves. If Mr. Walsheim asks you where you're from, let me answer. I'll field the questions."

Darren adjusted his aviator sunglasses. He had on the same dark blue jeans, black boots, and green vest that he wore when Ty had met him on the mountain.

"Do you think the vest is too much? I know it's a little over the top, but I like the rugged, in-charge look. It's what producers like to see. Plus, it has lots of pockets. And one more thing. Don't talk about my father. Don't mention the Karpet King."

Ty lifted his hand and touched Darren's arm. "Don't worry. I won't say anything. Only you talk."

"Right." Darren turned onto another street and followed a stream of cars. "Skater, this is my first interview. Sounds crazy, huh? But I've always worked for my dad. I've had school interviews, stuff like that, but I've never really gone up for a job I wanted. Not that I want this job." He glanced over to Ty. "Let's be clear about that. I mean, I looked at their website. Walsheim's company makes TV commercials like I do for my dad, but who wants to live in San Diego?"

A single word popped from Ty's mouth. "Park."

"Oh, yeah, the Safari Park. It's not in San Diego, just close by. Don't mention that either, nothing about climbing billboards or jumping under antelope signs." Darren laughed.

"But that's part of my plan, Darren."

Darren didn't give Ty a chance to elaborate. "Nothing about plans, either. We don't want to be coming off like outer space guys."

He drove into the lot next to the old building and parked the Jeep.

Ty looked up at three rows of mostly shaded windows.

"This be it." Darren leaned toward Ty. "Look at my chin. Is the spot red?"

Ty shook his head. "Gone."

* * *

Darren only had to knock once on door #7B.

"Come on in! We're expecting you." A strong, male voice reached through the door.

"Okay, this is it," Darren whispered. "No cave talk, no shamans, no emmydactyls. This could be a disaster but don't worry, not like the Greenberg mess."

Darren turned the handle. The tall white man and the short dark boy stepped into a room as drab as the rest of the building. Until Mr. Walsheim smiled.

"You must be Darren Davies," he said in a rich baritone, extending his hand across the metal desk. "Sorry, I can't stand. I'm on crutches." Darren shook his hand. "And who's the little feffer?"

"The feffer?" Darren glanced down at Ty. "My nephew, Ty." He caught Walsheim's odd smile and suddenly realized the difference in his and Ty's skin color needed some explanation. "My uncle Jack married a black woman who had children from another marriage." He nodded. "That's it."

"Ah, the blending. I love it! Although I think that would make him your cousin."

"Yes, of course. I just haven't seen the feffer in a while."

"Well, nephew, cousin, makes no difference. Nice to meet you, too, Ty. Have you ever water-skied?"

Before Ty could answer, Darren jumped in. "He's just out here for a summer visit."

Walsheim chuckled. "There must be water wherever he lives. Anyway, I bruised my foot on those stupid water skis. Hit a rock. Then the bruise got infected. So much for my midlife whimsies. Won't you both sit down, please."

Darren and Ty took seats on the two metal folding chairs across the desk from Walsheim.

Darren sized up the production chief as a robust man who looked like he'd never missed a meal or turned down a slice of pizza. Dressed in a blue suit jacket and white shirt open at the collar, he fully occupied the chair he was sitting in.

"Let's cut to the chase. I told you a little bit about what I wanted on the phone. Our in-house director got married and his wife wants to live back East." Walsheim leaned forward, resting his arms on the desk. "You're not planning on getting married, are you? No wedding bells dinging through your head?"

"No, sir."

"Good. I'm married, for better or for worse, as they say. They just don't tell you the odds when they slip that ring on your finger. Better or worse?" He chuckled again, and his small dark mustache spread above his thin upper lip. Darren guessed Walsheim was in his mid-forties. His thinning black hair was slicked straight back, like an old-time movie star. "Here's the deal," he went on, "I'm looking at you to be our next in-house director. Thirty-six hundred a month to start, some benefits, and you'll be with a company that's ready to swing into bigger things."

"In San Diego?"

"You betcha." He leaned back. "Walsheim Productions has been a business in San Diego for seventy-five years." He quickly reviewed how his grandfather had started the company as a print ad agency. Then TV came along, "and we jumped on the bandwagon."

Darren listened attentively as Walsheim explained the company expansion into training and industrial films and public service documentaries.

"Mind you, I'm not offering you the job. Let's be clear about that. Are you interested, that's what I want to know. That's why I left my number with your editor."

Darren hesitated, not sure how to handle the question. "Am I interested?"

"Yes!" Ty pounded his fists against his knees.

Darren shot a terrified look in Ty's direction. It was the first word out of the *wing*'s mouth since they'd entered the office.

The smile on Walsheim's face broadened. "Is he your agent?"

Darren fluttered his hands. "He's just hyper. He's not used to Hollywood meetings."

Walsheim switched his look between Ty and Darren. His smile never faded. "Look, I didn't come all the way up from San Diego just to see you. I'm casting a couple of parts for a public service ad. I'm looking at some actors." He nudged a stack of glossy photos in front of him. "But I've seen all those carpet commercials on TV, and I've always thought they were pretty cheesy-fun in a good kind of way. When that fellow in the editing room gave me your number, I thought, what the hell, why not talk to you?"

Darren took a deep breath and folded his hands on his lap. "I like documentaries."

"Documentaries?" Walsheim slapped the stack of glossies. "That's good, so do I."

"I'm learning more about the world, Mr. Walsheim. About different people. And I'd like to go out and show that."

"You're speaking from your heart, aren't you?"

Darren nodded rapidly. "Yes."

"No billion-dollar blockbusters?"

"No."

"No CGI crash and trash monsters?"

"No, sir. People. The faces, the feelings, the songs, the culture." Darren blurted out his own feelings, amazing himself at what was pouring from his mouth.

Walsheim raised his dark brows. "Have you always felt his way?"

"No, sir." Darren cleared his throat. "I'll be honest. I've always wanted to be a blockbuster." He shook his head. "I mean direct a blockbuster, but recently I've started thinking about other things." Darren glanced over to Ty. "Like where people are in the world, where they live, how they get along. That kind of thing."

"Really?"

"Yes. It's a big world. We don't even know how or where some people live. The River Gan isn't on any map, yet some people actually live there."

"The Gan, you say?" Walsheim gave Darren a puzzled look. "I don't believe I know that river."

"There are so many places like that we don't know about. People who have feelings and love, who worry about their kids and have to fight off disease and threats from other people and emmydactyls. And yet they survive. We've got to bring the world together, not tear it apart."

"Emmydactyls?" Walsheim raised his brows.

Darren gulped. "Just an all-purpose word." He glanced at Ty, who offered an encouraging nod. Darren turned back to Walsheim. "There are people speaking languages we don't even know exist!"

"My grandfather knew a few words of Swahili."

"Exactly. But how many people know the word for water in Swahili?"

"Fitzi."

"Really?"

Walsheim threw up his hands with a loud, barrel laugh. "I don't know. My grandfather only spoke German to me. Look," he leaned forward again, "when I was a kid, I wanted to be a magician. The next Houdini. I learned all the tricks." He snatched up a bottle of pills off his desk before Darren's startled eyes. "See this? Pain pills for my foot. Walawala!" He whirled his arms, pounded his hefty chest, and flipped open his empty pink hands. Darren and Ty heard the stamp of his foot under his desk. "Walawalawala! Where'd it go?"

"In there." Ty pointed to the right side of Walsheim's desk.

Darren coughed and cleared his throat again. "He's just being silly. Like I said, he's a little hyper in meetings."

"You said he's never been in meetings."

"Not in this building, not in Hollywood." Darren folded his arms and kicked out his long legs in front of him. "That's it. He's cave-schooled, I mean, homeschooled too much."

Darren watched the company chief turn his dark eyes to Ty and point to the center desk drawer. "You mean here?"

Ty pointed again to the right side. "No, there."

Darren forced a weak smile, shooting a look between Ty and Walsheim, hoping to get back to the business at hand. "I think he means in the desk drawer on that side. Our right, your left. He's just being a little silly."

"He means that?" Walsheim pointed to the drawer on his left. "That's your final guess?"

Ty nodded.

"You're not confused because this is a high-level Hollywood meeting?"

"No, sir."

Walsheim opened the drawer and pulled out the bottle of pills. "No one has ever guessed that before." He looked stumped and gazed curiously at Ty. "You little feffer. I'd bet a bunch of money you're from Cajun country. Mystical, those people. I've always wanted to go down to Cajun country. That would make a helluva documentary."

Darren's voice shot up along with his hand. He ruffled Ty's hair. "He's a feffer."

The production chief leaned back in his chair. "We've talked enough." He told Darren he was going to interview a few other fellows, some business obligations, a couple of Guild recommendations. "But I like you, even though the little twerp guessed my trick."

Darren saw Walsheim give a wink to Ty before he looked back at him.

"I like the cheesy fun you put into those commercials. You write them, don't you?"

"Yes, sir."

"Forget the 'sir.' Herbert Walsheim sounds too much like a Gestapo agent." He chuckled again and thrust his hand across the desk for a handshake. "Everyone calls me Herbie. So one way or the other, whatever I decide, I'll get back to you."

Darren took his hand back and placed it on Ty's head. "Say good-bye, Ty."

"Good-bye, Mr. Herbie."

Walsheim chuckled. "He's a gosh-darn Cajun feffer."

* * *

"Mr. Walsheim seems pretty straightforward." Darren drove away from the production building, feeling relieved but not convinced. "And he's open to making documentaries and expansion. But…"

"What?"

"San Diego is a lot farther from Hollywood, and Hollywood is where the action is for film."

"But you told Herbie about making movies about people and places where you don't even understand how they talk! That's not Hollywood."

"Since when are you an expert on the movie capital of the world?"

"I'm a feffer. Besides, I hear the wind."

Darren scoffed. "Everyone with an ear hears the wind."

"Sure, Darren, but not everyone listens to it." He reminded Darren that once he had told the *wings* how his world has wars, people starving, tearing countries apart over stupid ideas. He said the beasts in his world were bombs, bullets, crazy people. "But in Mr. Walsheim's office, you said you wanted to put people back together, show all the different languages and countries and how all people have feelings and love."

Darren turned onto Sunset Boulevard. glanced over to Ty, wondering if the little feffer had just said something profound or mystical, something that ran deeper into the forest and caves, into that world Sita had talked about and that he, born in the palm tree-shaded world of Beverly Hills, had never been in touch with. He let the thought slide into the sound of the Jeep and the silence between them.

He leaned back, keeping an eye on the traffic. "Now that I'm back in the car, lots of thoughts come into your head when you're driving and not looking at the guy across the desk. Besides, I don't know anyone in San Diego. It's a big city. Not as big as Los Angeles, but it's still big."

"You don't know anyone here except Dorsey and your father."

"That's not quite true. And, besides, here I know where everything is. I grew up here."

"I grew up in a cave, Darren, but I made a friend in another world. You can do it too."

"What about my father?"

Darren didn't look over, but he could feel Ty's glare, like a burning stick. Ty's voice dropped to barely above a whisper. "You don't get it. It doesn't matter who you are or where you are. The problem will always be the same."

Darren kept his eyes on the road. "Are you saying something I'm supposed to hear?"

"Don't be afraid. That's what I'm saying."

"You've got nothing to lose, Ty, nothing on the line. I've got a home up here, a career, a girlfriend."

"You've got a girlfriend who doesn't love you and a home your father bought!" Ty shouted. Darren was looping through traffic, but now he could really hear him. "And I don't know what a career is, but you can get one in San Diego!"

"Calm down." Darren had never seen Ty this angry. "You don't know everything. Adult life is more complicated."

"More complicated than what? I've got to save my people. I've got everything to lose, a mother, a father, all of my *wings*. I could take us back into another future where there're monsters ready to kill us. I've got everything on the line. My people, Darren!" He pounded the dash. "My people!"

"Then they should have sent someone older."

"They didn't send us. I had a vision." Ty crossed his arms. "What's a feffer anyway?"

Darren thought from one red light to the next and then to the next. He glanced over to Ty's waiting look. "Someone strong, brave, willing to go where no one else has ever been."

"Then, damn it, you can go to San Diego." Ty didn't pause for Darren's comeback. "You've got wheels, Darren. You know the road."

* * *

Darren and Ty stepped through the sliding glass doors at Home Depot and headed directly for the Garden Center.

They walked into a large, airy, sunlit room. Bags of fertilizer, weed killer, and mulch were stacked next to small potted trees and long tables filled with flats of flowers and plants.

Ty couldn't read the writing on the bags, but he smelled the moist scent of earth, the fragrance of the flowers, and a feeling deep inside him brought him back to his dark river cave and the windswept cliffs.

Darren chose three hollyhock plants. "They grow tall. No one will see the garage window." He told Ty he still had to get some wire mesh. "I'll meet you at the car. Do you remember where we parked?"

"Outside."

"Yeah, outside. But do you remember where outside?"

"I'll find you."

"Good. Ten minutes." Ty followed Darren's look over to a tall black man wearing an orange bib apron, sorting pots. "It's three thirty. The man in the orange apron will tell you when ten minutes are up." He checked his watch and grabbed a big orange shopping cart. "Twenty to four. If I'm not at the car, just wait there."

Ty had seen people with his skin color at the mall and on the Pier, but he had never talked to anyone who looked so much like a Kishoki elder. *All the man needs is a thick gray beard and shorter legs.*

"Can I help you?" He heard the man's voice call over to him. "Are you a gardener?"

"I want to make a garden." Ty explained that he wanted to plant a vegetable garden like he saw on the TV garden show.

"Most vegetable gardening starts with seeds." The clerk removed his gloves. "Come over here, I'll show you." They walked over to racks of seed packets. "Are you with a school garden club or helping that gentleman I noticed you talking to?"

"He told me to tell you 'twenty to four.'"

"Twenty-two-four?" The clerk wrinkled up his brows. "What's that about? Some kind of seed number?"

"I've got to meet Darren at twenty to four."

"Oh." The clerk chuckled. "You're talking about time." He glanced at his watch. "You've got a few minutes." He bent to pick a seed packet from the rack. "Gardening puts you in touch with the earth. And what grows from it gives us life. See what I'm sayin'?"

Ty nodded.

"Is this going to be your first garden?"

"Yes, sir."

"Acie." He tapped the laminate badge pinned to his orange apron. "And what's your name?"

"Ty."

"Well, Ty, the first thing you're gonna do is clear the soil, get rid of sticks, stones, any debris." Ty listened carefully as Acie explained what "tilling" meant and how deep to plant the seeds. "If you plant the seed too deep, the seed might germinate. You know what germinate means, don't you?"

Ty shook his head.

"It means the seed starts to grow when it's still in the ground. It'll die before it reaches the light." Acie smiled. "I like to plant in straight rows. Where're you livin'?"

"By the River Gan." *Maybe people the same color as me know where the river is.*

"Gan," Acie mumbled. "Shoot, I do a lot of fishin', but that's one river I don't believe I've put a boat or boots in." He glanced at his watch again. "I think it's about time you met your friend. Any chance you want to buy some of these seeds?"

"Maybe later, sometime."

The clerk chuckled. "Well, good luck on your garden. Don't forget." He raised three fingers. "Clear, till, plant."

"Thank you, Acie." Ty took a step through the Garden Center doors, still mumbling, "Clear, till, plant." He looked up and stopped. Sunlight flared off the windshields of what seemed to him like endless rows of cars. The brilliant light shuttered his eyes, and all the cars seemed alike. He and Darren had entered through the main doors of Home Depot, but the Garden Center faced the north side of the parking lot.

Where am I?

He couldn't locate the green Jeep. Ty wandered down lane after lane, looking for Darren. He heard a woman shouting across her car top. A big yellow car, like a tall box, beeped at him down the middle of a lane. Exhaust fumes burned his lungs. Dirty air teared his eyes.

Another car, low to the ground, bouncing up and down, drove past, screaming loud music. Ty was starting to feel dizzy. He gulped in deep, rapid breaths.

"Darren!" he shouted. "Darren!"

A truck screeched like a mountain bird, nearly hitting Ty as it pulled out of its parking spot. Ty dodged the rear of the truck, sending him flat against the back of a black car, setting off a sharp jumble of ear-splitting sounds.

The cave boy jumped away and stopped walking. *I've killed the deadliest beast in the forest. I've climbed the highest cliffs. I've gone farther along the River Gan than Star.* He looked up with tears in his eyes. *Here I am lost. There is no branch without leaves, there are no rocks piled against a tree trunk, there is no rain cloud on the side of a hill. There is nothing to guide me.*

The rapid blasts of a car horn startled him again. "Ty!" He saw Darren hanging out the driver's side window, shouting at him. "Get in here, feffer-head!" Darren pushed the passenger side door open, grabbed Ty's hand, and yanked him in. "I was certain you'd be back at the Jeep when I got there. From now on, you stick with me, no wandering off! I was worried." Darren maneuvered out of the parking lot. "What was so interesting about what the guy was telling you?"

"His name was Acie."

"Okay. Acie."

Ty didn't feel the need to say any more. He was still taking deep breaths, shaking from the parking lot confusion. Darren's tone of voice was hardly comforting.

"My mother was the only person I ever worried about before. Watching her die, not knowing what to do or how to comfort her." Darren shook his head, as if he were talking to himself. "I was a jerk. I just don't want to lose someone else." He looked over to Ty. "I don't want to be a jerk again. Hear me? Besides, Sita would kill me."

Ty kept his eyes on Darren. He could see tears rim the white man's eyes. He wanted to say, it's all right, but he wanted Darren to feel what he was feeling. His mother Su had taught him that this was the thing to do. She said it often about Star.

"Let's talk about something else, Skater." Darren breathed deeply and shook his head. "How did you know Herbie's trick?"

"In caves there is no light, only from the fire or cracks in the stone. We watch close, very carefully. We never know when a snake will slip under the hides or a poison bug will crawl into the cave. That's how I watched Mr. Walsheim."

Darren finally smiled. "Herbie."

"Yes. Herbie opened the drawer before he grabbed the bottle of pills because he knew he was going to get the bottle. Then he grabbed the bottle and jumped his arms around and pounded his chest. And what did he say?"

"Walawalawala. Is that Kishoki?"

It was Ty's turn to smile. "No. But he stamped his foot."

"His good foot."

"Exactly. That's when he closed the drawer with the pill bottle in it."

"Really. You saw all that, huh?"

"With cave eyes I see the world."

Now that he had smelled the earth and flowers, now that he had learned about seeds and soil, it was the River Gan Ty wanted desperately to see again. "Let's go back home," he said.

"I'm not cooking tonight, Skater, and I don't think there's enough emmydactyl meat in the freezer." He smacked Ty's knee and laughed. "One more stop and we're done."

Ty shook his head. "Everyone in America thinks they're funny."

"No, Skater. Just the politicians and talk show hosts." Then he fished a cell phone from his vest pocket.

CHAPTER 25

Darren's phoned-in food order was wrapped and ready to go when they walked into El Pollo Loco. Ty kept his eyes on the flames shooting up on the long restaurant grill, sizzling with pieces of chicken. The grill brought another unexpected pang of homesickness to Ty's heart. He started to rock from one foot to the other, moving less to the surrounding music than to something deep inside him, some restlessness or rhythm from long, long ago.

He watched Darren walk over to the cashier and pay for the take-out. He felt a pair of eyes on him and turned to smile at a pretty, dark-skinned girl.

When Darren came back, he shook his head. "What would Sita say?"

"She told me to see more of America, Darren."

They walked out of El Pollo Loco loaded down with large brown bags filled with Styrofoam containers. Ty breathed in the smells of refried beans, chicken, and salsa, but his mind was elsewhere.

"Let's go to the mountain."

"Mountain?" Darren backed up the Jeep and turned toward the boulevard. "What mountain?"

"The mountain where I saw you."

"That's pretty far from here. Everyone's waiting for the food."

"They're not going to die, Darren. Ko and Shum stuff themselves with Cheetos every day."

Ty was getting more restless. He had smelled the richness of the earth at the Garden Center and heard the music and seen the flames of the long grill at the restaurant. The invisible hands of sense memory were pulling him back into his world.

"Less than half an hour ago, you told me you wanted to go home. Right?"

"Right. But then I got this idea."

"It's a bad idea. The food'll get cold."

Darren turned his eyes to the road, but Ty sensed that what was bothering him had more to do with the mountain and less to do with hungry stomachs or cold food.

"Your father's commercial was on the mountain," he said.

"So?"

"Herbie is in San Diego."

"So what?"

"So I see the shadow of the mountain crossing San Diego."

"You're talking just as crazy as Sita again. You've never been to San Diego, and you don't know where it is. We're not going back."

"Darren, when I was going to go on this journey, my father wanted me to help him. He was at the river washing the meat of a ram he killed. I didn't go by the river. I didn't want to help him when the only thing I was thinking about was beginning my journey."

"Well, I'm not thinking about ram meat."

"No, you're thinking about Herbie's offer. Is that why you don't want to go to the mountain?" Darren looked away, out the side window. When he turned his gaze back to the road, Ty answered his silence with his own insistent demand. "I need to see the mountain."

"God, Ty!" Darren thumped the steering wheel. "This is crazy! We're not supposed to be doing this!"

"That's why we're doing it."

Darren bolted onto the freeway. Within minutes they were on another freeway, darting through an underpass, turning onto a road Darren called the PCH. "And we're not staying long, got that, Skater? Refried beans suck when they're cold. I don't even know if I can find the place again."

Ty lowered his side window and stuck his head out. He felt the warm ocean breeze against his face. The wind tangled his hair. For the first time since he had started his quest, since the first night he kissed Sita in America, his spirit felt free again.

Darren turned away from the coast and started the drive up the steep canyon road.

"Is this the kind of mountains you have back around the caves? Ty?"

Ty pulled himself in and stared blankly.

Darren repeated his question. "Look!" He waved his hand toward the craggy rust-colored face of the cliffs that surrounded them.

"We have big mountains."

"Bigger than this?"

"They touch the sky, Darren. Sometimes the moon."

"Everything touches the sky. The sky is just air. Everything touches it." Darren started to ramble about how the sky is every-where. "That's something that connects us, Ty!" The thought burst like fire across the front seat. "You and me! If we could stick our hands up, me on the roof of my house and you on top of your cave, we'd be grabbing a piece of the same sky. I'm almost twenty-five, you're fourteen. Time doesn't matter to the sky! Sing it!" He punched the air. "Time doesn't matter to the sky!"

Ty sensed Darren was bouncing through a jumble of emo-tions he didn't understand.

"Look," Darren gabbled on, "I'm not a weather guy, but you've got to figure that the clouds that pass over my house have to pass over your cave, over your people in those caves who have no idea of what a car or a toaster or a TV remote is. Right?" He glanced again over to Ty.

"Right, bro. Watch the road."

Darren skidded across the gravel shoulder before he veered the Jeep back into the lane.

Ty leaned back in his seat. "I'm going to make a garden, Darren."

"Up here? Now? Don't be crazy."

"A garden by my cave. I'll bring water from the river."

"Make the garden by the river. It's easier, Skater."

"There's too many big trees near the river, and the rocks along the river are too big to move."

Ty saw a ribbon of water cascading down the cliff-side, spilling into the creek far below. He wondered if this cliff-side stream, flowing into the Big River, somehow twisted through the rumbling waves and underwater currents and tunneled its way into the sunlit river where his father washed the meat, where the elders caught fish, and where he was born. Darren's words about the same sky hovering over his house and caves ran through his mind. *If it's the same sky, then it's the same water too.*

"We're close," Darren said. He was following an old red truck along the mountaintop road.

"Do a lot of people live up here?"

"Mostly artists and musicians. It's an old hippie stomping grounds."

"What's a hippie?"

"Just a collection of people who like to do things their own way, sing a lot, wear lots of colors, and hang out with nature." Ty caught his smile. "They'd probably like to family-up with you guys in caves." Darren turned off onto another road. "They call this Old Topanga Canyon Road."

The two-lane blacktop wound tighter. Giant oaks and huge rocks leaned toward the curves. Sunlight sifted through the leaves, spotting the road with pools of light. Time was swallowed up by a lazy, green and golden silence.

"It'll be a miracle if I find this place again." They passed a long pipe fence that surrounded a corral. "Hang on, this is beginning to look familiar."

Darren started uphill. A white wooden house and a stand of pepper trees came into view. He bore right again, onto an abandoned fire trail. The Jeep kicked up clouds of dust, banging over ruts and stones. Ty raised his window as Darren hung onto the wheel, bounced to the crest of the hill, and hit the brakes. Before he got a word out, Ty had jumped from the Jeep and was clambering up the last twenty yards to the ridge.

"Wait for me!" Darren shouted. "You're always jumping out of the Jeep! Didn't I tell you not to do that?"

Egg-shaped rocks poked out from the dirt and trampled grass. A range of mountains rose in the silver haze beyond the sparsely wooded hillside. Ty could see the gleaming blue band of ocean they had passed, but his eyes were drawn to a grassy meadow, scooped out of the rocky hills.

"We were there!" He pointed excitedly as Darren trudged up beside him. He smiled at a swarm of golden butterflies fluttering across the field. "*Uoki*. Look how many *uoki*."

The boy and man gazed silently at the lush meadow. Flowers wiggled their yellow petals in the furrows made by the mountain wind. Ty looked up at Darren. "We can go home now. We were here."

"That's it? I just drove thirty-five miles, almost got us killed, to look at a patch of yellow flowers and butterflies?"

Ty nodded. "We were definitely here. This was real. This wasn't a dream."

"Hell no, we were here." Darren lifted his glasses. "Look over there!"

Ty turned his gaze up the road to tire tracks the film crew vehicles had made almost a week ago.

"Proof positive," Darren announced. He pulled out his cell phone and speed-dialed home. "If anyone is there, pick up. This is Darren." He raised his voice into the voice mail. "Sita, pick up if—"

"I be here, Darren."

"Sita?"

"Sita, yes!"

Ty could hear her shouting excitedly through Darren's cell, knowing it was the first time she'd ever spoken into a phone.

"You'll never guess where we are," Darren bellowed. "On the mountain in Topanga where I first met you. We've got food. We're coming back now. Hang in there."

They drove down the mountain, leaving behind the dusty tire tracks and butterflies. By now, the late afternoon rush-hour traffic was snarling the highway, but Darren had a smile on his face.

Ty turned his eyes to the ocean. Plum-colored waves wove through the river current. The garden, the water, the wheels, he realized, were real things, as much a part of his journey and quest as they were of Darren's world. *All this is true. All this is really happening.* He turned back and caught Darren's eye. "I think we're brothers from another galaxy."

"Galaxy?" Darren whipped off his sunglasses. "Where'd you get that?"

"*Star Wars* talk, Darren." Ty smiled. "Inside we're brothers."

* * *

Darren followed the traffic through the McClure Tunnel, driving east into a haze of freeway exhaust and smog.

"Do you *wings* know the word soul? Soul," he repeated. "It's something invisible, but up there on the mountain, I was beginning to feel all that stuff the minister talked about when my mom died. He talked about her soul and I could feel it, I could really feel it up there."

"Spirit."

Crossing into the far right lane, Darren didn't notice that Ty had answered him.

"Spirit!" Ty shouted, a second time. "Spirit is like soul."

Darren nodded. "I think so. I don't read a lot of New Age stuff, but I think Indians use the word spirit and soul pretty much the same." He slipped between cars onto the Overland off-ramp.

Ty was holding the golden shell in his palm. "Man Who Stands Alone is a great spirit man."

"You got that from the spirit man?" Darren glanced at the golden shell. "So that's like a good luck thing, like a charm, he gave you for the trip."

"With the shell, I am safe."

"Does Sita know about this golden shell?"

"Sita knows everything, almost everything." Ty held up his thumb and forefinger. "She's this far from being a shaman."

"Yeah, that's what you guys keep saying." He raised his brows. "Or maybe a sha-woman. Get it? Sha-man, sha-woman." Darren caught a slightly alarmed look on Ty's face. "It's a joke, Ty."

"Shum is funny, Darren. Sometimes Ko is funny. You're not Shummy or Ko. Do you get what I'm trying to tell you?"

Wow, Shum and Ko aren't that funny. He let the thought pass and pulled into the alley behind his house.

"If the Spirit Man could tell you when you were leaving, I could get my father off my back."

Ty pushed the button on the remote door opener. "Your father isn't the problem. I got mad at Man Who Stands Alone and sometimes I made fun of him, but I promised to trust him and now I'm here. The mountain was real. You are real and so are my caves."

Darren stopped the car. They both got out.

"Your father is not the problem. He never was."

Darren laid a hand on Ty's arm. "What are you saying?"

"Herbie is real, and the journey you go on with him will also be real."

CHAPTER 26

"Ty's the one who insisted we go back to Topanga. It was his idea."

Sita was still fuming but, for once, she kept her mouth shut.

"I'm not blaming him. I mean, not altogether. I was the guy driving." Darren watched Sita load a large baking sheet with several pieces of chicken. "I think he's got a way of getting back to cave land. He thinks the golden shell will take him there. Something like that. Let me help you."

Darren slipped the baking sheet into the oven. "I'll be honest with you, I sort of believe you're from caves. I mean, I do. But—"

"But what?"

"I can't understand why you don't know where they are. Why someone isn't looking for you."

"Maybe someone is."

"But there are no Kishoki people, Sita. We Googled Kishoki. No River Gan. Nothing. *Nada.* Ty says all of this is real but…"

"But what? We're not in computers or machines, Darren. We're from long, long ago. Before machines. Before anything in this kitchen. When time was only the moon, the stars, and the sun."

Darren stared at her, speechless. *Why does she keep challenging me with crazy ideas?* When his thoughts finally jelled, he spoke slowly, carefully wording his questions. "You mean, you're saying you're not only not from this place, but not from this time, not from now?" His voice suddenly rose. "You're saying you were born before the automobile, before Napoleon, before history?"

Sita nodded. "I dream-visited this world before. I saw these things, TV and cars and people talking into little things in their hands. But only Ty and Man Who Stands Alone know this."

"Does everyone in your tribe dream like this?"

"No. I *star-step*. No one else does. Not even Ty." Sita turned to the window, to a faint blue glimmer of light in the sky. "I see this dream, but it's Ty's dream. Without him, we would still be sitting on the rocks by the River Gan."

"Wow." Darren shook his head. "Am I supposed to believe all of this?"

"Do you believe there's pancakes or chicken in the oven?" Sita turned away and emptied containers of salad into a wooden bowl. "What happened at your interview?"

"Great. It went great." Darren paused. "I think. He said he'd call me either way. He did a trick and Ty guessed it, so I don't know if that hurt us or helped us."

"Ty guessed a trick?" Sita dropped the salad container on the counter. "What kind of a trick did Ty guess?"

Darren explained how Mr. Walsheim hid a plastic bottle and Ty pointed to where it was.

"I think I know the trick." She paused. It didn't seem to Darren that she was happy with Ty's success. She looked back to the counter and changed the subject. "What if the boss-man said you got the job?"

"I'd have to move to San Diego. It's about a two-hour drive south of here."

Sita opened a smaller Styrofoam container. "What's this?" She tipped the contents toward Darren.

"Guacamole. Don't tell me you don't know what avocados are?"

Sita dipped her finger in the container. "Mmm…it's excellent." She dumped the guacamole into a small blue bowl. "San Diego is where the zoo is. Ty told me. Where the antelope are."

"Well, they're really at the Safari Park, which is close."

"So are you going to go?"

He told her again that Mr. Walsheim hadn't offered him the job.

"But if he does. That's the question."

"I don't know yet." Darren pulled the tray of chicken from the oven. "I have to think about it some more."

"I know you've thought about it, Darren."

He stopped and stared at the clever look in her eyes. "I don't know why I'm telling you this. Mr. Walsheim—he likes to be called Herbie—is a magician. *Was* a magician. Do you know what that is?"

She nodded. "A person who does magic."

"Sort of like a shaman."

"Stop it, Darren! I told you, shamans don't do magic. It's a lot deeper than that. It's not tricks!"

"Okay, I'm sorry. Anyway, that's what Herbie wanted to be, but he got involved in his father's business. And then he stayed there and he never got to be what he wanted to be."

"And you don't want to be like that?"

"I don't want to make carpet commercials for the rest of my life." Darren walked over to the counter and ripped open a bag of tortilla chips. "Look." He took a chip and dipped it into the small bowl of guacamole. "Try it."

Sita wolfed the chip down in one crunch. "Love it. I love it!"

He poured the tortilla chips into a plastic bowl and started for the dining room. "Let's go, sweetie. Chips ahoy!"

"Darren."

Her voice drew his look back.

"You've got to tell your father what you just told me."

"About the guacamole?"

"About what Herbie never did."

* * *

Darren swallowed down a forkful of mashed potatoes. He watched the boys jab their forks into the platter of chicken, pulling off pieces onto plates already heaped with mashed potatoes, corn, beans, and chips. "What's your best meal in cave land?"

"Meat," everyone answered at once.

"Everyone cooks together," Ty elaborated. "One animal, sometimes two animals. But each family takes meat for how many children they have."

"He means," Sita interjected in a superior tone, "the amount of food you take depends on your family's size. You call it proportional distribution."

"I seriously doubt you know what that means." Darren caught an icy glare pass between the two teenage lovers. "What else do you eat?"

"Snakes," Sita said, looking pointedly at Ty. "If we can catch them."

Ty ripped his napkin off. "I'm going for a walk."

Darren had no idea what was going on. "Don't go far! It's dark out! Captain Martinez has his eye on you!"

Ko looked up. "Ty can see in the fog."

"It's not foggy!" Darren shot back. "I said *dark*!"

"He can see better when it's not foggy."

"Better," Shum repeated in a quiet tone.

Darren turned back to Sita. "What's up with him?"

She shrugged innocently, but her voice dripped with sarcasm. "Maybe he's planning Herbie's next magic trick."

* * *

Ty looked at the streetlights, still amazed by their illumination. *If these lights were along the River Gan or ringed the Kishoki clearing, how much safer my world would be.* Beyond the streetlights, he saw a scattering of stars, none as bright as the silver darts across the forest night. He understood that these surface lights, from the streets, the buildings, and cars, loomed over the city like a watery gray cloud, dulling and hiding almost all of One Hand's creation. *These are the makings of the Antelope People, my people. These are the people who went ahead when we stayed behind. Would I trade the beauty of the night for the inventions of this future world?*

The question in his mind was left unanswered in the sound of footsteps behind him, the soft padding of feet that the forest had taught him to hear. He turned quickly.

"Why are you walking alone?" she said.

"Why are you following me?"

"You told Darren that the shaman is magic, and you made a big thing of Herbie's trick."

"I didn't tell Darren that the shaman was magic. He said that. He mixed up the two."

"I am a shaman-in-waiting, not a magician." Sita walked up beside him. "I see the light, not the shadows from the light."

"I know that." He turned and started to walk.

"Well, I don't want him to think I do tricks," she said, keeping a close step with him.

"I didn't want to have to explain everything to Darren. He doesn't have a clue what our lives are like."

"Where did you learn that?"

"What?"

She mimicked him in a singsong voice. "He doesn't have a clue what our lives are like."

"You're not the only one who can talk, Sita. Just because you talk more than anyone."

"You're jealous because I'm a genius in languages."

"No. You probably don't even know what that word means, just like Darren said."

He looked over to her. The streetlight caught her face. The beads, sequins she called them, sparkled on her yellow camisole. Her jeans with flowers on them hugged tightly to her hips. Even the colored stones on her wedgies were shining. *She's so beautiful.* But he quashed the thought with a firm command: "Go back to the house."

"I'm with you. You went to the mountain and saw the yellow flowers and you went to Darren's meeting. What else did you do without me, besides chew gum?"

"Home Depot."

"What's that?"

He knew she wouldn't go back. He took her hand and continued walking. "A gigantic store that has everything. I couldn't believe it." He told her about the cliff-high shelves of tools, the plants and flowers. "And a man, his name was Acie. He was brown-skinned, like us."

"So you met Herbie and you met Acie, and it's not even time to sleep. Incredible."

"Don't be jealous, Sita. Acie told me how to plant the seeds: clear, till, plant. But then I got lost; it was terrible."

"You got lost in Home Depot?"

"In the parking lot. I couldn't find Darren's Jeep. I started to feel sick. I wish I would have had your hand then."

"You'll know better to take me along next time." She swung his hand closer to her. "Do you still love me? With all the things you saw and all the places you went, do you still love me? That's the question, Ty."

"You told me to go with Darren and see more of America."

"Answer the question."

"I told you I love you. How many times do I have to tell you?"

She looked into his eyes. "How many leaves are there in the forest? Did you see any pretty Home Depot girls?"

Ty shook his head. "No, just Acie." He was relieved she didn't ask him about El Pollo Loco.

"We're in a different world, Ty. Don't you think that once we get back to the River Gan, whenever that is, that I want to remember those words, that you loved me in another world?"

He thought of the night at the campfire when all she wanted was the reassurance of his kiss.

"Of course I still love you. That's why I went back to Topanga. To see and breathe and touch the mountain. To know this isn't a dream, but it's not our world."

They walked to the corner and turned back.

"Herbie said I was a *feffer*."

"What's a feffer?"

"A real cool dude."

"Sometimes." She smiled and Ty felt her hand squeeze his fingers tighter. "I'm gonna be a shaman when we get back. I just don't wanna be thirty summers before we get there."

* * *

It was dawn. Su and Star awoke and quickly dressed. They washed their faces in a bowl of cool water and stepped outside. The sky was turning rose and milky white. They started up the steep cliff-side path.

Moments later they saw the tall yellow flowers that surrounded the shaman's cave.

"I will go," she said and took the first steps. Approaching the mouth of the cave, Su pressed her palms in front of her. "We come in peace." Her voice trembled. Her heart started to falter. "One Hand guides us." Only the morning wind filled the silence. "It is Su and Star the hunter."

"You are welcome." The sage's voice passed through the veil of shells. Su looked back to Star and waved him forward.

She had been to the one-eyed shaman's cave before, but never had she seen it so vibrant with light. The fire pit blazed and torches were burning on the walls. The crystal wands that hung like icicles from the cave roof glowed with incandescent splendor.

Man stood up from the bowl of his ebony chair. "Why are you here?"

"Our son is gone."

"Many nights," Star added, stepping to Su's side. "Ty is lost."

The Man pressed his chin down so that his thick white beard covered the colored shells and stones on his chest. Su saw his good eye, darker than a moonless night, shift between them.

"He lives far away."

Su clasped her hands. "What does that mean?"

"He is well. He sees many things. Learns many things. Wings are with him."

"Where?"

The Man stared at the fire pit. "Where time runs too quickly."

Su didn't understand his answer. Trembling more, she forced herself to ask the next question: "Will he come back?"

The shaman looked away. Slowly, he moved across the stone floor, past the antelope skull, to a crystal shrine glowing with red and gold flames that surrounded it. Folding his hands, he bowed slightly, whispered words the visitors could not hear. Then he dropped seeds on the shrine and removed something. "You take this. You ask the spirit. You ask One Hand." He walked back and handed the amulet to Su.

She and Star looked down at a golden shell in her palm.

Star raised his voice. "My son is near water?"

Man Who Stands Alone turned back to the fire. Su stared at the shell. "It will speak to me," she said.

225

CHAPTER 27

D arren shut the car door, leaned back, and folded his arms, holding down the flutters in his stomach. He wished his father had opened the windows instead of letting the AC run. The morning sun was already flaring off the Mercedes' hood. Cigar smoke was stinking up the car.

"I want those kids out of here within twenty-four hours, if not sooner. You can't have teenage kids hanging out at your house in a neighborhood like this." The Karpet King pointed a finger at Darren. "I told you before, it doesn't look good."

"Is that because they're not white?"

"Don't play the race card with me, young man!" Davies pulled the cigar from his mouth. "I was hiring blacks and beaners before you took your first pee on your mother's arm. All those little shots of Spanish you toss off don't impress me. We *habla español* at every one of our stores. It just doesn't look good for a grown man, a college graduate, to have teenage boys sleeping in his house!" He leaned back. "What's gotten into you?"

"Maybe something real."

"Real? What's real about three long-haired runaways and a jail-bait chick? Look, I offered them money. Are they giving you drugs?"

"No." Darren wanted to tell his father that the jail-bait chick was a budding shaman and that Ty was on a quest to save his clan, who lived in a time zone that predated Napoleon and written history. But he knew that if he said any of these things, it would only confirm in his father's mind that they were all taking drugs. He didn't expect when he ambled down the walkway in his black sweats and rumpled blue T that within minutes of saying "good morning" he'd be slinging accusations with his father and his temper would be getting hotter than the Mercedes' hood. "Of course, you already know what Dorsey's like."

Davies pulled the cigar from his mouth. "What are you talking about?"

"I met her six months ago at the grand opening of your Valley store. She told me that she was hired with a couple of other starlets to dress up the place for photo ops and publicity noise. And she heard about the job from Milt Haskins, one of your country club friends."

The Karpet King blinked. "That doesn't mean I had anything to do with her. She worked for an agency. They sent her over."

"I don't believe her or you, anymore."

The two men glared at each other. Darren could see the disbelief gather in his father's eyes, but what roared from his mouth was a sharp, biting attack. "You've never believed anything I've said. Never!"

"You're wrong," Darren answered coolly. "I believed you when you said Mom didn't kill herself, that she died of a medical overdose. I believed you when you said I was better off working for you than trying to make it on my own. I believed you when you said that shooting commercials for Karpet King was my ticket to the movie business. That's bull! You never wanted me to get into the movie business." Almost like a hiccup, Darren gulped for air. "The only good thing the commercials have brought me is meeting those kids on a mountaintop."

"Your mother died, God bless her, because she screwed up her medication. I never went to college. I busted my butt to get where I am. And I never saw you turn down my credit cards." He jabbed the air with his cigar. "If you don't get my business, who does? My new wife will get half, sure. But Evvy can't run a company. She couldn't close a deal if God came down and wanted her to carpet the stairway to heaven! You're it! You're the man." Davies rapped his knuckles against the console. "You're making commercials so you learn all aspects of the business. It's called marketing. That's part of my success. Karpet King, crazy rug on my head. And you're going to be wearing the crown next." He smiled. Tobacco juice wet the corners of his mouth. He smacked Darren's knee with the flat of his hand. "Now go in there and get those kids out before we get more neighbor complaints." The sharp ring of a cell phone stoked his command. "Karpet King!" he answered with a roar.

Darren waved the cigar smoke from his face, opened the car door, and got out, not bothering to respond to the perfunctory lift of his father's hand.

He marched through the house into the kitchen and gulped down a glass of water. The *wings* watched, without a word.

"Have you guys eaten breakfast?"

"I made hot chocolate." Sita smiled proudly.

Darren ignored her cheerfulness, even though he could tell it was well meant. His forehead was red, ringed with sweat, and the blotch on his chin felt hot.

"Do you kids have fights with your fathers?"

They shook their heads.

"It's not normal, is it?" Darren set his water glass down. "Unless you're fourteen. Of course, you are fourteen."

"What's 'normal' mean?"

He turned to Ty. "Like something that happens a lot of the time."

"Our fathers are our elders," Ty answered. "We do what they say."

"Did your father tell you to come here?"

Ty didn't want to lie in front of Sita and the *wings*. He tilted his head, hoping some honest idea would pop into his mind. "Yes!" he finally said brightly. "My mother told me to always follow my heart, and my father told me to always obey what my mother tells me to do."

Darren nodded. A smile crept to the corners of his mouth. "You're a smart kid, Ty, like Sita said."

"I said *sometimes*," Sita added quickly. "Like now. I think you should lie down."

"Maybe I would have a week ago, or a month ago, or last year. But I'm not lying down anymore."

"Won't you get tired?" Shum asked.

As edgy as Darren felt, he still couldn't repress a smile and ruffled the top of Shum's head. "It's got another meaning, Shummy." He pulled himself up to his beanpole height and took a deep breath. "Guys, follow me. We're going out back and wrap that mesh across the window."

He grabbed his Panama hat and was out the door.

* * *

Sita watched them leave. She understood that there was another meaning to Darren's remark about lying down, but she wasn't sure what it was. She repeated the phrase slowly several times. Her guides were with her. That was what Man Who Stands Alone had told her, how he knew that she might be the one to succeed him in the clan when he died. Everyone born had seen and unseen guides, he told her. But for some, for the gifted, the guides chose to make themselves known and to exchange wisdom for trust. So she repeated the words and slowly a smile rose to her lips as the hidden meaning of "lying down" became clear.

She jumped up on the counter and watched Darren and the *wings* nail metal bars across the garage window and fasten a piece of screen across the bars. Ty came out of the side garage door carrying a tall plant.

Sita raised the kitchen window. "Are those the plants you bought at Home Depot?"

"Hollyhocks!" Ty shouted back.

The first ring of the phone startled her. She took her eyes off the window and waited for the answering machine to pick up. "Herbie Walsheim here. I'm headed back to San Diego later today. If you get back to me before lunch, the number again is…" He rattled off a number and hung up.

Sita leaped off the counter and raced out the back door.

"Darren! Darren! Herbie called!"

Darren was on his knees, half hidden by the hollyhocks. "Huh?"

"Mr. Walsheim wants you to call him. He just left a message!"

"When we're done, Sita."

"No, now, Darren!" She came deeper into the yard. "He's going back to San Diego later."

"It's the old Hollywood brush-off. 'Nice meeting you. We went in another direction.' He probably called on his way back to San Diego."

"But maybe he didn't." Sita wouldn't let up. "Maybe he's telling you what you want to hear."

Darren stood and up tipped back the brim of his Panama hat. "Want?"

"Yeah, want." Sita could see the *nagya*, the unhappiness, above his head. "You're not going to know unless you call him."

"Call him." Ty dropped the spade in his hand. "Call him now."

Darren looked over to Shum and Ko. "Put the tools back in the garage."

* * *

Darren marched into the house with Ty and Sita a step behind. He didn't bother listening to the message. He pulled the crumpled sticky note from his pocket and tapped out Walsheim's number. "Hi, Herbie. Darren Davies here… An hour and a half? That's cutting it close."

Out of the corner of his eye, he saw Sita nodding her head emphatically.

"Sure, I'll be there… Bring him along?" His voice dropped. Darren said good-bye and hung up. He turned to Ty. "He wants me to bring you along."

Sita didn't wait a beat. "If he's going, I'm going."

"Don't be crazy. I can't bring a bunch of kids to an interview. This is a professional situation. He's going to think I don't have any adult friends."

"You don't really, Darren. Not like us."

"Besides," Ty said, "Herbie's got a sore foot. Maybe Sita's powders will help him."

Darren threw up his hands, getting excited again. "You're not going to start the shaman stuff in my job interview!"

"She healed my arm when an emmydactyl almost killed me and Shum's chest when the skinheads tried to kill him. You saw that!" Ty looked over to Sita. "I didn't get a good look at his foot, but I think it's a snap."

"Okay, we're wasting time." Darren turned to Sita. "But you've got to scrap the sunglasses. You can't go in there wearing rhinestone sunglasses."

"I promise I'll take them off when we get out of the car."

"This could be…" Darren's voice drifted along with his gaze. "This could be…" He repeated, but he didn't have the nerve to finish his thought.

Sita finished it for him. "What you've been waiting for."

* * *

Darren backed the Jeep out of the garage. He had reluctantly agreed to bring Ko and Shum along, unwilling to risk the chance of the Karpet King coming back and finding the two *wings* alone in the house.

"It's our opportunity," Ko said in a Spanish accent, "to see more of Amer-ee-canos." His coarse black hair, waxed with Darren's hair gel, was flat, shiny, and parted down the middle.

"You and Shum stay in the car." Darren laid down the rules. "Don't go anywhere. You can open the doors if it gets too hot, but that's it."

"Don't worry, Darren. We've got your back."

The director glanced over to Sita, sitting primly in her silk hoodie, her coral skirt, and brown sandals. "What happened to the wedgies?"

"It's a meeting, Darren. My first meeting in America, and I want to look professional. You don't want me looking like one of those beach bunnies, do you?"

"I'm the one getting interviewed, Sita. Please remember that."

"Are you scared?"

Darren kept his eyes on the traffic. "I'm not scared. He's either going to say 'yes' or 'No, nice meeting you and good luck with those carpet commercials.'"

"But you don't want him to say that, do you?"

Darren reached for the CD button, but Sita grabbed his hand and held it.

"Answer me first."

"Sita, it's my Jeep. If I want to listen to music, I will!"

"First, answer my question! You don't want Herbie to say 'no,' do you?"

"Maybe."

"Maybe you don't or maybe you do?"

He yanked his hand back. "Maybe I want you to get your hand off mine and be quiet!"

She turned away with a sullen look and stared out the window.

"This is Hollywood Boulevard," Darren called out, anxious to change the subject. "Look out the windows on my side. That humungous theater is called the Chinese Theater. It's famous. All the big movie stars have their handprints or footprints in cement in front of the theater."

"Footprints noted!" Ko yelled back.

The Boulevard traffic forced Darren to slow down. Sita leaned forward, craning her neck to catch a glimpse of the exotic Asian-style building.

"Man Who Stands Alone could live there," she said.

"People don't live there. They go to see movies like *Star Wars* and *Ice Age*."

"Soreee," she snapped. "This is my first go in Hollywood."

Darren couldn't help smiling to himself. Piled in the car with him were a wannabe shaman, a spear thrower, a burly street brawler, and a vision seeker, all claiming they lived in caves in some century before written history. *This is as crazy as any movie in that theater.*

"And all along these sidewalks," he continued, "there're shiny stars made of metal. And the names of famous actors are on these too."

"Han Solo?" Ko shouted out.

Darren explained that Han Solo was the name of the character in the *Star Wars* film but that Harrison Ford, the actor who played Han Solo, had a star.

He turned right on a side street and cruised into the parking lot only a block from the Boulevard. "We be here," he said, stopping the Jeep in a shady place at the rear of the building. "Don't open the doors, yet," he commanded. "Sita, off with the shades. Put them in the glove compartment." He glanced in the rearview mirror. "You guys stay here. Like I said, only Ty and Sita are going in with me."

"We roll the windows down, that's all," Ko growled. Dark Predator sunglasses that Darren had loaned him hid his eyes.

"You can't when the engine's off."

"Okay, maybe a short walk."

"No!" Darren smacked the steering wheel with both hands. "Doors open, that's it! No foot on the asphalt!" He glanced at his watch. "Okay, if it gets too warm, you can get out of the car, but you can't leave the parking lot. Only walk in the parking lot. In the parking lot," he repeated. He looked over to Sita. "I told you to put the sunglasses in the glove box."

"I look much older when they're on. You want an older woman in the mix."

"How many times do I have to tell you this isn't your meeting! It's not a shaman convention."

He looked to the rear seat, gave Ko and Shum a final warning, and got out of the Jeep.

He was already feeling jittery, and he hadn't even reached the stairway to the second floor.

* * *

Darren lifted his fist to knock when he heard a powerful but familiar voice on the other side of door 7B.

"Come on in!"

He looked down at his companions. "Don't forget," he whispered, "no crazy talk about caves, emmydactyls, or shamans."

Walsheim sat at his desk, his hands folded. "I thought I heard someone at the door. Welcome." He gave Darren a quick glance, but his eyes settled on Ty and Sita. "I see you brought the feffer, as I asked, and who might this lovely young lady be?"

"Sita," Darren answered in a straightforward voice. "She's Ty's cousin."

"Oh," Walsheim lifted his brows, "you brought the whole Cajun family."

"Ko and Shum are in the Jeep," Sita said.

"Conan Shum? Sounds quite Cajun. I love that dialect."

"No!" Darren shot a "shut-up" look to Sita and quickly explained, pronouncing each name distinctly. "Ko and Shum. Two of the feffer's friends. They're a little shy. They preferred sitting in the car."

"I can understand that. Meetings are more often than not boring for teenagers. Especially when they're used to the rugged Cajun bayou." Walsheim chuckled and motioned to the metal chairs across from his desk. "Please, have a seat. We've only got two chairs. I didn't expect Miss Sita."

"I would be honored to stand."

"No, no. I'd feel bad about that. Young Ty, why don't you look in that closet?" He pointed to a door in the back. "Maybe there's an extra folding chair in there."

Ty walked back and opened the closet door. "No," he said, with his head poked in. "There's this." He dragged out a three-step, rusty utility ladder.

"Well, that's good enough. Miss Sita can sit on the top step. Bring it over here and open it up."

A thick tendril of panic wrapped around Darren's heart. He had no idea if Ty knew how to open a collapsed ladder. "Spread the legs, Ty." He didn't want the situation to get out of hand before the meeting started. "Like we saw at Home Depot."

The cave boy stumbled across the floor with the ladder trapped between his legs.

"Open those legs, Skater! You're almost home!"

Sita bit her lip.

Walsheim raised his dark brows again. "Is my young magician having trouble opening a ladder?"

"I got it!" Ty jerked the metal legs apart and set the ladder firmly on the carpet.

Darren grinned with relief. "He got it!"

Sita quickly climbed two steps up the ladder and assumed a seat on the top. Darren sat down and looked up at her. She towered over Ty.

Walsheim clapped his hands. "Well, now, the Queen has her place, everyone is comfortable. Let's get this meeting underway." He turned to Darren. "I had one other candidate who interested me. He showed me a DVD with several of his commercials. You don't, by chance, have a DVD with you, do you?"

Darren cleared his throat and shook his head.

"Darren's commercials are on channel eleven," Sita announced from her perch.

Walsheim smiled. "Oh, yes, I've seen them." He leaned back and took a sip of bottled water. "This fellow's about your age, maybe a year or so older. Very ambitious, and I like that."

Darren returned a weak nod.

"On the other hand, he's just as flashy as his commercials. I don't honestly know if I could work with someone, you know, too hip for the Strip. I'm a little more old-school myself, and you seem more grounded." He looked over to Ty and Sita. "I thought to myself, no parent is going to let their kids in the company of a man they don't trust. A big brother, if you will. Am I right?"

"Exactly." The word popped out of Sita's mouth. "Our parents are delighted we're with Darren."

"Now, now," Darren interceded. "We don't want Mr. Walsheim to think I put you up to this."

Walsheim smiled. "Nothing like an endorsement. Are you going to be a movie star?"

Before Sita could answer, Darren swooped in. "She's just the feffer's friend, the cousin, like I said." His voice cracked. "She's had a very long trip, so we shouldn't pressure her. Big city. Bright lights." He threw a look to her. "She doesn't like talking."

"Oh, I could tell she was the quiet type. But like they say, still rivers run deep. Even in Cajun country." Walsheim slapped his desk, detailing how much he loved Cajun music and blackened catfish sandwiches. "You can tell I've had more than a few." He chuckled again, but in the next breath, Darren watched the producer's jovial face turn very serious. "So I'm caught between the two choices: the slick commercial man or the classic family guy. And this is how I'll make my decision. I'm going to show Ty a trick. If he guesses it, the job is yours."

"A trick?" Darren winced. "Not another trick?"

"Don't you like magic?"

"Oh, no, don't get me wrong. But…"

"What?"

"My job is hanging on a trick?"

"That's right, and it's a doozy."

Sita leaned forward and crossed her legs. "We like doozies. What kind of a doozy?"

"Sita…" Darren was trying his best to settle his nerves and stop Sita from talking. "Mr. Walsheim is going to show us the doozy."

"I performed this at the American Legion Christmas party when I was thirteen." Herbie removed three silver cups from the center drawer of his desk, each in the shape of a miniature dome.

Darren started to sweat. "I don't want to sound ungrateful…" The last word crumbled in his throat. "But isn't this a little arbitrary?"

"Only on the surface, my friend. Life has many layers."

"But it's my life," Darren squeaked.

"That's why I involved the Cajuns. They're obviously one of the layers."

"We're definitely a layer," Sita agreed.

Walsheim nodded. "In nice sensible sandals."

"On sale at Macy's. A bargain."

Darren shot Sita another look.

The producer pushed aside the stack of glossy photos and set each cup on his desk. "Everyone has guides. Sometimes, they arrive unexpectedly." He removed a penny from his pocket and held it up to three pairs of anxious eyes. "Now, watch carefully.

Walawalawala!" He whirled his arms, pounded his chest, and flipped open his hands with the same flare he had displayed at the previous meeting.

The three visitors stared in silence at his empty hands.

Walsheim stamped his good foot. "Walawalawala," he intoned in his deep baritone voice. "Under which cup is the penny?"

Silence. His phone rang. Darren's eyes shifted to the ringing phone. Herbie stared at it. Darren held his breath.

Walsheim reached over and clicked it off. "I'm not answering that," he said, keeping his eyes on the phone. "It's probably the competing director. But Ty gets first crack at the trick." He turned slowly to Ty. "Under which cup, young Ty?"

Ty pointed. "The first cup."

Walsheim answered just as quickly. "Sorry, cup three."

Darren threw his hands in the air and leapt to his feet, screaming, "You can't do that! I don't care how many layers life has. This isn't a cake! It isn't a game! You can't decide my life on a trick! I want this job! I want to work with you! I want to make those documentaries we talked about!" Darren's red face was scrunched up, his flat chest was heaving, and his long arms flailed in the air. "You can't decide my fate on a..." He groped for words. "On a feffer's choice! I'm ready to make the leap."

Walsheim smiled. "He's a very smart Cajun feffer." He tapped the first cup.

Darren swayed back and forth, trying to steady himself and focus on the producer. Ty leapt to his feet and threw his arm around Darren.

Walsheim lifted the cup, revealing the coin. "You see, he was right."

"He's a feffer," Darren squealed.

"I was anxious to see how much you wanted this job, Mr. Davies. I knew that working for your father, you'd be secure for the rest of your life, just as I have been since I went into the family business. Your reaction was the answer I needed and what I wanted from someone I'm going to work side by side with. Something you said stayed in my mind: we've got to bring the world together, not tear it apart. Passion!"

"Passion!" Sita echoed, clenching her tiny fists. "Passion in love! Passion in life!"

"Yes, Queen Sita!" The producer leaned back in his chair and told Darren he'd meet him again in San Diego in two days. "My secretary will call you with all the details." He offered his guesthouse, just a room and a bath. "But it'll do," he said, "until you find an apartment. I want you to get into the swing of things ASAP." He rapped his desk. "You made the leap."

"Yes, sir."

"Herbie."

The grimace on Darren's face softened into a smile. Ty let go of his arm and the young director reached out and shook Walsheim's hand. "Thank you, Herbie. You won't be disappointed."

"My disappointments were settled long ago."

Sita climbed down the ladder. She removed a small leather pouch from her hoodie pocket and sprinkled a few grains of mustard yellow powder into the water bottle on the producer's desk.

"Drink this, Herbie. Your foot will get better."

Herbie eyed the plastic bottle. "Cajun tonic. I love it!"

"Cajun tonic," Darren mumbled as the trio left the office.

He walked briskly through the hallway and down the steps, pumping his fists with excitement. The two *wings* on either side were just as thrilled.

"That powder isn't going to kill him, is it, Sita? He's my new boss."

"No, but it might send him into the future." She smiled. "Just a Cajun joke, Darren. Lighten up, you made the Herbie leap." She skipped down a stair. "Now we can get back to the River Gan and I can go shaman deep."

Darren grabbed the rail. "Shaman deep! What's that about?"

Sita looked up from two steps below. "Just think how many centuries there are, D! Maybe we'll find you in another life, without a cellie, a TV, or a fridge."

* * *

"Where are they?" Triumph turned to stomach-churning fear as Darren stared at an open door and an empty Jeep.

Ty and Sita answered with the same puzzled look.

"Ko! Shum!" Darren yelled. The three spread out in different directions across the parking lot. "I told them not to leave the parking lot!" Darren was in a rage. Any vestige of elation over his new job had vanished.

"I'll find them," Ty said. "I know my *wings*."

"Wait!" Darren raised his hands. "You're not going anywhere. Not without Sita and me. We can't let anyone else get lost." He checked his Rolex. "We were in the meeting for half an hour. They couldn't have gone too far. Right?"

Both time-travelers answered with military precision: "Right!"

They got back in the Jeep. Before Darren had started the engine, Sita retrieved her sunglasses from the glove compartment. "I feel much better," she said, adjusting the frames. "The sun was killing my eyes."

Darren gave her a "don't be ridiculous" look. "We'll go back the way we came. Ko was very curious about Hollywood Boulevard." He made a left turn onto the Boulevard. The traffic was just as backed up going west as it had been on the way to the meeting. "Sita, you look out your window. Ty, you look out the side window in back of me. As soon as you see them, shout it out."

The last word hadn't left his lips when Ty exclaimed, "Han Solo!"

"Don't shout unless you see them."

"But that's where they are, Darren!"

"The star? The Han Solo star?"

"Yes!"

"That's what he means," Sita said, adjusting her glasses. "Ko's a Solo freak."

"That's the Harrison Ford star. I'm pretty sure it's on your side of the street, Sita." Darren cut sharply into an empty parking space. "Let's get out. We've got a better chance of finding them if we're on the ground." He turned to Sita. "We stay together. You hold Ty's hand."

Darren put coins in the parking meter and they started up Hollywood Boulevard. Ty pulled Sita along, tugging at her arm each time she stopped at a clothing store window.

"A girl can't even enjoy a little window shopping," she complained. "They haven't walked back to the River Gan. We've got time."

Darren was checking out each bronze star they passed, asking every other pedestrian, "Do you know where the Harrison Ford star is?"

Sita managed to hop-skip from one bronze star to the next. "Ty," she shouted, "I'm *star-stepping* and I'm not even sleeping!"

"Just keep up!" he shouted back. "This is no time for Kishoki jokes."

At Highland Avenue they waited for the stoplight to change. Sita pushed her rhinestone sunglasses up on the bridge of her nose. "I've got a feeling we're close," she said.

The "walk" sign blinked. They crossed the street linked hand in hand. Darren's long, loping strides pulled them along.

Fans milled around different polished stars, each inscribed with the name of a famous actor or entertainer, some living, some long dead. They looked down at the gleaming stars as if a part of the person were really there. "Harrison Ford!" Darren shouted. "Harrison Ford!"

Twenty feet later, they were standing with a small cluster of Asian tourists staring down at the polished Harrison Ford star.

"Big name," someone said, laughing. "Big foot!"

"Foot?" Darren shrieked. "That's it! Foot!"

He nearly yanked Ty's arm out of its socket as his galloping steps brought the trio under the soaring canopy that shaded the theater concourse. They stopped.

Darren watched Ko step back. Shum stepped forward, trading places in Harrison Ford's footprints. The spear thrower smiled, looking up, meeting Darren's flabbergasted expression. "Ko's very smart. He found Han Solo."

Ko, in his Predator sunglasses, his arms crossed, his hair slicked back, grinned like a pint-sized Vegas gangster. "We nailed it, Einstein. We can go back to the Jeep now."

"Now?" Darren's panic crashed into outrage and disbelief. "I told you not to leave the parking lot! You found a pair of footprints in a city of ten million people, but you can't find your way back to the River Gan! Is this the way *wings* obey orders?"

"Darren," Ty swiftly intervened. "Han Solo is important to them, like you getting the job was important to you."

Sita smiled. "Listen to the trickmaster, Mr. Davies."

* * *

Except for sunlight flooding through the windows, the Baskin-Robbins shop was empty. The *wings* crowded around a small table, celebrating Darren's new job. The director pulled up a chair and set his cappuccino blast on the table. "So, little feffer, how did you know which cup to choose?"

"It's an old trick my mother taught me. Herbie stuck a coin under each cup, like my mother did with a nut and a gourd."

"It's called the nut-gourd trick." Shum nodded, slurping up a spoonful of mint chip banana split.

Ko had almost finished devouring his cookies and cream/rum raisin banana split. He nudged Shum and made a "zip it" sign across his lips.

"Any cup you tap, a coin will fall," Ty continued. "It doesn't matter which one you choose. He hid the first coin, the coin he showed you, in his sleeve when he threw his arms around and shouted 'walawalawala.'" Ty explained that if Darren had said number one, Herbie would have tapped number two or three and shouted, "Two" or maybe "Three." The person wouldn't hear the coin fall. If Darren had said "Two," Herbie would have tapped one or three. Unless he wanted the person to win, the person would always guess wrong. Ty snapped his fingers. "Baby trick."

Shum smiled. "Baby trick."

Darren was impressed. "So when you chose number one, it really didn't matter."

"Exactly. Herbie only wanted to see how you would…" He looked to Sita. "Don't help me. I'll get it." Ty tapped the table twice. "React. He wanted to see how you would react. That's why it was really you, not me, who chose the right gourd."

Sita leaned back and clapped her hands. "Ty is one smart feffer."

"His mother is very smart," Shum added. He raised his plastic spoon. "Let's stay in America until we finish all the flavors. Then we'll know which ones to take with us."

"Where are we going to keep ice cream so it doesn't melt, Shumster?" Ko looked over to Darren. "Sometimes he doesn't think past his knuckles."

Darren reached for his drink when his cell phone rang. He glanced at the incoming number. "Hi, Dr. Greenberg. What's up? … What did my father say? … I understand… Probably not right away. I'm moving, but thank you for all your help." He slipped the cell into his vest pocket. "Dr. Greenberg's dropping me as a client. He thinks I should see someone more into flying saucers." He looked between Sita and Ty. His voice was calm, and a smile crept into his dark eyes. "He thinks you're dangerous."

Sita hunched her shoulders and leaned into the table. "Do you think we are?"

"I think I'm the luckiest guy in the world."

* * *

On the way home, Darren's rousing voice led the *wings* through a rough rendition of a Freddie Mercury song: "We are the champions, my friend…and we'll keep on fighting to the end. We are the champions… We are the champions of the world!" The *wings* muddled through the lyrics, laughing and buoying up Darren's spirits even more.

"Wow, doesn't it look great!"

"What?" Sita looked around.

"The neighborhood." Darren laughed. "I don't think I've ever seen it look this good."

But as he made the corner turn, a dark specter of danger loomed ahead. The black Mercedes was parked in front of his house. He didn't bother going into the alley. He pulled up behind his father's car. Before any of the *wings* had unbuckled their seat belts, Darren was in the house.

* * *

Through the kitchen window, he glimpsed his father in the backyard. He tapped the counter twice, breathed deeply, and, much like the final call from Greenberg, he felt a sense of peace as he walked outside.

"Looks like you did a damn fine job fixing the window." The Karpet King's gaze shifted from the screened window, half hidden by the hollyhocks.

"I had some help."

"Local handyman?"

"The *wings*."

"*Wings*?" Davies took the cigar from his mouth. "Those kids? I told you I wanted them out of this house."

"They're leaving."

"Good."

"And so am I."

"What the hell does that mean?"

"I got a job. I interviewed for it and I met with Mr. Walsheim today, and he gave me the job."

Davies raised a brow, stumped by Darren's answer. "Walsheim?"

"He owns a film production company in San Diego."

"San Diego." Davies squinted. "You can't drive to San Diego every day. That's five hours on the freeway. Do you realize how much that's going to cost me in gas?"

"I'm not commuting. I'm moving there."

The Karpet King caught the eye of Sita and the *wings* standing in the kitchen doorway. "And those hoodlums are going with you?"

"Yes. In a way."

Davies took a step toward his son. "You can't go. They can go. They damn well better go!" His gruff voice rose. "But you can't go!"

"I'm twenty-four years old, twenty-five in a couple of months."

"And you're my son. You're working for me. That's the only job you've ever had. Being my son and working for the Karpet King!"

"I'm sorry, but..." Darren paused, pulling every ounce of courage from his soul. "But that's over."

"You won't have this house, damn it!" Davies punched the air with his cigar. "I'll sell it!"

"Go ahead." Darren started back to the house.

"Wait!" Davies knocked his fists against the empty air. "You won't have the company credit card or the gas card." His face turned crimson, seething with rage. "In fact, you won't have any cards. And no car!"

Darren turned back. "The Jeep is in my name. Remember? It was a gift after I made your first great Karpet King commercial."

Davies struggled for words. "Okay, the insurance for the car. You're under the company policy."

"I'll buy insurance. Mr. Walsheim is paying me."

"But you're going to have my company someday. You're the next Karpet King!"

"That's not what I want. I never wanted the carpet company."

"Fifteen hundred a week." The Karpet King lurched forward. "I'll pay you fifteen hundred a week! That guy in San Diego isn't paying you that kind of money."

For the first time in his life, Darren felt not anger but sympathy for the man he had feared since he was a child.

"Two thousand. Two thousand dollars to stay on board."

"I'm sorry. It isn't the money anymore." He left his father's plea hanging in the backyard stillness. Darren took two quick steps toward the kitchen doorway, brushed past the *wings*, and disappeared into the house.

The Karpet King stood alone, speechless, staring at the grass. He knocked the ash off his cigar.

Sita walked up to him and placed her hand on his arm. "Mr. Davies, Darren loves you."

He looked down coldly. "Who are you to tell me?"

"I'm a shaman-in-waiting. Your history is in my heart. He will always love you, but—" She raised her eyes to him.

"But what?"

"You have to let Darren be who he wants to be."

Davies pulled away from her hand as if it were ice. "You can't talk to me like that."

Again she looked into his cold, dark eyes. "But I have."

The Karpet King clamped the cigar between his teeth, took a step toward the side of the house, and walked back to his car.

* * *

Darren sat in his office, coming to grips with his future. He called Marc to make certain his final Karpet King commercial was ready for airplay, and he arranged for a U-Haul rental. He held a lengthy call with Walsheim's secretary, making sure he had addresses, phone numbers, employment form data, and general information. She said she would email him everything.

"Thanks, Joyce. I'll definitely be there in a big ol' U-Haul. Twelve o'clock sharp. ... The Cajuns? ... Herbie told you all about them, did he? Well, they've got to get back. Long trip, that kind of thing." As he said good-bye, he heard a light knock on his office door.

"Sita, Darren." She peeked in. "Ty and I are going for a walk. Don't worry. Just around the block." She told him that Ko and Shum were watching some kind of big machine on the magic crystal. "It drives like a car but it only has one wheel in front and two wheels in back. I think it's called a tractor." Her gaze shifted to a few open boxes. "What are you doing?"

Darren was going to tell her about the arrangements he'd made. Instead, he folded his arms and leaned back. "You know, this is the first time I've had an argument with my father and my skin didn't break out."

"Because you weren't fighting with him. You were fighting for you."

"Shaman speaks and Darren listens." He got to his feet and closed the corner window. "Do you have any idea what a mess I was when I met you? I thought I knew everything. I pretended I did. Pretty girlfriend. Directing job. House in West LA. But you saw through all that. You saw the hollow me, through eyes half my age." He paused, deciding whether or not to share a phone call. "I called Dorsey. I wanted to tell her about my job and that I was moving to San Diego, but she didn't even listen. She was so excited about a part she just got. Finally, I said good-bye and hung up." He sighed a breath. "And now I'm saying good-bye to you. I'm going to miss you. All of you."

"We will miss you too, Darren. We are here because of you."

"No. You are here because Ty had a vision to help his clan."

"That's true. The vision has a seeker, but it has to have a home." She laughed, a little trill of laughter that brought a blush to her cheeks. "Who knew the home would have a dishwasher and a magic crystal?"

"More shaman wisdom." He turned his gaze to the dark computer screen. "Look at that. We searched the world for the Kishoki. We never found them."

"The computer is new, Darren. We are old." She giggled again and her blush came back. "You will find us in your heart."

Sita smiled and left the room.

In his whole life he had never talked to anyone the way he was able to talk to Ty and Sita. He didn't know why. Cajun, Kishoki, Antelope, it didn't matter who or what they were. He knew, in some way he couldn't explain, they were older than he. Older in time. Older in wisdom. Older in the spirit of their souls.

Then a new thought came into his head: *I've got to take their picture before they leave.*

* * *

Ty and Sita walked past houses where lights had already been turned on. Water sprayed across trimmed front lawns and flower beds.

"Smell the grass," Ty said. "It's the same smell along the River Gan."

"Look," she said.

Ty followed Sita's gaze to a housewife watching them from her doorway. "She's like the mothers watching us from the mouths of caves."

Hand in hand they turned the corner, walking lightly, as if the cement beneath them was a trail of forest leaves.

"I can't see our shadows," he said.

"Because we are leaving. Time is turning us into ghosts."

Ty laughed. "Not so fast. I've still got to talk to Darren about something. Besides, I'm hungry. Ko and Shum are going to want to eat too."

"Maybe I will make dinner tonight."

"Can you?"

"If Darren helps me. I know how to use a stove now."

"Hell, mo'fo. I could buy you a stove and put it on my credit card."

"Don't talk like that!" she reprimanded him sharply. "You didn't come here to learn gangbang talk like those stupid skinheads."

"Sorry." Ty felt a crunch in his heart. He knew she was right. "Will a budding shaman kiss a stubborn seeker on Darren's block?"

"Will you promise to never call me mo'fo again?"

"I promise."

They kissed.

"And will you kiss me on the corner of..." He looked up at the street sign, but he knew it was hopeless. "I can't read."

"The street with no name," she said.

He wrapped his arms around her. The sun was setting, and they kissed again.

The harsh blast of a horn startled the teenage lovers. A low-riding gold car, like the one thumping music Ty had seen in the Home Depot parking lot, drove by. The driver thrust his arm out and flipped a thumbs-up sign.

"What does that mean?" Sita asked.

"We're on our way home." Ty grinned. "What else could it mean?"

* * *

"It's called mushroom casserole."

Sita held up a large Pyrex dish between her hot-pad-mittened hands. Her stained red apron drooped past her knees. The *wings*, seated at the dining room table, returned uncertain smiles.

After one tasty bite, Ty lifted his glass of milk. "This is for Sita. The best cook in America."

Ko raised his stubbled chin, adjusted his Predator sunglasses, and lifted his glass. His voice, for the first time since they left the River Gan, was neither a grumble nor a growl addressing her. "Thank you, Sita. It's the max."

"Max!" Shum echoed.

"Thank you, Ko," she said.

Sita didn't take off her apron until they had all gone to bed. She blew out a candle on the bedside table and snuggled up to Ty.

"Okay, skateboy," she said, wrapping her arms around him, "as we say in Kishoki, cut to the fish head: Do you really have a plan?"

"Feel the golden shell." His voice was an ardent whisper. "It's getting warmer, like someone is pulling us back. Like time in another golden shell far away is reaching for us."

Sita placed her hand on the golden shell and closed her eyes.

"Is it Man Who Stands Alone?" he asked anxiously.

"No, no," she answered. "I see your cave. I see the golden shell in your mother's hand."

CHAPTER 28

S ita and the *wings* stood at the living room window. A bright
morning sun splashed across the front yard.

"That's one big car." Shum grinned, looking out to the street.

"It's called a van," Ty said. "Darren told me. We're going to
help him put all his stuff inside it."

The *wings'* eyes were fixed on a big white van with a jagged
orange streak across the door. Darren was opening the back doors
and dragging out large flat pieces of cardboard.

"Shummy." Ko nudged his *wing* mate. "If Einstein thinks he's
gonna drive us back to cave land in a van, he doesn't know the
Kishoki roads." They slapped hands.

Ty ignored Ko's silliness. He leaned to Sita and whispered,
"That's our ride to the zoo park. That's where the antelope are."

* * *

Darren plopped the cardboard down on the living room
floor. "Okay," he said. "We're going to make boxes. We need this
too." Darren held up one of the tape dispensers. "I'll show you
how to use it." He got down on his knees, clopping around the
cardboard in an old pair of jeans and a baggy white T-shirt.

"Second big job!" Ko shouted. "First, we put glass in the
garage window. Now, dudes, we're making boxes!"

Darren shook his head. "If you need me, I'll be packing up
stuff in my office." He walked out of the room thinking to himself,
How could I have ever doubted that they were from another world?

* * *

251

Ty and Sita worked in the kitchen, cramming the coffeemaker, toaster, a pot and skillet into a box they had made. Darren had told them that once he got his San Diego apartment, he'd come back for the rest of his stuff.

"I feel like we're packing too," she said with a wan smile. "When I touch these kitchen things, even though I want to go back to my world, I still feel sad. Just when I'm beginning to know how to use them, they are being taken away." She set down the basket and started folding dishtowels into it. "I want to be a shaman, Ty. That's who I am. And I know that only in my world can I be that. Here I would only be one more teenager at a mall or like the girls we saw at the beach in bikinis. My world is on the River Gan. That's where I will be who I am. That's where you will be who you are, where you will change things better for the Kishoki people." She rested her hands on the basket. "That's why we need to go back, but that doesn't mean I can't feel a little sad."

Darren loped into the kitchen lugging a blue and red box. "I forgot to bring these in. Vitamin-plus energy drinks. You guys have got to start drinking healthier. It's never too late."

He set the box of drinks on the counter. Sita watched him take a deep breath.

"It's kind of an emotional day," he said. "Packing up all my stuff in the office. But I know I'm doing the right thing." He took a step back. "Let's load the van."

* * *

Bare-chested, with his T-shirt rolled up and wrapped like a headband around his forehead, Ko wheeled the dolly stacked with boxes down the front walkway.

"Wheels are the future!" Ty shouted back from the van tailgate.

Darren waved a hand. "I'll do the office boxes, Ko. Wait for me! The computer stuff needs special handling." The words had barely popped from his mouth when another voice caught his ear.

"Mr. Davies!" The mailman was walking toward him, pushing a mail cart and waving a book-size cardboard box. He handed Darren the package and glanced at the U-Haul. "You're not moving, are you?"

"Charger town, Curt. San Diego. As soon as I get a place, I'll put in a forwarding address."

"Is your dad opening a store down there?"

"I'm going solo. No Pop, no more carpet commercials. New job, new everything." Darren's eyes lit up with a smile. He told Curt to leave future mail in the door slot. "My dad'll pick it up. He's always over here. Maybe he'll sell the house."

Darren watched the mailman amble over to the next house. He looked down at the box in his hands. It was from Amazon.com.

"What is it?" Sita asked.

"Just a book." Darren knew inside the box was *The Caves of Ajanta*, the book he had ordered in his futile attempt to locate the *wings'* homeland. He tossed it in the back of the van. "Let's finish packing."

It felt like summer was over and everyone was packing up and going home, but summer in LA was just beginning and so were the fortunes of an ambitious young director and a crew of intrepid time-travelers.

"Darren," Ty stacked a box and wiped the sweat from his cheek. "On the way to San Diego tomorrow morning, could we stop at the ocean? We'd like to see it one last time."

"We're driving straight down the 405, Ty. It's way out of our way." He reminded Ty of how he had promised Herbie he'd meet him at his house at noon.

Ty frowned. "It's the Big River, Darren. Don't you remember how we drove down the mountain and that's the first thing we saw?"

"Of course, I remember, but I can't be late on my first day of work. It's not professional."

"Definitely not professional," Sita agreed. "But we could consider adjustments."

Ty looked back to Ko and Shum waiting for an answer. He shook his head *no*.

Darren saw the disappointment on the *wings'* faces. "Okay, okay." He glanced at his watch. "It's almost dinnertime. We'll stop for some food near the beach and then we'll hit the Big River."

* * *

"Sita!" Ty looked in the living room and kitchen. He raced back to the hallway. "Sita?" He opened the bedroom door.

"Sita?"

The room was dark but for the light of the candle sitting on a bedside dish.

Sita sat on the bed. Her rhinestone sunglasses covered her eyes. She spread her arms. "My Macy gifts from Darren." Surrounding her were all the clothes, the skirt, silk hoodie, and camisoles.

"I'm saying good-bye to them," she said. "Ty? When we get back to the caves, when I don't have these jeans and camisoles, will you still think I'm beautiful?"

"More beautiful. The most beautiful of all the *kanta-wings*."

"Don't tell Man Who Stands Alone. I know you say that to make me feel good, but a shaman, even a shaman-in-waiting, should not feel so insecure on one side or think so much about herself in pretty things on the other side."

In that moment Ty loved her more than in all the moons and suns, winters and summers that they had been together. He opened the bedroom door, and Sita blew out the candle.

"*Wings*, we're going to the Big River!" Ty shouted. "Last night, last taco in America!"

CHAPTER 29

Dusk and smog turned the sky a brilliant orange as the Jeep sped down the Santa Monica Freeway toward the ocean. Sita sat next to the window in the backseat, along with Ko and Shum. A big stuffed panda rested on the lap of each of boy.

"They can't see anything," she complained. "Why did they take them? I can't move. It's just dumb!"

"That's not nice," Darren said.

"I didn't mean dumb. I meant…" Sita paused. "*Leshko*. That's right. It's a Kishoki word."

Darren glanced in his rearview. "Meaning?"

"Inconvenient," Ko answered, in a voice muffled from behind the panda's head.

Darren left the freeway, pulled into a Del Taco drive-thru, and ordered tacos, burritos, and drinks.

Less than half an hour later, they sat on the shoreline sand eating their food. A thin veil of gray clouds, like old lace, skirted the purple twilight.

Darren looked over to a handful of teenagers sitting around a campfire. One of the boys played a guitar while the others sang in a language none of the *wings* understood.

"What is it?" Shum asked.

"Spanish. They're probably kids from Mexico or their families are from there."

"South of America," Ko couldn't help adding.

Ty pushed aside a few Styrofoam boxes and got to his feet. "We'll clean up when we come back."

Darren shot him an anxious look. "From where?"

"Just to touch the Big River." Ty took Sita's hand.

Shum and Ko jumped up. They all walked down to the ocean shore.

Darren looked over to the Mexican kids at the campfire. The words of a Spanish song floated through the air. He looked back at the *wings* walking along the shore. Within shouting distance of each other were two groups of kids from two different lands. The Latino teenagers were from a country only a few miles from the city in which he was soon to live. The *wings*, Darren knew, were from another world where somewhere there was a River Gan and a land of cliffs and caves.

The white wavelets licked at Ty's sneakers. Sita let the cold ocean water run over her sparkly wedgies. The clouds had drifted away, leaving behind a starry sky.

The songs and music of the guitar could still be heard. The flames of the fire reminded Ty of the fire pit in his cave. He knew this was another sign that very soon they would be going back.

He looked over to Ko and Shum. They had marched into the ocean until the waves reached their knees.

Ty walked with Sita for a few yards along the shoreline. He looked at the moon. "This is the water of the River Gan," he said. "We are here and we are there, and time is in the golden shell." He turned to Sita. "Now you must say it."

Sita repeated the words as Ty had spoken them. Then, together, with the moonlight on their faces, they said, "Tomorrow we will go home."

"How?" she said.

"Tomorrow, you will know."

* * *

They were quiet on the way back to Darren's house. Ko and Shum hugged their pandas and fell asleep in the backseat. Sita kept silent, but she was filled with nervous energy. She knew that the words Ty and she had said at the ocean marked the end of their journey and the beginning of Ty's mysterious plan. But how would they travel into the past on a golden shell or from a zoo park?

Sitting in the backseat, she could only see the side of Ty's face. He was looking at the stream of headlights and lit windows in cliff-tall buildings. Sita heard Darren talking about San Diego, how big the city was, and about some money he could give the *wings* until Ty worked out his plan. "But you've got to punch the ticket plan *mañana*," he said. Then she, too, fell asleep.

She awoke as the car slowed down and came to a stop. Darren had stored the U-Haul in the garage. She saw the glow of the porch light in front of the house. She opened the Jeep door. *Last night in Darren's casa.*

* * *

Ty gathered everyone in the living room and spoke only in Kishoki.

"*We have one more thing to do.*"

"*What one more thing do we have to do?*" Shum looked up, surprised.

"It's our last night in America, dude," Ko growled in English. "It's movie time."

"No." Ty waved his hands and looked over to Darren. Again he spoke in Kishoki. He told the *wings* that they must thank Darren for feeding them and keeping them safe and that they must ask One Hand to watch over Darren in his new life in San Diego.

He instructed Sita to translate some of this to Darren and told the *wings* that she, as the shaman-in-waiting, would conduct the ceremony.

Sita stood up in her ocean-wet wedgies and cleared her throat. "I know you want a movie," she said. "But this is more important. This is the Kishoki way." She sent Shum to the bathroom to bring back towels and told Ty to place one of the dining room chairs in the middle of the living room, where Darren would sit. Then she went to the kitchen and heated a cup of oil, mixing in a teaspoon of her ochre- and lavender-scented powders. Balancing the five utility candles in one hand and the cup of oil in the other, she returned to the living room.

Before Darren sat down, Sita had Ty lay the towels flat under the chair.

"Sit," she told Darren. "I'm going to pour this olive oil over your head. Don't worry, it's warm."

"You gotta be kidding!" Darren threw up his arms. "It's going to get on the Persian rug! My father will kill me! He's already pissed off. Now he'll send a hit man down to San Diego and have me whacked!"

Ko growled, "Don't be a baby."

"You father will never know," Sita added. "Besides, you told us the rug wasn't really Persian. It was a Chinese rip-off."

"You don't even know what a rip-off is!"

"I know you and I know your father. That's enough." She turned to Ty. "Give Ko and Shum candles and Darren too. Then light each candle, including mine and yours."

Sita signaled Ko to turn off the lights.

"You, Darren Michael Davies, are now a part of the Kishoki clan," she said in the darkness. "We are your ancestors. You are one of the Antelope People who went ahead when we stayed behind. We have found you and we bless you. The circle is complete.

"Close your eyes," Sita continued. The shaman-in-waiting poured the warm olive oil over Darren's head. Then she began a chant in Kishoki: *"Let our brother have the eyes to see, the ears to hear, and the lips to speak all that is good and true in the sacred light of One Hand's world."*

The *wings* joined the chant, following her in a circle around Darren. Around and around they went. The light of the candles danced to the words of their chant. The *wings* shrieked, stamped their feet, and patted Darren's head. Olive oil ran down his cheeks and over his closed eyes. Melting wax dripped on his fingers. He remained silent and still.

Sita stopped, stamped her foot twice, and the boys blew out their candles.

"Can I get up?" Darren asked in a quavering voice. "I can't see."

"Shum, turn the lights back on," Sita ordered. "Ty will take you to your bedroom, Darren. Remember, you must sleep with the oil on your head."

In the living room, Sita and the *wings* sat quietly, waiting for their hearts to slow and their blood to cool.

"I'm going to miss him," Ko mumbled. "He was like the father I never had."

"You have a father," Sita said.

"Not in America. In America I'm a *kleshko*, an orphan."

"North of the border," Shum whispered, "we're all orphans. We just need a way back."

CHAPTER 30

"Let's go! We're rollin'!" Darren shouted. He had gotten most of the olive oil out of his hair in the shower. His raven-black locks looked like they'd been moussed up for a punk concert.

The *wings* straggled into the living room, already dressed in their leather jerkins and boots.

Darren looked over to Sita. "Lower the hood on your cape. We don't want you mistaken for an evil munchkin."

"Will we eat on the way?" Shum asked.

"No Sugar Pops, no hot chocolate," Darren stated flatly. "We're on a tight schedule. And Shum," he continued in a commanding tone, "you can't take your spear."

It looked to Darren as if Shum was about to fall over. The *wing* gasped. "What if we meet another emmydactyl?"

"You've got a better chance of meeting Captain Martinez again before you meet another emmydactyl in San Diego."

"Wait, Darren. Shum's right."

Darren looked over to Ty. "Are you siding with him?"

Ty was concerned over the kinds of dangers they might face on their way back.

"That's definitely a risk," Darren agreed. "But you can't walk around America carrying a spear."

Sita jumped in for the first time. "You can carry a gun in America, but you can't carry a spear, is that right?"

"Look, I don't want to get into an argument about guns." Meeting Herbie in San Diego and still not a clue about Ty's secret plan was heating up Darren's nerves. "If you cut the spear in half, you can take it. Maybe you can hide it under your jerkin."

"Done!" Ty shot back.

Darren hustled the boys back to the garage. He took down a saw from his tool rack. "Ever used one of these?" He handed it to Ty. "We saw them at Home Depot."

"Right," Ty answered firmly. "It's in my DNA."

"Don't be crazy. Where'd you hear that?"

"Ko."

"I ripped it off the TV, Einstein."

"Okay, Ko. I'm not mad, I'm letting you say that. We probably won't ever see each other again."

With the Predator sunglasses shading Ko's eyes, Darren couldn't tell if the regret he saw on the *wing*'s lips was real or not, but he took it to be a silent apology. He looked over to Ty, who was sawing Shum's spear in half, impressed with the way Ty handled the saw.

"My father's got tools too, Darren. Cave tools. We just don't have a Home Depot."

Shum slipped the pointed spear-half under his jerkin. "How does it look?" He stared back at the silent ring of faces.

"You can't tell," Ko said, boosting a sly, clubby smile.

Shum took a wobbly step. "I can't walk either."

"Hunch forward between each step," Ko advised, raising his shoulders and bobbing his head.

Darren had seen enough. He hurried the *wings* back to the house.

Ty called Shum and Ko into the living room. The boys hitched on their bedrolls.

"I'll meet you in the van," Darren said. "I'm bringing it around to the front of the house. When you close the door, make sure it's locked." He spoke directly to Sita, confident she would follow his directions.

Ty, trying to be as fair as possible, instructed anyone wearing sunglasses to place them on the fireplace mantel. Sita and Ko stepped forward. Shum wanted to take his panda bear.

"No way," Ty ordered. "The panda goes on the mantel too."

Shum had to rest his bear on its side to keep it from rolling off the mantel.

Then the cave boy leader intoned a prayer. The *wings* stood silently, heads bent, hands at their backsides.

"*We came here on the light of the golden shell and so we will return.*" Ty spoke in Kishoki, with his eyes closed. His voice was clear and carried forth like the sound of an oracle. "*We found the Antelope People and all the magical things they have made. Now we go back to teach our people. We do not have the tools, the inventions, to make such things, but we have our minds, our hearts, and our imaginations. May we be safe on our journey home.*"

Ty watched Shum step to the front. Like a young Kishoki warrior placing an eagle feather before the sacred fire, Shum laid the TV remote on a shelf below the magic crystal.

"Good-bye, Han Solo," Ko whispered.

Ty raised his arm, turned sharply, and his eyes fell on Sita. "We go. The plan begins!"

Shum, Ko, and even Sita didn't know the details of his plan, but Ty, in full command, was confident that they posited in him the same faith that led them to begin their journey.

He watched Sita lock the front door. The *wings* waved good-bye to the *casa* and all the miracles it embraced.

* * *

"Safari Park?" Darren sat in the driver's seat, shaking his head in a state of shock.

"That's where we must go," Ty said resolutely. "That's the plan. You told me the zoo park was close to San Diego."

Darren didn't know what he should have expected. He had to be at Walsheim's house by noon. "Can't you guys take a taxi or a boat?"

"Don't be ridiculous," Sita butted in. "We're talking space-time continuum."

Darren glanced back as if she'd just announced she was marrying the U.S. president. "Your golden shell has to be in the park, is that what you're telling me?"

"We have to hear the antelope," Ty answered firmly, again. "That is the message from the golden shell in my father's cave."

"Why didn't you tell me you talked shell to shell?" Darren grumbled. "I could have said hello to your parents." He turned the ignition, still frustrated. "We've got to make up a story." He glanced in his rearview mirror. Sita and the *wings* sat on boxes in the cargo cabin, trying to get comfortable and listen at the same time. "You can't walk into Safari Park looking like you guys, with bedrolls on your back."

Pulling away from the curb, he glanced in his side-view mirror. Sunlight flared off the glass. He couldn't see, but as he moved forward, the sun slipped from the mirror. Darren saw the dark specter coming toward him. He saw the car's side window lower, like a giant mouth opening. The black Mercedes stopped parallel to the U-Haul.

The Karpet King leaned across the console. He pulled the cigar from between his lips.

"Leaving, huh?"

"We're on our way. The house is locked. The Jeep's in the garage." Darren's voice was as dry as reeds in a summer wind. "I'll be back in a few days to pick it up."

From the height of the van seat, Darren looked down at his father. The face was jowled, with the look of an old lion. Cigar smoke curled through the open window.

Finally, Davies spoke. "New haircut, huh?"

"Just a little gel."

"You're doing the right thing, son. Start out with nothing, like your father. Blaze your own trail."

The words shocked Darren, slammed against his heart: *You're doing the right thing.* He had never heard his father say those words before.

"Thanks, Dad."

"I love you, son."

"I love you back."

It was that simple. No hugs. No more than a smile. A lifetime of anger and remorse gave way to words as magical and life-giving as the spark of a firestone. *You're doing the right thing.*

He watched the Mercedes drive away, a sleek black ribbon that curled around the far corner and disappeared. Darren shifted into drive and pulled away from the curb.

"Did your father say good-bye?"

"More like hello, Ty. For the first time in my life."

Less than ten minutes later, the U-Haul was riding the 405 Freeway, heading south.

"We're doing it, Ty. We're on our way." Darren's voice was upbeat again. "I've been thinking about this. When we get to Safari Park, I'll buy you tickets." His plan, he explained, was to tell the guard that the *wings* were a part of a Young Adventurers' Club. They had to pick a period in time, in the 1800s, and their task was to feel what it would be like on a safari. "Can you remember that?"

"We're part of a Denture Club."

"No!" Darren smacked the steering wheel. "That's very funny, but that's not it. Dentures are for your teeth. This is Adventure Club. Everyone say it."

"We're the Adventure Club."

"Right. And you're imagining it's the 1800s."

Ty turned his head to Sita. "What's the 1800s?"

"Long time ago, *masuqa*." Sita smiled. "But we're longer time."

Traffic came to a crawl. Darren pulled down his sun visor. He recalled how Ty had climbed the wall to a picture of an antelope on a billboard advertising the park and how Ty had told him that the Kishoki were once part of the Antelope Tribe.

"Don't think you can grab those animals and ride them back to your caves. You'll get arrested faster than you can guess a Herbie trick." Darren tapped the wheel and sped into the next lane. "We're movin' now, guys."

"Rollin'!" Shum shouted.

"Cold can't stop us!" Ty shouted.

Sita joined the voices of Shum and Ko. "Cold not stop us/claw not stop us/river brings us home/river brings us home."

They sang over and over the Kishoki song they had sung at the campfire when they began their journey.

Darren merged onto the 78 Freeway. He raced the U-Haul down the middle lane, followed the Escondido exit, and wound his way through the wavy grid of small-town streets. Soon he was on a country highway, surrounded by open fields and rolling sun-lit hills.

"See that, Ty?" Darren pointed to a sign on his left, lettered in black: *Parking – Safari Park*. "This is it."

He turned onto an uphill road and parked the U-Haul in a lot designated for campers. Then he dutifully locked the van doors and led the *wings* up the paved road to the park entrance.

How can this place take them home, Darren wondered, *wherever that is?*

Shum pointed to one of the small houses, a wood-shingled ticket kiosk with a straw roof, at the park entrance. "We could build this house."

"We have many things to build," Ty agreed.

"Good, I'm glad you guys are learning, but right now, wait here." Darren directed his warning especially to Ko and Shum. "Don't go anywhere. Nowhere. You stay with Ty and Sita."

He bought four tickets for the Safari ride. "This is the path to the tram," the clerk said, moving his finger down a squiggly brown line on the park map, finally stopping at a small yellow square marked "elevators."

"Elevators?" Darren winced. *This is definitely more complicated than the Santa Monica Pier.*

"That'll take them down; then they follow the path past the lions."

"Any antelope?" Darren asked nervously. "The billboards feature antelopes."

"Oh yeah, they'll see all kinds of animals."

"You're sure?" Darren's voice started sounding more aggressive. "I mean, about the antelope."

The clerk raised his chin. "Look, mister, I don't feed, herd, or house the animals. My job is ticket sales." His wrinkled face grew larger as he leaned toward the speaker hole in the glass that separated them. "There's a line behind you, so make up your mind."

Darren bit down hard on his teeth, as if the force of his bite would channel the right decision. He knew Walsheim was waiting for him. He knew he was on the brink of the first breakthrough job in his life. It was insanity to think he could go with the *wings*, but he also knew that if Ty could get lost in a parking lot, the *wings* could just as easily get lost in the massive park. "I'll take another ticket."

Darren checked his watch and walked back to the *wings*. "We're set. Everyone stay together. I'm going with you." He led them under a huge canopy. "It's the Young Adventurers' Club safari," Darren told the turnstile attendant, handing him five tickets.

The gray-haired attendant pumped his fist. "Gets them away from those crazy fantasy games." He shot a look to Ko. "This ain't an insult, but the porky kid looks like he came straight out of a jungle adventure."

Darren nodded. "He's Einstein's grandson."

* * *

Huge overlapping trees and lush groves of bright, flowery plants bordered the path. Ty and the *wings* were in a land as green and checkered with shade and sunlight as any forest trail along the River Gan.

"Look, look!" Shum pointed to a large blue bird with a hooked beak.

Sita turned their eyes to another bird whose yellow and red beak looked like a bright cone stuck on the end of its face.

They passed a waterfall, a lagoon filled with ducks, and crossed a wobbly wooden bridge. Ty stopped to point out small deer with tiny ears and huge black eyes. "*Fooksies*! Just like the animals the hunters bring back to us."

"Cavendish dik-diks," Darren corrected him, reading off the printed marker. "Let's go, guys. My meeting with Herbie's at noon."

Slowly, unconsciously, they were returning to a familiar world.

The *wings* finally said good-bye to a tree-high cage of black and brown gibbons.

"Bye, George," Shum and Ko shouted together as the gibbons swung effortlessly through the trees, just like in the *Curious George* cartoons they had adored.

"Hold it! Hold it, right there!" Darren held his cell phone inches from his eyes. "Ty, put your arm around Sita. Ko move in a little. I want to get a picture of all of you."

They smiled like school kids on a holiday.

The *wings* followed Darren's brisk pace to a shaded platform packed with tourists. He rushed the *wings* into a huge elevator.

When the big steel doors closed, Ty whispered to Sita, "Don't be afraid. I've been in one of these before."

Darren watched Ty take Sita's hand. He looked over to Ko and Shum staring straight ahead, squeezed together in the crowded box. When the doors drew back, the two *wings* bolted out before any tourist had taken a step.

Darren glanced at his watch, calculating the drive time to San Diego. He dragged the boys and Sita away from an outpost of lions dozing on gigantic boulders, surrounded by a deep, dry gorge.

"Big cat." Shum shook his head slowly in awe of the golden animal collared with an imperious brown mane.

"It could swallow a thousand rats, Shummy, and still eat a pizza."

"Probably pepachoni."

"Donuts." Ko giggled.

"Bagels," Shum shot back. And they low-fived for their last time in America.

Sita grabbed Ty's hand and followed Darren to the tram station.

* * *

Darren didn't know how hearing an antelope voice or riding a tram through the park was going to bring the *wings* any closer to their caves than riding a bicycle with a flat tire would get him to San Diego, but by now he knew there was an invisible curtain of time beyond which he understood nothing. He looked over to the long line of visitors already assembled on the platform.

"You're going to be okay?" he asked one final time, handing Ty the tickets. "I mean, like when you pointed to Herbie's drawer, you're that sure?"

"Walawalawala." Ty smiled. "We're gonna make the leap, Darren."

"Right." Darren swallowed the feelings welling up in his throat. "Follow the line of people. I'll watch until the tram takes off."

Sita reached up, wrapping her caped brown arms around Darren. He wasn't expecting a show of emotion from the *wings*, especially from Sita, whose feisty opinions and arguments had always seemed contrary to his privileged life. He ruffled her shiny black curls.

"Shampooed," she said. "Last time."

"If I ever need a shaman, I'll call you in the sky. Or I'll go over to Macy's and look for you in the Juniors' department."

"Imagine us in the caves," she said. "That's where we'll be. Maybe you'll dream of us and the dream will come true."

Darren felt in his heart a flood of warmth, a good-bye he was only able to express in the mute stirring of his lips and the silence of his eyes.

"We love you." Shum's voice rose, as true as the flight of his spear. "You're family north of the border and south of Mexico."

The rumbling sound of the tram pulled Darren's attention away. He saw five connected cars stop at the platform. Each car, filled with tourists, was canopied with a metal roof and open on the sides. He looked over to Ty, but the *wing*'s eyes were fixed on a blue-uniformed attendant pulling back a bolt on the small knee-high doors of each carriage.

When the cars were empty, the line of waiting people rushed forward into the tram.

"Go," Darren urged. "Go now!"

Ty and the *wings* reached the head of the line just as the tram filled up. The young lady attendant, in a khaki park uniform, lowered a bar and placed a metal gate in front of it. Ty and Sita stopped.

Darren winced again. "Damn."

* * *

"The tram is full," the attendant told Ty. "You have to wait." The cave boy's smile vanished with his sinking heart. "Don't worry," she continued. "The next tram will only be a few minutes."

Her green eyes shifted to the bedroll on his back. "Are you going to sleep overnight in the tents?"

"We're members of the Adventurers' Club," Sita answered quickly.

Softly, in Kishoki, Ty told the *wings*, *"You sit together. I counted four seats in each row. I will sit in the first seat by the small door. When I give the signal, you follow me. We must be very quick."*

"What's the signal?" Shum whispered.

"Amskray."

"Amskray," Shum repeated. "Sounds familiar."

Ty watched the next tram pull up to the boarding platform. A flood of tourists exited the cars.

"Enjoy," the attendant said. She removed the metal gate and raised the bar.

Ty quickly led the *wings* to the last car. He took a seat directly in front of a knee-high door. The *wings* sat together next to him. Shum's spear poked through his jerkin.

"Shummy!" Ko whispered, frantically gesturing for him to push the spear point back down.

* * *

From a distance, Darren watched. Tourists, still waiting for the next boarding, blocked part of his view. He saw the tram slowly move forward. He saw Ty and the *wings* seated in the last car, and he thought he saw Ty catch his eye. He started to lift his hand to wave but dropped it as the vision-seeker's head turned away. All he could see was a long ginger braid against an eagle emblem on the back of a leather jerkin. Then the car and the jerkin disappeared.

* * *

The tram slowed to nearly a stop. The *wings* heard the woman driver's voice stream through the overhead speakers: "On your left," she announced, "roaming in their grassy habitat, are the giraffes."

270

"Big neck," Shum squealed. "Really big neck!"

Ty joined the *wings'* laughter, all amazed at the animal's giant chocolate spots and unique body shape. Ko had to motion Shum to push down his spear again.

As they approached the next station, the overhead voice directed the visitors to a great brown rhino.

"I don't see anything," Sita cried out. "Where is it?"

Ty pointed to a huge brown boulder, much like the giant boulders that surrounded the animal. "See, it's the one moving just a little. That's it!"

As fascinated as Ty was by the exotic creatures, half his mind was somewhere else. His chest felt like it was on fire. He was swallowing hard. He believed in the golden shell and in his plan, but what if the antelope weren't in the fields? Could all the animals be seen from the tram? What if the antelope, the spirit of his ancestors, had been moved or died? Ty had placed his faith in a rooftop billboard that Darren had told him would be wiped clean and replaced by another advertisement in one or two full moons. Had Darren taken a different road or had they passed that same corner in another full moon, Ty knew the sign might not have been there. He knew that wherever he would be, he would not be sitting in this Safari Park tram. *I saw the message because Darren took that road to the Hollywood building. Darren must be part of the plan.*

"Is that destiny or chance?"

"Is what destiny or chance?" Sita raised her voice above the surrounding chatter.

"What's happening to us."

The tram rumbled up the narrow trail to an oblong lagoon.

"Destiny, *masuqa.*" Sita grabbed Ty's arm. "Look!" She pointed at long-beaked black-and-white pelicans sunning themselves and diving off a small island into the sunlit water.

Ty and the *wings* heard the driver's voice pointing out pink birds with curvy necks and stick-thin legs she called "flamingos" and then "ostriches," whose long necks and tiny heads looked like a snake had wiggled out of their bloated white stomachs. Ko and Shum pounded their knees with laughter. Ty smiled nervously and tapped his right foot against the tram floor.

"I love the color of the flamingos," Sita said, in the last words of English she would speak in America.

Ty was barely able to get a few words past his dry lips. His foot kept tapping the floor, unconsciously repeating the rhythm of music he had heard watching the flaming grill at El Pollo Loco. It was the restlessness of a rhythm coming back from long, long ago.

But where are the antelope?

The tour guide's voice called attention to a field of huge brown animals with curled horns. "Cape buffalo," she called them. Climbing the peaks of the Kishoki cliffs, Ty had seen these same animals roaming across plateaus between the vast stretches of forest. He felt he was getting closer.

The tram slowed down again. He heard the guide announce: "Look on your left. These are the grey antelope."

The words thundered in Ty's brain. He grabbed the car's side rail. "Sita," he whispered, "let's amskray!"

Sita turned to Ko and Shum. "Amskray!"

Ty released the latch on the short car door and jumped from the tram. Sita, Ko, and Shum were on the heels of his journey boots.

Racing across the tracks, Ty could hear passengers shouting: "Kids overboard! Stop the tram!"

He and the *wings* rushed up to the wooden rails fencing the antelope. "These are antelope," he said in a breathless gasp. "They are the sign of our people who went ahead when we stayed behind."

Shum boldly removed the shortened spear from beneath his jerkin.

The anxious voice of the tram guide rose above the tram hysteria. "Emergency at Station Six. Four kids jumped off the last car. All in leather. A girl in a cape. They've got a spear."

"This is Control Center. Do not approach. Security is on the way. I repeat, do not approach. They might have other weapons."

The *wings* barely heard the responding voice. Words had slipped into an unknown tongue.

Fearless and calm, Ty touched his chest. His fingers burned from the heat. Park voices died on the wind. All he heard was the low, crackly bark of the antelope. He turned to the *wings*. "*Close your eyes and repeat: We have heard the sound of the antelope. Darren is gone. We are gone. We trust in the golden shell to take us home.*"

The *wings* closed their eyes and repeated the chant. Above them, clouds drifted across the sun. The sky turned slate, as smoky gray as the shoulders of the grazing antelope.

CHAPTER 31

"M y stomach hurts," Ko groaned. "It was the emmy-dactyl's blood. I had two fingers too much."

"Look at my spear," Shum kept repeating, his dark eyes bugging out in bewilderment. "Half of it is gone!"

"It probably broke off in the beast's rump, Shummy."

The two boys trudged through the shallow waters of the River Gan. They had no memory of America, no panda bears or pizza. All they could recall was their magnificent victory over the forest's most fearsome beast.

A few yards ahead of them, hand in hand, Ty and Sita maneuvered around the river-slick rocks and fallen timber.

"You remember?"

"Yes, I remember," Sita said.

They remembered every smile and frown on Darren's face, Herbie's tricks, shoes in shop windows, cell phones and TV, the Westside Pavilion and Santa Monica Pier, crazy Dr. Greenberg, skateboard rides, the tastes of ice cream, burgers, Chinese and Mexican food, the Karpet King, baseball and bubble gum.

"The fight in Westwood," he said.

"*Star Wars*," she said.

"Home Depot."

"Even Dorsey's dress," she said.

Every molecule of life had a place of memory in the tissue, the nerve belt, and heartbeat of these two souls. It was their journey, their quest into a vision that Ty alone imagined and Sita had guided with a shaman's gift.

"I want to do more," he said. "I know what I want to do."

Ty ducked under an overhanging bough and pushed aside a branch. Birds fluttered from the tree. A swarm of insects buzzed through the leaves. Ahead of him, he saw two figures standing in knee-high water.

"Pa!" he shouted, throwing up his hands. "Pa!"

The hunter Star and the man next to him looked up the river. "Ty!" Star dropped his spear and splashed through the water toward his son.

Ty heard the roar of laughter from the hunter's lips. He felt the embrace of his father's muscled arms and the hunter's rough reddish beard against his cheek.

"Many suns rose and fell," Star said. "You were many suns gone."

Ty heard more shouting. He saw Ko's father jumping up and down in the river, splashing Ko and throwing his arms around him.

Four time-travelers and two grateful fathers were rooted in water, in the river mist that reaches the clouds, brushes the stars, and returns again with life-giving rain. They stood together in the fluid, unending cycle of life.

* * *

In the firelight of the cave, Su covered her son's face with kisses, fed him roasted meat, and asked him repeatedly, "Where did you go, Ty? Where?"

"I went where my dream took me. I went over the sun and stars."

Su read into his words the meaning of the golden shell in her hand, but Star shook his head sadly.

"How can you jump over the sun or kill an emmydactyl with a boy's spear? Our son is suffering from river fever," the hunter lamented. "The same fever that turned his hair the color of the cliffs when he was a baby."

"But Ma said you and Sita's father found a dead emmydactyl in the river."

Star nodded grimly, dismissing Ty's retort. "The scales on its chest were ripped apart. Another beast had killed it."

"You didn't see any cuts from Shum's spear or from our knives?"

"There is no one else in the forest, Ty. I am a hunter. My father was a great hunter. There were cuts on the emmydactyl from the sharp rocks in the river. You cannot kill an emmydactyl with baby knives." His eyes crimped with sadness. He turned to Su. "Make our son a medicine tea. When the fever goes, he will talk sense again."

* * *

In Sita's cave, her mother, Yan, was just as filled with grief and disbelief.

"Do my tears mean nothing to you?" she sobbed. "Ty doesn't listen to his father. He doesn't listen to the elders and laughs at Man Who Stands Alone. What do you want with a dreamer?"

"He is more than a dreamer, Ma."

"A storyteller. Does that make him any better, Sita? The elders' laughter still rings in my ears from his crazy story about singing by a fire pit and killing an emmydactyl. An emmydactyl! The deadliest beast in the forest no Kishoki has ever killed! He makes a fool of Ko and Shum for letting them repeat this fantasy."

"It really happened. I saw it happen."

"Stop! Do not make me think you are crazy too. It is enough you tell me about being a shaman." Sita's mother wiped the tears from her eyes and brought Sita a plate of food. "Ty will never feed you or your children. They will die like leaves in the cold season."

"He will do more, Ma. You will see. He will feed you, my sisters and brother, and all the Kishoki children." She watched her mother stoke the fire, and she added, defiantly, "And even the children of my children!"

* * *

As foolish as Star found his son's talk, Ty still convinced him to try the net he had woven like the web of a baseball glove.

"Ty, you made this before. The fish wiggle through the net."

"That was with vines." Ty ran his fingers across the leather webbing. "If this doesn't work, I'll carry water from the river until your hair turns white."

"I will die of grief for my son before my hair turns white." He grabbed the net from Ty's hand and stormed out of the cave.

At dusk, Star ran up from the river with a basket hanging from his shoulder and the leather net in his hands. "Ko's father always missed," he gasped, as spontaneous praise hurtled from his lips. "He could never spear a fish. Now, we call him Big Catch Wei. Look!"

Ty peered into the basket, brimming with a slick mound of silver and pink fish.

"The net works!" Star shouted, slapping Ty's shoulder. "It works!" His face beamed with a proud, paternal grin. "Now that the fever has left your head, you can think again."

The bearded men no longer laughed at Ty. He and Shum were honored with white feathers at the Council of Elders.

"This is just the beginning," Ty confided to Shum. "I have bigger plans."

"Bigger plans!" Shum trumpeted as they left the Council cave, without a clue as to what Ty was talking about.

* * *

"Now you understand," Man Who Stands Alone said. "Your *star-steppings* were not simply nighttime fantasies. They were real voyages into time." He gazed at Sita, sitting cross-legged on the dirt floor of his cave. The flames of the fire pit separated her from his jeweled vest and all-seeing eye.

She had returned to her schooling with Man, studying the sacred rituals and wisdom that would someday bring her the mantel of the first woman shaman.

"And time curves just like wisdom, back and forth. It plays with our memory." The shaman waved a branch of sage over the flames. "At times we learn from the future and sometimes we learn from the past."

Sita nodded. "Wisdom sits at the edge of the cliff looking out."

"Only when love comes along like the wind does wisdom take flight."

Sita smiled. "You are so right."

The shaman threw the sage stick into the fire. "And still, you never stop talking."

* * *

Together with Ko and Shum, Ty cleared shrub and stones along flat sections of the cliff. His father scoffed, accusing Ty of spending too much time on cliffs where only weeds and flowers grow. "Your fever has come back," Star grumped. "You are more stubborn than your mother."

Ty saw his mother stamp her foot. She didn't challenge Star, but Ty knew that she believed in her son. She had already begun drying gourd and squash seeds and digging up tubers and plants for the future garden.

Ty turned away from Star and spoke directly to Su. "First we clear the land. Then we till, then we plant. Acie taught me this."

"Acie? Who is Acie?" Star demanded, knotting his vest. "He is not a Kishoki."

"He's one of the Antelope People from over the sun."

"There you go, talking about jumping the sun again." Star threw up his hands. The veins on his forehead bulged. His voice filled the cave. "You are a hunter, just like your father and your father's father!" He grabbed his spear. "This is what we know. This is how we eat. The flesh of the ram, the deer and the fish!"

Ty looked at his mother. Her face glowed with a wily smile. "I understand more than your father's noise."

* * *

Ty and Ko surveyed the long rows of tilled soil. The ginger-haired boy looked over to his friend, whose face beamed with pride. "Ko, what are you thinking?"

The grumbling *wing* looked at the terraced cliff. "We are making food."

"For the whole clan, Ko."

"No Ko anymore. Call me Han."

"Han?" Ty gave Ko a baffled look. "Why?"

"I hear Han in my dream." Ko nodded, with a big moony smile on his face. "Ko is an old time name. Han means new life. Soon I will marry a *kanta-wing*."

Ty remembered how Ko and Shum had wandered down Hollywood Boulevard and stood in the footprints of Harrison Ford. He wondered if some tiny remnant of memory could have stuck in Ko's mind.

He wrapped his arm around his *wing*'s shoulder. "Han it is."

"But how will we bring water to the seeds?" Shum jumped up from the log he was sitting on. "Only the river and the sky have water."

* * *

Star was even more outraged and incredulous. "From the river to the cliffs?" he scoffed. "The water will fall out of the pots before you are half way up. We are better off pissing on the seeds."

"Star!" Su's voice rose above her husband's. "Put your mouth to bed."

Ty turned to the cave entry. Su had taken down the hide and was glaring at Star. "He is my son too," she said. "I carried him and fed him with my blood."

Ty saw the dark gleam in his father's eyes as he turned away from his wife. The hunter lifted his fist to his heart. "You will be a great hunter! That is my will."

The words echoed in Ty's mind with the sound of other voices. He thought of Herbie and of Darren, men who had bent their dreams to their fathers' wills. He didn't protest Star's wish. "Can I use your tools?" he simply asked. "I will make you a gift."

"You were my gift," Star roared, "until the river fever turned your thoughts against me! Even the shaman did not think Su could have a child, but she did. For what?" he screamed. "For what?"

* * *

The following day, armed with a burning torch, Ty searched through the animal bones stored in one of the caves. He brought home a very long, straight bone, tapered along its length. With Star's file, he made small consecutive grooves on the beveled edge, keeping in mind the image of Darren's saw he had used to cut Shum's spear.

Along with Shum and Han, he went into the forest, looking for fallen trees.

"We will make wheels," Ty said.

Shum dusted off his hands. "What's a wheel?"

Han poked him. "Wheel, Shummy!" Then he looked up at Ty with the same puzzled gaze. "What's a wheel?"

Ty cut into a slim tree with the bone saw he had made.

At dusk, Star stared at four large, equally round discs, each the width of his extended thumb. "Too big for fire pit," he squawked, waving his hand dismissively.

"It's not for fire, Pa. It's for something that will make your anger disappear."

The elders stood with folded arms, eyes filled with curiosity and mouths gabbing about what foolish scheme the teenage *wings* were up to.

Ty scooped up the discs and carried them down to the river. In the *wings'* cave, Ty pounded a dent in the center of each disc.

With a rock and sharp bone knives the *wings* chipped and whittled a smooth hole through each disc. They gathered long thick branches, cut them to an even length and laid them out side by side on the flat clearing ground. Then they wove a leather strap through the branches to hold them together.

Ty sent Han to find straight, narrow branches. "Like this," he said, pointing to the hole in the wooden disc. "Not too thick."

He watched his trusted *wing* disappear into the forest. He wondered what had changed in Han, and why. He looked over to Sita, who had come to watch the *wings* at work.

"Something happened inside him, in America," Sita said. "Something happened in his heart. The heart doesn't know time or distance."

Ty shot a wide-eyed grin. "Maybe the roller coaster shook his heart."

Sita laughed. They hadn't spent much time together since their return. Sita, sequestered with Man who Stands Alone on the summit cliff, and Ty, working in the forest and river cave, had hardly seen each other.

"What did your mother and father say?" Ty asked.

"My mother cried from the day she saw my empty bed. She told me not to see you again."

Ty dropped the stick in his hand. "What did you say?"

"I told her she cannot stop the sun from crossing the sky."

Ty smiled. "Good Sita."

***

The next morning, Ty sawed two of Han's branches and inserted the ends of each through the holes in the discs. "Wheels," he said, looking up. "Now, we set the platform between the wheels."

In the clearing, Han helped Ty lift the sturdy platform onto the axles.

Sita watched with Su and a handful of elders. Star stood to the side, eyeing the contraption with dubious scorn.

The visionary *wing* dragged the platform around the clearing with a strap attached to the front branches. The platform rolled along just as Ty had imagined it would. The wobbly wheels held the ground, but on the third revolution, Han saw the platform spin off its axles.

"Look out! It's falling!" he shouted.

Star shook his head, grumped and walked back to his cave. Su wiped tears from her eyes with the back of her hand.

Sita ran over to Ty. "You have to keep the platform attached to the axle. Then it won't come off." She took his hand and led him into the cave of bones.

Even in the gray light of the cave, Ty could make out the sun-bleached glow of the round animal bone Sita held in her hand. "This is what you need," she said. "Put a hole through this part." She pointed to the bulbous end of the bone. "Then, put the stick through the hole. That way, the platform won't sit on the axle. The wheels will be free to turn, but the platform won't slide off because it's attached to the bone."

The *wings* chiseled holes through the four bulbous bones Ty and Sita had found in the cave. They drove the axles through the bone holes and slid each wheel into place on the axles, binding the ends of the axles with vine and sap.

"This is it." Ty sighed with relief. He wiped the sweat from his forehead. "We're ready to roll."

"Ready to roll!" Shum shouted at the dusky sky.

In the clearing, Ty and Han placed two large vessels of water on the platform.

The moon was rising when Ty finally yanked the cord. In a great circle, past the astonished looks of the elders, he pulled the flat cart, forcing their eyes to follow his ever-increasing pace.

A loud voice rose above the rumble of the wheels. Star was rushing toward the clearing, waving a huge stone club. "I'm going to smash this foolish toy! We Kishoki are hunters!" he yelled, stumbling across a pair of broken axles the *wings* had left behind.

Su rushed to intercept him before he could get off his knees. "No, no! You can't kill our son's dream!" she cried, holding Star back with all her might and her heart.

"He is dishonoring my ancestors!"

"Your ancestors left us long ago!" She yanked the club from his hands. "We are the people who stayed behind." She pointed the club toward the clearing. "Look! Look!"

Ty caught his father's eye. He raced faster. The wheels held. Not one vessel tipped or drop of water spilled on the dusty Kishoki ground.

He saw his mother beating the sky with triumphant arms. Han and Shum howled and slapped their hands.

Ty slowed his pace and wiped the dust from his eyes. He turned to Sita. He saw her mouth slightly open. No sound reached his ear, but he could read the word on her lips.

"Walawalawala."

CHAPTER 32

Ty's success brought more volunteers to help clear and widen the path from the river to the terraced cliff-side.

Only he and Han were strong enough, working side by side, to pull the heavy carts, loaded with water jars, up the steep path.

"We'll build more carts with larger platforms and bigger wheels," he told his *wings*.

They irrigated the soil. The seeds and tubers sprouted. The sprouts blossomed into plants. Food rose from the moist mother earth.

With the first harvested crops, the elders began to see the benefit of planting and growing food. The doubt and scorn that once filled Star's eyes turned to a fatherly pride.

"That's my son. That's Ty."

He sat across from Ty at the fire pit and sipped his tea. The autumn wind beat at the hide covering the mouth of the cave.

"Teach me how to jump over the sun," he entreated his son.

"Wheels," Ty answered. "Follow the wheel. The wheel is the world."

* * *

The hunters still hunted. Women still foraged for berries and herbs, but Ty's fishing nets and gardens increased the scope of the clan's diet and fortified their food stock against the bitter, imprisoning winters.

Wild animals came to forage on the crops. Some were killed for their meat. Others were domesticated. The process of breeding began.

"Now we eat well," Su said, hugging her son. "Even in winter our children do not die. They grow strong."

Ty never claimed his father's dream of following in the great hunter's footsteps. When he and his *wings* pulled his carts through the clearing, loaded with vessels of water from the river, firewood from the forest, crops from the cliff-side, even bunches of children gleefully riding on cart-laden piles of hides, Ty knew he had brought the elders more than a meal. He had brought them the gift of his imagination.

Sita wore the red stone Ty had promised her on his return from their journey. He found broken pieces of amber, filed them down, and polished them. With hardened sap, he attached thin bone frames.

"I love 'em," she said, pushing the ersatz sunglasses up on her nose. "They're priceless."

Unlike Man Who Stands Alone, who wore iridescent feathers over one eye, Sita was the shaman who wore shades.

They walked together along the River Gan. Dusk was settling on the water. Birds still twittering in the trees and the splash of fish leaping in the shallows were the only sounds filling the silence.

"More noise in America," Ty said.

Sita took his hand. "More of everything."

"No," he whispered. "Here there are more stars and more silence."

She turned and stepped closer to Ty. "Will a seeker kiss a shaman-in-waiting on the banks of the River Gan? You promised once," she reminded him.

Ty closed his eyes and kissed her.

"And will we ever see the street with no name again?" she asked.

"It depends on where your potions take us. You told me there were many centuries. Is it possible we could visit another one?"

Sita nodded. "Darren has a computer, *masuqa*. He knows the places of the world."

"But we know how the world works. Maybe we need each other."

* * *

Darren sat in Mr. Walsheim's one-room guesthouse, surrounded by unpacked boxes. The long drive, the sad good-byes at Safari Park, and unloading the van had left him exhausted. He sipped a cappuccino and scrolled through the photos on his cell phone until he reached the last picture he'd taken, the photo of the *wings* at the tree-high cage of gibbons. The screen was ghostly white. Only in his mind's eye did he see the faces of Ty, Sita, Ko, and Shum.

A knock on the door brought Darren to his feet. "Come in."

Walsheim's congenial smile lit up the dusty room. "You made it." He glanced at his watch. "Right on the button." His gaze drifted across the stacks of boxes. "I take it the feffers went back to Cajun country."

"They left on…on a train this morning."

"Look at this." The portly producer stood grinning with his arms stretched out, right leg raised, bearing all his weight on his injured foot. "Queen Sita's potion pulled off a miracle, and Mr. Ty knew all my tricks. They were amazing." Herbie took a step back to the open door. "See you in my office at two o'clock. On the button. You've got directions to get there?"

"Yes."

Darren watched the door close. He looked down again at his cell phone. The screen, still blank, glowed with light. He smiled at the image of Herbie with his arms outstretched, balancing on one leg, like a crane. "Cajuns or Kishoki," he whispered. "All I know is that I loved them and that my life is new because I met them."

Quietly, he started to unpack his boxes. He took out the cof-feemaker, skillet, and toaster, items Ty and Sita had packed in the kitchen. Something dinged and rolled on the floor. The glint caught his eye. He picked up a small golden shell and stared at it in the palm of his hand. *Could I reach them,* he wondered, *just as they reached me from the River Gan?*

QUESTIONS for DISCUSSION

How does growing up in caves, as opposed to growing up in a single-family apartment or home, affect the way the teenagers think?

Does growing up in a clan, in contrast to modern, individualized social units, enhance a sense of communal loyalty or create jealousies? Does clan life heighten a sense of security? In which kind of society would you prefer to live?

Is Sita, a spiritual seeker, wrong for being attracted to styles and fashion? Or is this simply a part of her spirit, a natural expression of her love of beauty and color?

What affect does skin color have on the various characters in the book?

How does one resolve the tension between loyalty to one's family and one's personal dream? Can it ever be resolved? To whom do you think you owe allegiance?

What do you think Darren owes his father? Materially? Emotionally? Does he owe him anything?

How does Ty's courage affect Darren? Do you think that Darren will continue to express the lessons of Ty and Sita's wisdom?

Wealth can be a tremendous advantage, but how in the novel does it also show how it can erode one's character? Would you rather grow up in wealth or in the *wings'* imperiled existence?

How does Sita's female perspective influence Ty's decision making? Is she smarter than Ty or simply more verbal? How does Ty express his intelligence?

Why do the teenage boys taste the blood of the emmydactyl? Is there any modern equivalent in our rituals of victory?

Is there a difference between love and loyalty, and how is it expressed in Ty's attitude toward his father? Toward Sita? In Darren's feelings for his deceased mother?

Do groups of people with drastically shorter life spans necessarily experience a deeper understanding or maturity earlier in their lives?

About the Author:

Ken Luber, writer and teacher, lives with his artist wife, Kathleen, in the mountain village of Idyllwild in Southern California. He has a BA from Ripon College and graduate work at the University of Iowa Writers' Workshop, and he is a graduate Fellow of the American Film Institute. Ken has traveled the world and written and directed television, film, and theater. He is also the author of *Everybody's Shadow*, a book of poetry. His first novel, *Match to the Heart*, is available on Amazon.com, e-platforms, and bookstores. Ken is presently writing a new novel, *Falling From the Sky*, and is working with his composer on the finishing touches to *Esperanza – the Musical of Hope*. www.esperanzathemusical.com.

CPSIA information can be obtained
at www.ICGtesting.com
Printed in the USA
FSOW02n2357141116
27355FS